Savage Woods

Books by Mary SanGiovanni

Chills

Savage Woods

Savage Woods

Mary SanGiovanni

LYRICAL UNDERGROUND
Kensington Publishing Corp.
www.kensingtonbooks.com

LYRICAL UNDERGROUND BOOKS are published by

Kensington Publishing Corp.
119 West 40th Street
New York, NY 10018

All Kensington titles, imprints, and distributed lines are available at special quantity discounts for bulk purchases for sales promotion, premiums, fund-raising, educational, or institutional use.

Special book excerpts or customized printings can also be created to fit specific needs. For details, write or phone the office of the Kensington Sales Manager: Kensington Publishing Corp., 119 West 40th Street, New York, NY 10018. Attn. Sales Department. Phone: 1-800-221-2647.

Lyrical Underground and Lyrical Underground logo Reg. US Pat. & TM Off.

First Electronic Edition: September 2017
eISBN-13: 978-1-60183-750-9
eISBN-10: 1-60183-750-X

First Print Edition: September 2017
ISBN-13: 978-1-60183-751-6
ISBN-10: 1-60183-751-8

Printed in the United States of America

This book is dedicated to my Sprout and my Seedling—my love for you is taller than the trees, longer than time, and fiercer than the elements.

ACKNOWLEDGMENTS

I'd like to thank my parents and sisters, my brother in-law, my Sprout and my Seedling for their support and understanding; Brian Keene, Matt Hayward, and Anna for their technical (and general) awesomeness; and Martin Biro and the folks at Kensington for their hard work.

PROLOGUE

In the part of the Pine Barrens that the locals called Nilhollow, the canopy of elder trees kept out all but the smallest patches of sunlight. Though late summer still dawdled, dragging hot, dry feet across the highway, roads, and suburban yards beyond the woods, it was cool in Nilhollow, almost cold beneath those trees. The branches waved unevenly in the odd breeze, whispering messages of rustling leaves among each other. The ferns below tittered as well, a faint gray-green undulation traveling from one frond to another. The wind itself shifted sullenly through the forest, atavistic in its sounds, its dull roar rising to a thin whistle and falling back again as it carried the messages of those it moved through.

The lesser, the elemental spirits of the trees, were restless because even in sleep, Kèkpëchehëlat, the ancient one who had gone insane, was restless. That this greater elemental might dream in its imprisonment would not have surprised them. Its thrashing did not alarm them only because it was still asleep, for now. However, they rustled and whistled and swayed among themselves about what would happen should it wake up. Once revered as a forest god, it was very strong, like the trees and rocks they protected, more so than all the other *manëtuwàk* in those woods, and if its dream-sounds were any indication, it would wake up with rage guiding and driving it.

They supposed that the Kèkpëchehëlat eventually would do just that.

Time, they had come to know over the centuries, meant that circumstances changed. Things fell apart. Plants in the *tèkëne* sprouted, grew, died, rotted away. Animals were born, grew, died, rotted away. The far-moving ones had come, had honored the *manëtuwàk* and tried to live alongside them with respect, and they, too, grew, died, and rotted away. Falling apart was the nature of things. So were all changes . . . even strange ones like the Turning of the Earth.

The Turning had come up from a crack in the ground, and it spread like a smoke, an illness, a superstition, all-pervasive and all-powerful. That which was not driven away was swathed in it, swallowed by it, and changed by it.

All of Nilhollow had Turned before the shamans of the far-moving ones had intervened. They couldn't reverse the effects, but with powerful binding-magic, they had stopped the Turning from expanding and engulfing the whole Pine Barrens.

The ax-wielding ones who had come next did not know or care about the Turning of the Earth. They gave little credence to the warnings of those they perceived as savages, feral as the lands around them, or their stories of the *nihillowewi tèkëne*, the murderous woods, whose preternatural origin and effects had been the source of so much terror. They learned quickly enough to stay away, though. The loss of their animals and their children, the soul-sickness, and the wide-scale spilling of blood taught them to stay away.

For a long time, only those who wanted to be lost—or those whom others wanted to lose—came to Nilhollow. Often the madness in the earth and air and water got into them, and they did terrible things to themselves. Sometimes, even in sleep, the Kèkpëchehëlat still wielded shadows of its rage.

The lesser *manëtuwàk* had not been put to sleep with magic, like the Kèkpëchehëlat, but they did often sleep, sometimes for days, sometimes for centuries. They slept until a dull roaring of beasts in the distance woke them for good. With the passing of even more time, their bindings grew looser, allowing them more movement. From the edge of the *tèkëne*, they could now see as well as hear those roaring beasts, hard-shelled and very, very fast on their round, blurred wheel-feet, which swallowed the ax-wielding ones whole, carried them away, and spit them out again.

Time had changed the earth all around them, as it did so often.

Few who passed through now seemed to remember the old ways of the far-moving ones. Long forgotten were many of the words and gestures that kept the Turning of the Earth from spreading and the elemental creatures bound there in check. There were weak attempts from time to time, solitary movers who stole into the groves at night to try, but too much had been forgotten, too much lost. So the old bindings had begun to fall apart, too. In time, the *manëtuwàk* of Nil-hollow were freer and freer to move through the rest of the woods again, and able to exert more influence, by degrees, over those who invaded their home.

Of course, if they could be completely freed, the ancient *manëtu* who had gone insane, the Kèkpëchehëlat, could be freed as well. It had grown twisted, as gnarled as the roots and branches of the surrounding trees, and in its state, it would not remember the old ways, either. All would be swept up in its madness. Its rage-sickness.

Things would change, die, rot away.

The *manëtuwàk* wondered if they should be afraid.

ONE

"You know, I read this article online the other day that said that black holes can move. They just, like, bounce around the universe, all random, ya know? And if they bounce our way and get close enough even just to wobble the revolutions of planets around the sun—*BAM!* We're all hoovered into nothingness."

The herald of this revelation, one Todd Mackey, scratched at the day-old strawberry-blond scruff on his chin and jaw. He squinted through the early morning haze, which bent the rays of the rising sun in odd angles through the forest surrounding the campsite. He and his brother Kenny were only into the second morning of their "guys' weekend" and already he was feeling unusually and uncomfortably enveloped by the trees, with their mantles of needle-green. Down there on the ground, with the forest growths and thicknesses far more pressing an issue than galactic vacuums eons away, Todd didn't much believe in, understand, or care either way about the movement of black holes; it was just talk. But he needed it, to forget the bad feeling he had. He wanted conversation, however inane.

The Nilhollow area of the Pine Barrens was Kenny's idea. He had told Todd the spot would be perfect—cool, quiet, and best of all, pretty much all to themselves. Unlike a lot of the rest of the Pine Barrens, Todd didn't know much about the Nilhollow part of it, other than what little he and his brother had seen online on camping websites. He knew it encompassed some six-hundred-plus acres, maybe a mile square (although math was never really Todd's bag) in a central area of Brendan T. Byrne State Forest, somewhere within the neat borders of Mt. Misery Pasadena, Glassworks, and Butler Place Roads. Like the rest of the surrounding forest, it was comprised of mostly pitch pines, bracken ferns, and just enough sand in the soil to remind him of the Atlantic Ocean not too far away. Despite the extensive hiking trails in the surrounding areas to the west and south and its location amid a prominent forest of the New Jersey Pinelands National Reserve, Nilhollow was difficult to damn-near impossible to find on any of the Pine Barrens, Brendan T. Byrne, or even old Lebanon State Forest maps. There were no nearby campsites out there, and the closest place to park was still going to be quite a hike from the road. It would be an adventure, Kenny had told him, and Todd was always up for an adventure.

The stories they heard from campers and locals in the Burlington County diner they stopped at along the way proved a little strange, but neither brother was inclined to put too much stock in them. Most of it was typical *Weird NJ*–style, clichéd stuff about cursed grounds, unexplained hiker deaths and disappearances, lights in the sky, that sort of thing. There were some even more bizarre stories, too—some of the missing people turning up inside-out and hanging from trees— but those were told in the same vein as the urban legends about UFOs and Lenni-Lenape spirits, and were not something the brothers were going to let stand as a deterrent. Hell, Nilhollow's unmonitored wildness, with its almost forbidden paths and their dark history, was at least fodder for campfire conversation.

However, for Todd, actually being there and feeling the place around him had gotten under his skin a bit more than he'd expected. Something about Nilhollow was just . . . all wrong. He could see why ghost stories might have gotten a foothold there.

For starters, the brothers had discovered the first morning that hunting was a waste of time, because animals went to great lengths, or so Todd was convinced, to avoid the area. That might have been due to a pervasive and lasting smell, faint to the boys but maybe stronger to the wildlife, of dead things rotting in wet, dark places, underneath thin shrouds of forgotten earth.

Shadows were too long in Nilhollow, and seemed to shift and dart with an anxious and aggressive purpose of their own. In the day, no birds chirped in the trees; no crickets chirped at night. It had taken him a while to notice, as is often the case when perceiving the absence rather than the presence of something. Once he did, though, he couldn't *un*-notice it. That was not to say there were no sounds at all; that was another problem, and one that had wreaked havoc on his sleep the night before. In the silvery hours just before dawn, while he lay awake in the darkness, there certainly *were* sounds, and they seemed to come from all around the tent—strange, sad, high-pitched crying alternating with deep bass warbling, like nothing Todd had ever heard before.

His brother, who slept like the dead, had heard nothing.

The worst of it, though, was that from the moment Todd had set foot on the path that led to the clearing, he had felt the off-kilter quality of the place, as if the whole area was shifted slightly off-track from the rest of reality around it. It was a kind of natural unnaturalness that felt . . . old. Very old—older than any Lenape tribes or their burial grounds, possibly older than human souls. It gave him the sensation of being watched, too, by someone or something as distorted and changing as the leafy shapes and shadows, as looming as the trees. But more than just being watched, it made him feel touched somehow, even pressed down on, which in turn made him feel sort of violated and at the mercy of the Barrens around him. He wasn't the superstitious or even really the imaginative type, nor did he scare very easily; Todd dealt with the world in terms of what he could see, hear, and touch, not what he felt. So the fact that he sensed those things as distinctly as the clothes on his body, a tangible thing he could not just ignore, made him all that much more uncomfortable.

Kenny claimed he felt nothing. Todd wasn't sure that was entirely true, but he didn't push it. Kenny had an annoying habit of deflecting his own fears and insecurities on others if people called him out on them, and Todd just didn't feel like arguing about it.

"No fucking way. Bouncing black holes? Come on, man." Kenny, who had given up any aspirations of bagging so much as a rabbit that weekend, stretched out on his back in his sleeping bag and lit a joint. Todd grimaced; years of athletic training, workouts, and good eating made the idea of smoking up seem like such a waste, but Kenny grinned defiantly at him. Neither said anything about it. The brothers were close; their summer's-end camping weekend was tradition, their catch-up time before Kenny's fall semester started, so personal quirks were put aside. Nothing got in the way of their weekend.

"It's true, man," Todd said, a small grin in return finding its way to his lips. "They move around, sucking up stars and planets and rocks and shit as they go—just bouncing around the universe like giant Dustbusters."

"I thought like, gravity kept them in place or something."

"There is no gravity in space, dumb-ass. That's why things float out there."

"Then how do you explain why the planets don't just go flying off into space? What keeps them going around the sun?"

"Centrifugal force, man."

"Caused by gravity," Kenny said triumphantly.

"Whatever. That's only because there are things that are bigger and more powerful, like the sun, for the planets to go around. The black hole is the most powerful thing out there—and if there's nothing bigger to keep it in place, then hell yeah, it's gonna move." A little impressed with his own train of logic, Todd looked at the jagged slivers of sky visible through the treetops. It was pearlescent up there, soft-looking. And it seemed very far away, like the light at the end of a long tunnel. "One could be heading right this way now."

Kenny scoffed and rolled over onto his side. "Doubt it. So what's the plan for today?"

Todd shrugged. "I dunno. Hiking? Supposed to be cool, I think. In the sixties, maybe."

Kenny nodded. The brothers were silent for a moment, and then Kenny's face lit up.

"Let's look for the vortex. We can hike there."

"The what, now?"

"The vortex. Well, paranormal researchers would probably call it a vortex, but it's not—not in the traditional sense. It's more of a chasm."

"Uh, meaning what? What's the difference?" Todd frowned at him. Already he didn't like where this was going.

"Well, a vortex is usually, like, a portal to the spirit world, right? A place where the veil between life and death is thin or torn through. Could be magnetic forces, pockets of gases coming up out of the ground, or hell, just people tripping their asses off. Damned if I know. But there are usually reports of all kinds of stuff near a vortex—ghosts, UFOs and little gray men, eerie lights."

"That sounds like a lot of bullshit," Todd said. It didn't, though. Not here in these woods, with the trees leaning in to listen and the heaviness of the air breathing down his back.

"No more than your bouncing black holes," Kenny went on with a sideways grin. "I'm just saying this isn't a vortex like that. None of that stuff the websites or even those old folks in the diner were talking about. It's a different experience. It's—Don't look at me like that, man. I'm serious. It's just this place in the woods where they say the land started to go bad. Makes people see things, hear things. Makes people do things, too. Crazy shit, man."

"I didn't know you were into that paranormal shit," Todd said. He was stalling. The more his brother talked, the worse an idea hiking out there seemed.

Kenny shrugged and looked away. "Didn't say I was. But I've heard a few things. From . . . friends. Friends of friends."

"Oh yeah? Who?"

"No one you'd know." He had an odd, flustered expression on his face, a look unused to being there. "Figured it might be something to do to kill a few hours, at least."

Todd raised an eyebrow. There was more to that story, whatever it was, but he wasn't sure he wanted to know the rest, and Kenny clearly wasn't interested in volunteering it. It did suggest, though, that maybe Kenny knew more about the nature of this place than he had let on.

Kenny continued. "They say it's a hole, like this little chasm—"

"I thought you said it was a vortex."

"I did. Psychic vortex. Physical chasm. Try to keep up." Kenny knocked the glowing head off the tiny remains of the joint and poked at it until it went out. "So what do you say? The Nilhollow vortex-chasm?"

"I don't know."

"It's just a hike."

"From the middle of nowhere to . . . deeper into the middle of nowhere. Why are you so dead set on going?"

Kenny squinted at him through a ray of sun. It cast an odd expression over his features. "Why are you so dead set against it? Scared?"

Todd scoffed. "I'm not afraid of a hole in the ground."

"Okay, then. So strap on your balls and let's go."

A low whine echoed through the trees as the brothers squared off. Todd could tell that even though Kenny would never admit it, he felt as strongly about going as Todd felt about the wrongness of those woods, though he couldn't imagine why Kenny cared so much. Nevertheless, the dynamic with Todd and his brother had always been that the desire to act always seemed to overrule an inaction, whether the motives were shared or explained or not, so finally, Todd agreed.

"Well, let's go then," he said to Kenny, gesturing off toward a wild and pathless tangle of woods. "You're wasting daylight."

Kenny grinned. Todd couldn't tell whether it was relief, excitement, or nervous energy that flooded his brother's features. It may have been a little of all three.

Todd found that as they got ready to go, his anxiety about their surroundings began to wane. For that, he was glad. He supposed the distraction of actually doing something, of taking charge of himself in his environment, restored some sense of control. They yanked on their hiking boots and loaded up their backpacks with water, Power-Bars, knives, and other essentials, secured their food in a bundle that they hung from a nearby high tree branch, and then headed away from the campsite. By the time they'd gotten their sleeping bags rolled up and bundled inside the tent, he found he was even kind of looking forward to finding his brother's ghost chasm, or whatever it was supposed to be.

"You know," Kenny said with a grin as he led the way down a sloping path toward some shadowed underbrush, "some say this chasm bounces. It's like your black hole, right here on earth."

Todd laughed, shoving his brother lightly. "Yeah, whatever. A magical, bouncing black hole in the ground."

Kenny shrugged, the mirth suddenly gone from his features. "That's what they say."

"So how do you know how to find it?" Todd asked.

Kenny glanced back at his brother with a knowing smile. "Those friends I mentioned."

Todd shook his head. "Still think this is bullshit," he muttered, but Kenny didn't answer.

For a while, the only sound was the crunching of the underbrush beneath their feet and of Kenny humming softly out of tune to himself; they'd gone off-trail through a dense expanse of pines, and the deeper they went, the more it seemed Kenny was going out of his way to find the hardest route to get there. It was maybe half an hour or so in before it occurred to Todd that Kenny was leading them without a GPS or map. He seemed to know exactly where to go, as convoluted as it was. At least, Todd hoped his brother knew where he was going. He'd mentioned those friends again, but Todd knew most of Kenny's friends from school and around the old neighborhood. He'd never heard any of them talk about the Pine Barrens, let alone Nilhollow. Furthermore, he couldn't imagine even the combined brainpower of any of those potheads could provide so detailed a set of directions to such a remote location that Kenny would be able to find it without a map or compass or anything. So who were the friends, exactly, with such intimate knowledge of the place? Todd was just about to ask him when they broke through into a small clearing littered with dead pine needles and cones. Kenny stopped short and Todd, who had been watching the unfamiliar ground beneath his feet to avoid a spill, nearly plowed into him.

"What?" he asked, waiting.

Kenny exhaled with what seemed to Todd to be a mixture of relief, satisfaction, and awe, and dropped his backpack.

"Here it is," he said with uncharacteristic reverence. "The Nilhollow Chasm."

The Nilhollow Chasm wasn't a hole, exactly; it was more of a jagged tear in the earth. As they approached, Todd saw that it only ran about six or seven feet long and was no more than three feet wide. Peering in, though, he suspected it ran pretty deep—so deep, in fact, that beyond the jutting rocks and tumbles of dirt was nothing but black. He thought that if he were to drop a quarter down there, he might never hear it hit the bottom. That idea was followed immediately and inexplicably by the thought that if he were to drop anything down there, something from beneath the earth might very well reach up and grab his arm, sinking shining black claws into his skin and muscle, and drag him in. He might never find himself hitting bottom, either.

It was a crazy thought. Stupid. Still, he took a step back from the edge.

"So," Kenny said, spreading out his arms to indicate the breadth of the area. He stood right on the cusp of the chasm, inhaling that stale air deeply. "What do you think?"

Todd looked around. At first, nothing struck him as being any stranger than where they'd set up camp. When he looked closer, though, he saw it—a subtle difference in the healthiness, the *natural-ness* of the surrounding flora, as if the essence of Nilhollow's weird-ness started right where they stood. Along the circumference of the clearing, the branches of the trees grew twisted in painfully odd an-gles, with most of the bark a rot-gray color. The pines and oaks there were sparser, an odd, washed-out gray-green not indicative of life or vitality but rather of illness or poison. That was the impression they left on Todd—a kind of unwholesomeness, a landscape barely able to fight through its strangled existence. The surrounding brush was strange, too. Had they just tramped through all that? How hadn't he noticed how . . . *infected* everything looked? The thin grass, pale yel-low in some places and nearly colorless in others, clung to the ground in clumps like fists determined to claw their way to that chasm. From beds of desiccated ferns, odd thorny bushes grew, black and talon sharp. There were no sounds of bugs or birds, no frogs, no crunching of leaves beneath anonymous hooves or paws. There was nothing but a silence heavy with expectation, a silence so dense as to almost be a low hum. It seemed as much inside his head as out, a heavy, cottony feeling that dulled his thoughts. He felt tamped down, in a way. Run through. He swayed a little where he stood, aware in the periphery of his mind that something . . . someone . . . something had changed. It hurt his head, though, to try to focus, to bring any kind of sharper awareness to himself and his surroundings.

The low hum seemed to be getting louder. It sounded to him vaguely like the churning up of something, a kind of atavistic crunch-ing and turning over of living things into oblivion. And beneath that, there were windy whispers that clotted his ears. In the whispers, he thought he heard a myriad of voices, anxious and insistent.

That faint death smell was stronger here.

Todd was sure in that moment, standing there, feet away from that narrow chasm with the hairs on his arms and the back of his neck on end, that whatever was wrong with Nilhollow had originated in there, in the clearing. In the chasm.

That was when Kenny turned on him, and with a grim smile, buried the sharp end of a stick about an inch or so into Todd's shoul-der.

Todd staggered back, as much in surprise as in pain. The sight of his own blood made him feel a little queasy. "Ken, what the fu—"

Kenny punched him in the mouth. His eyes flashed wildly, turned entirely black and shining for just a moment, and then returned with a murderous fervor. "You arrogant, ungrateful son of a bitch," he snarled.

A flood of anger replaced the pain in Todd's jaw. "Dick," he said, a trickle of blood dripping from the corner of his mouth. He swung at Kenny, landing a blow squarely on his brother's eye. Kenny tumbled back and then, tripping over a root, fell on his ass. His hand slid toward the edge of the chasm in a spray of pebbles that tumbled into the darkness. He looked up at Todd with a dazed expression, as if awaking in a strange bedroom. The fire in his eyes was gone.

"What the hell is wrong with you?" Todd swayed where he stood. The blood trickling down his arm was getting sticky. He swiped at it with the hem of his T-shirt and grabbed the stick. The slightest pull sent electric sparks of pain through the length of his arm.

"Why'd you hit me?" Kenny mumbled. "What—what happened to your arm?"

Todd gaped at him. "Are you kidding me? You—you fucking stabbed me and then punched me in the face. What the fuck you been smoking this morning, huh?"

"What? No. I-it wasn't me," Kenny said. "It wasn't—it was—"

Todd flopped down in front of him. Kenny was sweating profusely, his skin flushed. His injured eye had grown quickly and alarmingly bloodshot. It was swelling to a waxy red. Todd frowned, feeling a little guilty. He hadn't thought he'd hit Kenny so hard. "What the hell's going on, bro? You okay?"

"What time is it?" Kenny asked absently. "Where's the car?" He retched and turned suddenly on his side, vomiting onto the grass. What came out of him was clear and kind of jellylike, with threads of loosely clotted blood, and it smoked as it hit the ground.

"Oh my God, oh my God. What the fuck?" Todd dropped to his knees and put a hand on his brother's shoulder with the intent of helping him up. "We've gotta go, man, get you help—"

"No."

"Look, you're sick or something, Ken—"

"No!" Kenny's voice dropped to a growl Todd had never heard before. Kenny rolled onto his back and glared up at him. "I'm fine." His eyes closed for several seconds as Todd gaped, then he opened the uninjured one. When he did, there was nothing in it that Todd recognized as his brother.

They regarded each other for a moment, breathing heavily. Todd was aware that the cottony feeling in his head had dissipated a little, but not enough for rational planning. The car . . . yeah, getting to the car would be good. But where had they parked it? For that matter, where was the campsite? Hell, where had their backpacks gone? And what time *was* it, after all? He thought he might be hungry . . . or maybe thirsty; he couldn't tell which. As he rose to his feet, he absently tried to pull out the stick again, but fresh fireworks of agony set him off in a flurry of oaths.

Kenny coughed and sat up. There was blood on his chin. The emptiness in his un-swollen eye, the hollowness of his whole expression, unnerved Todd.

The heavy earth scent of old, wet leaves rotting filled Todd's nose and throat as he breathed in, and he started coughing, too. "Ken, something's wrong here. We gotta go—"

Kenny leaned forward as if to get to his feet, but stopped. He looked up at Todd in surprise. At first, Todd couldn't wrap his mind around what his eyes were seeing. A root or vine from the depths of the chasm behind Kenny had wrapped itself tightly around his arm. The flesh beneath was already bright red and a little shiny. Kenny clawed at it with his free hand. It took another root snaking up from the chasm and wrapping itself around Kenny's waist before Todd was jarred to action. He dove for Kenny's free arm and pulled. Kenny's grip on his own arm felt like a steel vise, and Todd had the crazy notion that his brother's fingers would punch right through to his muscle. He pulled. Kenny's eyes were wide. His mouth gaped open, but no sound came out. Another vine had wrapped around his neck and was now working its way down Kenny's throat. His face was bright pink, and he'd begun to make little gagging sounds. From his pocket, Todd snatched the pocket knife he always carried and flicked it open, immediately going to work on the vines. He stabbed and sawed, stabbed and sawed, and finally broke through the one on Kenny's neck. It burst open in a spray of that same clear jelly that had been in Kenny's stomach. It splattered on Todd's face and he flinched; it reeked of rotting leaves and bad earth, and it burned a little on his skin.

The moment of distraction gave the vines a chance to yank Kenny nearly out of Todd's grasp, but he clasped his brother's hand at the last moment and held tightly. Todd sank the blade of his knife up to the handle in a vine that was working its way toward his ankle, and the vine jerked back, then whip-lashed his face. The sting across his eye socket was immense; his vision blurred and Todd lost his grip on Kenny. He fell onto his back just as another vine whipped along the other side of his face, splitting his lip and biting into his cheek. In the next moment, Todd was aware that his mouth felt too large, somehow lopsided. The blood that spilled down his neck confirmed the tear at the corner of his mouth into the meat of his face.

Then Kenny started screaming.

And that, thought Todd as he lay dazed on his back, seemed surreal. His brother shouldn't have been able to scream. The remnants of the vine around and down his throat should have made it impossible to get enough air. He shouldn't have been able to scream. The thought played in a mental loop, eclipsing the horror in front of him. He shouldn't have been able to scream, but there it was, an ungodly wail, a howling whine that broke through the haze in his head and the pain in his face and body until Todd understood.

It wasn't Kenny screaming. It was whatever was below him, in the chasm.

The vine around Kenny's waist yanked him backward toward the yawning maw in the ground—and it did seem to yawn, or at least to waver in width as Todd watched it. Kenny's eyes, still wide, now looked glazed over, as if whatever had been behind them was winking out. The vine jerked him back again, and this time, Kenny's ass disappeared in the hole. It looked to Todd like Kenny was sitting in an inner tube, floating down the grass on that hot summer morning, and the absurdity of the comparison made him laugh—just a bark before the pain from the jagged flaps of his torn face put an end to that. The good side of Todd's mouth was turned up in a smirk, though, as Kenny sank through that imagined doughnut-hole of inner tube, his knees smacking against his chest. Kenny made no move to reach out to him, but a flicker of understanding registered in his eyes before they glazed over again. They didn't close, and somehow, that made Todd want to giggle, too.

The vine that was wrapped around Kenny's arm gave a sharp

yank and Kenny toppled sideways, a spray of blood painting his face before that, too, disappeared down the gap in the earth. His other arm flipped up in an exaggerated good-bye wave before the Nilhollow Chasm finally swallowed Kenny whole.

At that point, Todd did start laughing despite the pain—long, loud brays of harsh, dry laughter that eventually became crying.

TWO

The last of the police reports that Julia Russo filed against her ex-boyfriend, Darren, was right before she got lost in the woods.

If anyone had told her at twenty that her taste in men was only going to get worse over the next decade and a half, she might have laughed it off, at least outwardly. In her own mind, though, it wouldn't have surprised her. She had never had good luck spotting what others called "red flags." She'd come to think of those little odd and sometimes jarring behaviors in other people, particularly in men she dated, as simply personality quirks, many of which she made an effort to accept for a number of reasons.

For one, Julia's parents had long drilled into her head that she was not perfect—far from it, in fact. Each day had been an inevitable catalog of all Julia's personality flaws, everything from the way she did her hair (a shoulder-length face-frame of shining black with a dip always over her eye) to the way she dressed (things that were too tight, too short, or too low-cut). She was, at times, too thin or too chubby. Her job as a corporate administrative assistant was a dead end. Her apartment was a disaster. Her sense of time was nearly nonexistent. Her parents' list of her shortcomings was quite extensive, and it drilled into her the idea that if she wasn't perfect and yet still wanted to be loved, the very least she could do was try to accept the flaws of others. *Give what you want to receive*, she'd heard once, and it seemed like a pretty good general rule to live by.

She also didn't much care for confronting people about how those quirks affected her, another lesson she'd learned from her parents. To voice a concern, to stand up for herself, to offer a constructive criticism, all met with icy silence followed by a cold shoulder. Confrontation was another surefire way to lose affection.

The irony of her parent's criticism of her love life, she'd come to realize, was that they had driven her eventually to date Darren, someone as critical and prone to withhold love as they were. Darren, who at first had seemed so completely opposite her parents—so nurturing and loving and patient, so enamored with all the unique qualities that defined her, so very attracted to her looks and physique.

Darren, who had spray-painted *WHORE* across her garage door while she was out with her old college roommate in a noisy restaurant one night, because he had called her six times and she never heard the phone. Darren, who had once tried to burn her hands by holding them tightly against a mug full of hot coffee.

Darren, who'd received the restraining order and then buried an ax in her front door.

Their relationship had been strained for a long time, probably longer than Julia had truly realized. It had only been maybe three or four months into the relationship before the first of the quirks appeared. These came in the form of mildly critical and condescending comments toward her and disdain of her relationships with others. He didn't quite call her fat, but he'd shake his head and comment that it was a good thing he was so accepting of her body and the weight he saw she'd gained. He didn't outright accuse her of cheating, but he'd get so mad when he even thought she was looking at someone else, or paying too much attention to another man at a party. His tone of voice, his implications and suggestions, and his disapproving looks said far more about his thinking her stupid than any name-calling could. And those things made her second-guess her own words and actions. She began to watch everything she ate, even when he wasn't around. She watched what she said, avoided eye contact with most men, even watched how she dressed. Suddenly, all her endearing quirks had come to annoy him, as they inevitably did everyone, she supposed. She was, after all, flawed, and maybe she wasn't quite seeing the impropriety of her behavior. Maybe she was letting herself go. Maybe she really *was* embarrassing herself, and him, too. She tried to be more on top of her looks, more conservative and tasteful in her dress, more thoughtful and sensitive to his needs, more careful, more observant of how she conducted herself. She tried to be more.

It wasn't enough, and over time, she let him convince her that she had changed, as all women eventually change, revealing their shallow self-centeredness, their capacity, like feral and predatory things, to lie and manipulate their way into men's beds and wallets. All women, he told her, were that way underneath. It was a survival mechanism to be so, because they were essentially weak and worthless. They wanted men to think for them, take care of them, put them on pedestals, but that only gave them a sense of entitlement to run roughshod over everybody and everything.

Apparently, to Darren, she was no exception, though she tried so hard to be. She just kept screwing up. It took time and patience he didn't have with her to learn all his rules, and when she did, those rules seemed to arbitrarily change. She just couldn't quite get the hang of preventing his anger and disapproval, and that seemed to prove to him what an immoral, broken, conniving, weak, flawed creature she must be—despite the little voice in her head telling her that *he* was the one who had changed.

Sometimes he could be outright cruel, displaying an unpredictable and upsetting streak of heartlessness that the little voice desperately pleaded with her to see as more than just a quirk. However, he hadn't been outright abusive—at least, she had not truly recognized the behavior as such. He just lost his temper sometimes. He yelled in her face, pushed her around a little, shoved her into walls and furniture, grabbed her arm too tight—but he didn't hit her.

Until the day he did. She didn't like to think about it. The day it happened, she knew that she had to get out of that relationship. She might have been accommodating to a fault, but that had been too much to accept. She mustered up all the pride she had left and told him it was over. In only two days, she had deleted his number from her phone, mailed back whatever stuff he'd left at her apartment, and threw away anything she could find that reminded her of him. She felt nothing during the process except the sting of self-reproach and the echo of pain from his fist against her face.

That was how she was, how she'd always been: Julia wasn't oblivious to other people's flaws, only too tolerant of them, and for too long. She accepted quirks until they weren't quirks but acts of betrayal. Once that line was crossed, enough was enough and then she accepted nothing about the person anymore. That decision was usually final. It certainly was with Darren; she didn't need anyone, least of all the little voice in her head, to tell her that a punch in the mouth was a slingshot from the land of quirks to outright abuse. She was done with Darren for good, and she told him so, then made it clear there was not and would not be anything else to say on the matter.

That was when he went from unpleasant to scary.

There were the phone calls, which she let her voice mail pick up. Sometimes the messages would be sweet and loving, achingly so. In those messages, he reminded her so much of the man she had started dating, the man who always told her how pretty she was, how smart and talented she was. He told her he missed her and loved her, that he thought about her all the time, that he'd made a mistake, many of them. But there were other messages, sometimes during the same week or even on the same day, that were left in a different tone entirely. In those messages, she was a worthless bitch, useless for everything but the hole between her legs. She was a heartbreaking, soul-crushing cunt, and he should have known better than to trust anything that can bleed for a week every month and not *die*. In those messages, he swore he'd hurt everyone who ever was or got close to her—family, friends, coworkers, and especially anyone she slept with . . .

After she changed her number, the emails got worse. In between ranting screeds about her, he signed her up for spam, porn, even dating sites. She didn't understand his reasoning regarding the dating sites at first, but when she started getting strange visits from men, claiming they'd found her profile on a rape-simulations fetish site, she started to get it. That genuinely scared her. It had been hell trying to convince the site to take down her profile, but threats of lawyers finally put an end to the sluttyslave69 account, and the passage of a few weeks ended the visits from strange men.

Still, the damage was done. She began checking obsessively four or five times a night before bed to make sure that the doors and windows were locked. She pulled the curtains shut during the day as well as at night. She seldom went out after dark, and when she did, she made a security guard or a coworker walk her to her car. She slept with a letter opener under her pillow and a small kitchen knife just beneath her bed.

The police told her they couldn't do much except to take down her statement and file a report. Stalking laws were nebulous at best, and the local police were ill equipped and minimally trained to handle those sorts of things. There were no threats, after all—no damage to property, no physical violence. She hadn't kept the voice mails—

just seeing his name listed in her Missed Calls made her feel a little queasy. And they told her it would take some time just to prove the emails were actually coming from Darren.

When the phone calls and emails had begun to die off, next came the gifts. "Gifts" was the word the police used, but to Julia, they were anything but. The flowers maybe were, the living ones, with the note which read, "I'm sorry" in his tight, sharp little script. The dead flowers came with notes, too—little things like "I'm watching," "He won't protect you, bitch," and finally, "They're as dead as you are." After that last note, the police finally started taking her seriously. They went out to visit him and tell him to knock it off.

And then Darren became really dangerous.

Julia couldn't quite say she felt better as she drove home from the police station that afternoon. She wanted to; she wanted to believe that the cops would go out to his house or his job at the investment firm and arrest him this time instead of just scold him at the door. She had often lain in bed fantasizing about the police cuffing him in front of that insufferably protective mother of his, or his coworkers, some big show where people would finally be forced to see the monster beneath his polished veneer. She wanted to believe Detective Colby's reassurances that Darren would be in custody by the end of the day.

However, there had been too many times where Darren had slipped like a thief through some loophole or other, had paid a fee she couldn't dream of affording, and been let go with a warning. Detective Colby said none of that was a waste, that it was all a cumulative means to an end, and Julia did believe the detective honestly felt sympathy toward her and wanted to help. However, it often seemed that all Julia's efforts to protect herself from Darren's growing anger and frustration were met with an uptick in those violent emotions that meant harassment, nightmares, sleepless nights . . . and more gifts.

The dead rats laid out in the shape of a heart on her driveway.

The slashes in her tires, filled with bent nails.

The pig blood splashed all over the windshield of her car. *Where did a guy like Darren even find so much pig blood?*

When she bought the security camera, he moved out of view, leaving her a hole dug in the vacant lot across the street, shallow but wide enough for a body, with a crude wooden cross jabbed into the ground at the head of it. In permanent marker, he'd scrawled her name, her birth date, and that day's date.

All were violations of the restraining order. All of them he'd done just outside the range of the security camera.

But then he'd buried the ax in her front door . . . and she caught him on the security video doing it.

Each prior time, the police came out to look at what he'd done, took pictures and samples for evidence, carefully marked and packaged and removed everything, then hauled her in to file another report. They needed hard evidence, they told her, which could take time. Fingerprints, a hair, a fiber—anything. Julia honestly believed that at that point, they wanted a reason to put Darren away as much as she did. And when Julia called to tell them she'd finally caught Darren in the act, her triumph overshadowed by fear and frustration, Detective Colby was probably more excited than she was. She'd come in with the tape, as he asked, and he'd looked fit to do a jig right there in the office. They'd get him this time, and she would be safe. Free.

God, she hoped so.

As she turned onto Mt. Misery Pasadena Road, she wondered what, exactly, she could have done differently to make Darren leave her alone. She was pretty sure that despite his voice messages to the contrary, it wasn't *she* who was sending mixed signals. She didn't quite understand why he so fiercely wanted to hold on to her. Why couldn't he just let her go? It seemed that he had bled his obsession into every facet of her life. Everywhere she was, everything she did, his presence overshadowed it all.

She was still navigating the fog of these thoughts when a car pulled out behind her. She noticed that he was tailgating her, but it was immediately relegated to the same secondary sub-compartment of her mind that other road conditions were. She didn't recognize the car, a bronze-colored Honda CR-V, and so didn't pay all that much attention to the driver—not until he backed off, slowed down, then sped up enough to hit her car hard, jarring her bones and sending her drifting off onto the shoulder of the road. She tugged on the wheel to right herself, and pulled over, shaken. She was about to get out of the car and confer with the driver on the damage when a glimpse of him in the rearview mirror froze her.

The man who sat behind the wheel of the Honda looked a hell of a lot like Darren. It was hard to be sure beneath the tinted band along the top of the windshield and the dark sunglasses he wore, but Julia recognized that grim, joyless smile, that hostile drumming on the steering wheel by hands that wanted to hurt something, that lock of black hair and the way he tossed it off his face.

It was Darren; she was sure of it in her soul. She started the car again. Before she could pull out onto the road again, though, he floored the gas and rear-ended her, then backed up slightly and slammed into her car again. She heard the ugly whine of metal bending and denting, and the crunch of broken glass as Darren backed up, preparing to hit her again.

The impact in her bones right down to her teeth was nothing compared to the cold sweat on her skin and the sick ball of fear in her stomach. What the hell was he up to?

She jerked the wheel and stepped on the gas pedal, and the car lurched back onto the road. He wanted her to panic and get out of the car, but she wouldn't do it. He could run her over, leave her broken and bleeding on the side of the road, just a mangled piece of debris. Or maybe he had a gun and was planning on shooting her the moment she was free of the car and in range . . .

His rage was different this time; she knew it—could feel it as surely and jarringly in her bones as when he'd hit her car. He wasn't just planning to punch her this time. He was going to obliterate her. She forced herself to take deep breaths until the need to vomit slowly passed.

Julia pumped the gas again, and the car made a rattling noise like something was loose somewhere, but it kept moving forward. A hard thud jerked her head and neck forward painfully, and her car skidded across the oncoming traffic lane onto the far shoulder. For a moment, she felt helpless, picked up and carried by a wave of grinding metal. Then the car rolled over something and huffed as if exasperated by all this trouble. Julia wasn't great with cars, but she was pretty sure that sound of displeasure meant that something had punctured her tire. She was tempted to power down the window and peer out, but the thought of Darren taking aim at her and her head exploding like a melon all over the side of her car kept her from doing so.

Julia realized then that she should have called the police the moment she thought she recognized Darren behind her, or from the very first ramming of his car into hers at least, but frankly, she had been too surprised to think straight. Sure, Darren had a bad temper, and he was clearly not above crude and threatening little acts of vandalism to scare her into coming back to him. But this was much more intimate, more hands-on, and it had all just seemed so surreal. The idea that someone she had been so vulnerable and intimate with could be capable of such violent anger toward her made that sickness in her core spread to her head and limbs. What had gone so terribly wrong?

She pulled her purse onto her lap and rifled through the small pocket in the front. She had her cell phone out and had dialed nine and one when the shattering of glass made her scream. She flinched away from the shards as they rained in on her. When she finally dared to look up, Darren stood by the jagged remnants of the driver's-side window. With one hand, he reached through the broken window and grabbed her cell phone, which he dropped to the ground and stepped on as she watched. In the other hand, he had an ax.

He has an ax.

She gaped for a minute, mostly at the ax, still unable to convince herself this was really happening.

"Why?" she asked him, though no more than the shape of the word formed on her lips. No sound came out. Then she looked him in the eyes.

There was no real outward display of anger or hatred, but there was nothing even remotely resembling the spark of love or understanding, either, or even the simple flicker of humanity. His eyes were dead spaces, twin voids. There was no Darren in there—not the man she'd fallen in love with, certainly, but not even the man he'd become those last few weeks. That Darren was still human, however flawed and unbalanced. What drove this version of him from the seat of his mind was something else.

His expression never changed. He looked perfectly calm. His mouth was a thin fault line in the placid geography of his face. His eyebrows were neither knitted nor arched. He was not breathing heavily. He wasn't showing signs that any of this was affecting him at all. If he had, she might have entertained some hope of pleading with him.

He opened the driver's door—she hadn't thought to lock it in all the confusion—and grabbed her arm, yanking her out of the car with her purse still clutched tightly to her. His grip was inescapable, though, the muscles straining like a bundle of steel cables in his arm.

The world blurred for a moment and in the next, she was on the ground with the wind knocked out of her. He balanced the ax against his shoulder and took a few steps toward her. The thought that crossed her mind was that he was going to chop her up. He didn't want her body identified, so he was going to dismember her. He wanted her to rot right there at the edge of the woods, with wild animals carrying away whatever pieces were left. She felt sick.

He hadn't spoken a word, and that scared the hell out of her—so much so that when he hoisted the ax over his head, it took her a few seconds to react. She heard the sharp voice of the wind zipping around the blade as it sliced through the air toward her, and that, more than anything, sent her rolling out of the way. She came to a stop near some bushes and felt something soft like skin against her arm. She turned and discovered her arm was still tangled in the long, thin strap of her purse. Julia considered for a moment swinging the purse at him, trying to trip him up or throw him off balance, but it wasn't quite big enough or heavy enough for that. She pulled it to her anyway, gripping it like a medieval flail, and scrambled backwards into the brush.

He was coming toward her. She clumsily got to her feet and took off into the woods. Then he finally spoke.

"Julia," he called. "I'm going to kill you. Chop you down like a tree." And apparently, this thought struck him as incredibly funny, as he burst out laughing in a way that Julia had never heard before— mean, exaggerated laughter that sounded ugly, echoing, and hollow.

She broke through the brush onto a dirt animal path and took off running, doing her best to dodge the occasional rock or root jutting from the ground, or branch reaching out to whack her in the face. She heard great, heaving breaths behind her, which, given Darren's workout habits, seemed exaggerated for her benefit. She also heard the occasional thump as Darren swung the ax into a tree, followed by a grunt and a laugh as he pulled it free again. After a few minutes, he gave up the big-bad-wolf huffing and puffing and began to hum. She didn't recognize the song, but the way his voice ricocheted between the trees made her intensely uneasy.

Julia slowed, gasping for breath herself. She'd never been much of a runner, partly due to teenage years smoking cigarettes and partly to shin splints, and she didn't think she was built for much more sprinting through the woods. She considered her options: He could follow her easily as long as she stayed on the path, just as she could follow well-known and well-worn hiking trails.

Or she could take her chances in the woods. The supposedly haunted woods.

Was he still following her? Surely even Darren had to know this was crazy. Maybe he had just meant to scare her. Maybe he was already back at his car and ready to drive off, and it was enough to leave her terrified and lost in the woods. Or . . . maybe he was closing the distance between them, creeping between the trees like a hunter. *Or a crazed lumberjack*, she thought, followed by the Monty Python lumberjack song lyrics running through her head, and she fought hysterical laughter of her own.

"Julia! Julia, you beautiful slut. Come back."

So he hadn't left, then. Her stomach turned. He began humming again. She had no idea which direction it was coming from.

She had to pull it together, and quick. She was in the Nilhollow area; she knew that much. It was mostly unmapped wilderness, so far as she was aware. That meant potentially not great circumstances for her, but it also meant not great circumstances for Darren, either. She could disappear.

Disappear. The word rolled around her mind. The state park's forest area was huge. She very well *could* disappear.

"Julia, you're making me angry. Come back, now. Let's talk, okay? Hurry up. Chop chop." His voice exploded in another fit of laughter. "Chop chop!" She didn't dare turn around, but he sounded closer than she had hoped.

Taking a deep breath, she veered off the path and into the woods. She had managed to crunch and crash her way through several feet of dense ferns and other brush when a root caught her toe and she fell face-first into what she assumed was a thicket. She lay there, tears blurring her vision and blazing hot trails down her cheeks, breathing hard but as quietly as she could, and suddenly felt angry. The anger eclipsed her fear and her hurt, both physically and emotionally. It swallowed up everything. This situation was fucked a hundred ways to Sunday, as her police friend Pete's partner, Vince Perry, always said, but she'd be damned if she was going to lie there like a wounded deer, mewling until he found her and hacked her to pieces.

It was the first time it occurred to her that maybe she should kill

Darren. Just kill him and be done with him and all the trouble he caused. It was not that the idea of Darren simply disappearing, going to jail, or delightfully dying of a heart attack hadn't occurred to her during those endless days of frustrated helplessness—it sure had. This time, though, she seriously considered that she might have to do it herself, in self-defense if it came to that, and the idea made her feel both numb and strong at the same time. Maybe not here and now, while she had the disadvantage of being weaponless, but maybe someday. It was an odd feeling, like the breaking of something inside her—or the sprouting of something new—and she couldn't quite say she disliked it.

Julia rolled under a thick clump of ferns and waited, listening.

For a long time, all she heard was the occasional snap of a branch. She couldn't attribute any of the noises to Darren for sure. Maybe he finally had given up and gone away. She hoped he had, but she knew him better than that.

Then she caught a whiff of his cologne on a passing breeze; it instantly brought a welling of mixed feelings that she wrangled and forced down. He was close. She also thought she could smell the moist, sickly sweetness of sweat on her own skin, and wondered if Darren could, as well. Her heart pounded silently in her ears. She closed her eyes, held her breath, and waited.

"Julia," he called. He sounded like he was still on the path, maybe looking for her footsteps or some other indication of the direction in which she'd gone. "Julia, you bitch! You're really pissing me off now. Where the fuck are you?"

She willed the ferns around her to cover her, to hide her away from him. Acutely aware of every breath, every heartbeat, she tried to determine whether the crunching sound of footsteps was moving closer or farther away.

How many times had she been just like this, keeping her breaths shallow, avoiding his wrath, hoping he'd just get tired of terrorizing her and go away? How many times had she hoped the earth would swallow her up, just so she could get away from him? Tears escaped the tightly shut lids of her eyes, but she didn't dare move even so much as to wipe them away. It had often been like this, she realized—to lesser degrees, sure, but most of her relationship, most of her time, had been wasted in this very same kind of dynamic. She had been afraid of him, afraid of what he'd say or do, enough to pull away just a little, but not enough to break from the ground on which he wished to keep her. Ever since the police station, she'd been wondering how things had come to this, how things could possibly have escalated to such disastrous proportions. She had been a fool, she realized, swallowing the lump of bitterness in her throat, to have thought her relationship with Darren had been anything else than a steady coast downhill to where she was right now.

His next words, mumbled cursing, seemed right above her head. She was sure he must be able to see hear, or at least hear her heart, her breathing, *something*. To her surprise, however, the footsteps seemed to be retreating. Her shallow breaths caught in her chest. Was he . . . ? Yes! Finally, he was moving away from her. She said a silent thank-you to whatever forces in the universe might be listening as first his mumbling, then his movements, faded to silence.

She didn't move, though—not yet. She didn't want to do anything to bring him back. In fact, she wasn't sure she could move, even if she wanted to. It was warm under those ferns and peaceful, and for the first time in a very long time, she felt . . . well, not quite *safe*, not out there where he could come back and find her, or she could be stepped on by some bear or something. But she felt she was where she belonged at that moment, where she ought to be. The danger had passed. She had won. She would just stay there, then, for a few minutes and wait for her heart to slow down and her breathing to right itself. She was okay now . . . not a lumberjack, ha ha, but she was okay. She felt very tired, her limbs weighed down by the trauma of the day, so she closed her eyes. Just for a few minutes, she'd rest her eyes. She was okay. She was okay . . .

She fell asleep with the ferns above shielding her eyes from the rays of the setting sun, and dreamed of being watched over by eyes formed in the shapes among leaves, her hair stroked by tree branch-fingers. In the dreams, finally, she felt safe.

While Julia slept, the *manëtuwàk* watched the ax-wielding one stalking through the woods. He was an angry, howling beast, a thing as yet untouched by Nilhollow and already riddled with the same blood-hate and insanity as anything that lived in its depths. For that reason, he fascinated them a little. Out of curiosity at first more than anything, the *manëtuwàk* protected the sleeping one, shielding her from the other's notice to see what he would do, but what he did was swing that abominable ax, sinking it into the flesh of their trees and carelessly wrenching it free, then cursing the wilderness.

All the while, the *manëtuwàk* grew angrier and angrier.

It was their anger that finally wore through the last of their bonds. They felt good to be free, and more alive than they had in a very long time. The Kèkpëchehëlat still slept, but *they* could wander the whole of Nilhollow. They could reclaim their *tèkëne*, all of it—the trees, the grass, the ferns. And they could focus their full attention on the new ax-wielding one cutting into their trees.

They rustled the branches above the narrow path excitedly, moving on the breeze along the forest's undergrowth, converging around the ax-wielding one as he stomped, angry and directionless, along the path. He alternated between muttering and occasionally shouting in his odd, ugly language, and fuming silently.

He stopped, seeming to listen or perhaps sniff the air for signs of danger. He could sense them, just like deer had sensed the far-moving ones of long ago, but it didn't mean he could escape them. He turned suddenly, staring through them, unable to see more than suggestions of their faces and limbs in the leaf cover above or the waving fronds of ferns so close now to his legs. They were not strong enough to take a physical form just yet; they were still weak from having been held down for so long and because the Chasm was not nearby. However, they were not so weak that they couldn't shift the direction of the path so that when he turned back around, it was heading off even farther away from the sleeping one.

The ax-wielding one frowned, clutching his weapon more tightly. He moved farther down the newly drawn path, and they followed behind. They managed to shift the path again, clearing and redrawing it at only just the periphery of his notice, and he kept following it, deeper into Nilhollow, closer to the clearing where the Chasm was. They could feel him acutely, a foreign, almost unnatural thing among them with his seething hate, his desire to kill the one he thought of as "the bitch," whatever that meant. He was like the Chasm and yet not like it, and it was whispered between them, over his head among the foliage of the towering trees, that maybe they should just push him in and let whatever had split the earth in the first place deal with him. He had already ceased to be a source of fascination, and had become a rather intense beacon for their enmity. The pine trees bristled at his approach. The cedars and oaks rustled in hostile anticipation.

Every so often, he would turn around as if he could feel them, could hear the meaning in the words they whispered in the wind. Perhaps he could; some of his kind were more susceptible to sensing the *manëtuwàk*, particularly since the opening of the Chasm. It was shortly after one of these pauses where he scanned the tree line around him that the ax-wielding one stepped off the path without realizing it. More accurately, the path had been swept away beneath his feet, and he seemed not to notice that he now clomped through the sticks and roots.

The *manëtuwàk* leaned in closer, scratching at his face with thin, woody fingers, catching up his clothes, toying with him. They chose to move cautiously, so long as he still held the ax. They suspected that even in their state, it might be able to hurt them, as it had in the past. From time to time, he buried it in a tree and the *manëtuwàk*, now able to feel as well as move, cried out. With the intensity of their connections to the trees restored, their collective rage surged forward, a sudden, sharply cold wind that the ax-wielding one certainly felt. He shivered, and although he did not drop the ax or quit his feverish mumbling, he moved more cautiously, without swinging the ax at anything but the air.

It was not enough for them, though. The *manëtuwàk* pushed a tree root up in front of him and he tripped, swearing as the ax thumped to the ground in a fine spray of dust, with him alongside it. He cried out when one of them took the opportunity to sink a jagged branch into the flesh of his calf, just as he had sunk the ax into the trees, and rip it out just as carelessly. He scrambled away from the spot, away from the ax, his eyes wildly darting around every so often as he examined the jagged tear in his leg. Blood filled it and spilled onto the ground, and not far off, the Chasm shuddered. He spit out a word, a name, as if the one behind the name had injured him, then slipped off the over-layer of his upper clothing and tied it tightly around the wound. He spied a long stick and snatched it, then clumsily got to his feet, hopping and wobbling a little before righting himself with the help of his new crutch. He searched the ground around him, ostensibly looking for the ax, but the *manëtuwàk* had dragged it out of sight.

With a muttered word of anger, he turned back toward the direction from which he'd come. Seeming to have given up his search for both the ax and the sleeping one, he hobbled a few feet but then stopped, his head snapping around. It had finally dawned on him that he was lost; his helpless frustration seeped from him like sweat, and they could smell it. He was also beginning to feel genuine fear, though not of them—not yet. He was not in control, and clearly, he hated that.

He chose a direction, and with the help of the stick, he swung his weight forward in a graceless hop. He'd nearly made it back to the spot where the ax was hidden when the stick flew out from under him, skittering across the forest floor. He cried out as he tumbled forward face-first and smacked his forehead against a protruding root. His blood rushed to fill the dent in his head, and he groaned, swearing, as he rolled over.

The *manëtuwàk* held back. That time, they hadn't touched him... but at that moment, they felt the approach of the one who had.

It had taken its tree-form, the size of a small oak. Sheathed in gray-brown bark, its head, shoulders, and body were formed from knots of solid wood entwined with thick, curving branches that roughly defined sinewy musculature and features not unlike the far-moving ones. It glared at the ax-wielding one from twin impressions in the head filled with pale blue lightning. Its arms, also tightly corded with vines, ended in large, rough hands with long stick-fingers. Thin, jagged branches grew from its back and the top of its head, ending in sparse foliage that trembled with its rage. Its powerful legs were wrapped in roots and vines that it could uncoil and dig into the ground at will.

The lipless slit of its mouth parted, and it roared so loudly that the surrounding vegetation shook. The *manëtuwàk* pulled back, out of fear as much as respect. The one who had wielded the ax belonged to the Kèkpëchehëlat now.

He blinked a few times when he saw it; perhaps he thought the blood in his eye was blurring his vision, or that he'd whacked his head so hard on the root that he was hallucinating. But when the Kèkpëchehëlat, the once-mighty elemental god of the woods, roared at him again, he screamed.

Its movements were uneven, even jerking as it worked its power through physical limbs it hadn't used in thousands of years, but it came at the cowering one who had wielded the ax, with a speed that seemed to surprise the man. He scrabbled backward on his hands and feet until he thumped against the trunk of a nearby tree. The Kèkpëchehëlat closed the distance in seconds and loomed over him, its head tilted as if in consideration of the weak little thing bleeding at its feet. Then it reached down and hoisted him in the air by his good leg. Holding him up so their eyes met, it shook him a little and he struggled, screaming. His body twisted and squirmed as he tried to free his leg. His terror did not overcome his anger, that blood-hate in his body that held him in an even tighter grip, and he pounded his fists against the wood of the Kèkpëchehëlat's hand, when he could reach it. The whole time, he shouted a word they had heard before, and understood: No. "No, no, no, stop, no, fuck you let me go, don't kill me, no!"

The Kèkpëchehëlat grabbed his flailing leg with its other hand, and pulled the two limbs in opposite directions. There was a terrible wet wrenching sound and a crack like many twigs snapping at once, and the one who had wielded the ax came apart down the middle. The Kèkpëchehëlat dangled the two pieces in the air a moment, splattering the ground beneath with blood before crushing one of the halves in one hand, then tossing the crumpled mess to the ground. It studied the other half a moment, then pulled off the arm and what was left of the head and dropped those, as well. Then it threw that final, dismembered piece against a nearby tree. With a wet slap, it hit the bark and flattened against it, then dripped, bit by bit, onto the ground until the whole mess landed with a plop.

Having lost interest, the Kèkpëchehëlat wandered away. It was awake now and free. It was crazy, because it had long found sustenance in what it dug from the depths of the chasm. And its rage was a blazing sun compared to that of the one who had wielded the ax.

The *manëtuwàk* knew to stay out of its way.

Vines wrapped around what was left of the body and dragged it beneath the undergrowth, where the *manëtuwàk* set about disassembling it and giving over its parts to the wilds.

THREE

Julia awoke to tickling on her arms. She opened her eyes. It was dark and a light breeze brushed her skin, drawing out goose bumps. She squinted to make out the familiar shapes of her furniture. It was getting to be that time of year, she supposed, when the summer warmth of the day dissipated into a fall chill at night; she'd have to get up and close the window. Or maybe, if she could just find that extra blank—

The day came back to her in one nauseating rush. She sat up quickly to discover the tickling on her arms was due to bugs crawling all over her—a little winged thing with needle-thin legs, a spider, some ants. She cried out and slapped them away, shaking out her clothes, her hair, standing up and brushing at her legs and face. For a moment, Darren and his ax didn't matter. She hated bugs; they filled her with a shuddering loathing unlike anything else.

When she was satisfied that she'd gotten them all, she sank back to the ground, tears in her eyes. Her skin crawled. Her left arm ached where she'd slept on it, and the bruises from her encounter with Darren were already turning purple. And she knew that her path of blind wandering made in the daylight would be just about impossible to retrace in the dark. She was lost. She was like the others now, an Internet news article, a footnote on a forum somewhere about people who'd gone missing in the Pine Barrens, the land of the Jersey Devil, portals, and mysteriously missing hikers as well as the mafia's biggest body-dumping ground. It was not that she believed much in New Jersey's urban legends, but an open mind about people usually led to an open mind about other things. Particularly when one was alone in the dark in a strange place, a deeper, more primal and instinct-based part of the brain took over, and that part of the brain believes it all.

It didn't help that said part of the brain reminded her that the part of the Pine Barrens in which she found herself lost was the Nilhollow area. The word itself was a muddied derivation of an old Lenape word for "murderous"—murderous woods, they'd called it. She remembered that from third-grade history class. It was a place where the Lenni-Lenape, and later the European colonists, left their crazy, their criminals, their sick and dying. It was there that people practiced dark and ancient rituals, and there that so many had literally gotten away with murder. It was there that Julia was lost.

In spite of all that, or maybe because of it, her strongest and most preoccupying feeling was that of naked vulnerability, which made the other things, the physical things at least, almost peripheral. She had the specific and uneasy feeling of being watched from the darkness between the trees. In her mind's eye, she could imagine a dozen or more pairs of eyes, animal in the thinking that went on behind them, curious and vaguely hostile. She scanned the area slowly, trying to make out the eyes or any other distinct shape—deer, squirrels, owls maybe. Men with axes. She couldn't see anything at all, not unless she counted the odd clustering of leaves that suggested a face. It was funny, the way the human brain looked for faces in things, as if being alone in any environment so alien as to not have other people was intolerable. It was funnier still that the brain could find those faces—eyes, mouths, even hands—in the contour of a tree trunk, a clump of bushes, or a fan of leaves. She supposed it was a comfort thing, a mechanism of the brain to sooth anxieties and fears by imposing the familiar over the unknown. She didn't find it soothing, though, that so very many foliage-faces and tree-bark scowls seemed to crowd her, watching, waiting to see if she'd scream in helpless anguish, cry, run in circles trying to escape them . . .

Julia stopped and took a deep breath. Her thoughts were erratic, strange, disjointed. She needed to think—take another deep breath, assess the situation, and think.

She felt around for her purse and found it nearby under a clump of ferns. She grabbed the strap and dragged it to her lap, opening it to rifle through—

He has an ax. He smashed my car window with an ax . . .

—and see what she had with her. The phone was gone. Darren had seen to that right away.

In her makeup bag was a compact with a mirror, a lipstick in dark wine and a lip gloss of shiny pink, an eye-lining pencil, a tube of mascara, a pair of tweezers, some makeup brushes, and a couple of small palettes of eye shadow. *Well, great,* she thought. *At least when they find my body, I can have my face on.*

She shivered. Have her face on—it was an old phrase her grandmother had used to mean putting on makeup, but in the context of her situation, it felt morbid. She had a sickening feeling that if it got to the point that people found her dead body, the animals would have already gotten to her face. Makeup or not, there probably wouldn't be much to identify her except scattered teeth.

She felt those tears of panic welling up in her eyes again, and she wiped at them good and hard with the hem of her T-shirt. She was *not* going to die in these woods. She'd been through too much, survived too much, to even entertain the thought another moment.

She dumped the rest of the contents of her purse onto the ground in front of her. A bunch of crumpled-up old gas station receipts fluttered out among some paper clips. Her wallet and a small bottle of water hit the dirt with soft thumps. There was also a travel-sized bottle of ibuprofen, a business card for the lawn guy, a heavily creased pamphlet about domestic violence awareness, a pen with TD Bank's logo along the side, and a couple of batteries. It struck her all as useless junk, meaningless crap that people carried around every day, thinking they *needed* it all. It was funny how the whole meaning of the word "need" had shifted for her. She didn't need to get her nails done or need a new pair of shoes or a glass of wine, not there in the woods. And she didn't need any of the junk she'd thought so indispensable as to carry in that purse, she thought bitterly.

She was about to hurl the pile into a nearby bush when a voice inside her head told her to stop. Perhaps it was the voice of instinct, more urgent and less refined than conscience, a long-dormant part of her that was kicking in now that she was lost in the wild.

Maybe it wasn't just useless junk, the voice suggested. Maybe some of it, at least, could be used for something. Just maybe it was all about looking at things a different way.

She scooped all of the contents back into her purse except the compact, the mirror part of which she held up to the feeble moonlight trickling through the treetops. She couldn't quite angle it right to use it as a source of illumination. She sighed, tucked it into the front pocket of her purse where her phone had been, and zipped it all up.

If, God forbid, she hadn't made it back to her car by morning, she might be able to use the compact for something else. She knew people made fires with mirrors, and she had paper for kindling. Or she could break the mirror and use the shards for something. She didn't want to think like that, though. She hadn't wandered *that* far in. She was sure that with a little bit of hiking, she could find her way back. Traffic was sparse on the road where her car was parked, and the woods seemed to be dampening sound anyway, since she couldn't even hear crickets or tree frogs . . . but still, it couldn't be too hard to find the path and just follow it back to the road. Then she'd flag someone down, hopefully a cop, and get him or her to call a tow truck.

That Darren could be waiting for her back at her car briefly fluttered across her mind, but she shooed it away. Now was no time for thoughts like that. First things first: She needed to find the path.

Swinging her purse on her shoulder, she headed back in the direction from which, in her best estimate, she had originally come. As she walked, it dawned on her that she could avoid going in circles by marking the trees. She dug into her makeup bag and grabbed her lipstick. The next sizable tree she found had rough, heavily lined grayish bark, but she managed to draw a big wine-colored X on it. Satisfied, she moved on. Ten feet or so later, she marked another tree, and ten feet beyond that, another. It made her feel resourceful to be taking control of the situation. Ten feet more and she marked another tree, and when the overgrowth forced her to bear left, she marked that tree with an arrow.

After fifteen or twenty minutes, she felt a tinge of unease that she hadn't found the path yet. It hadn't taken her so long to get to that thicket as it had for her to get to this point, and there was no path in sight. However, she told herself she'd been running scared—she could have covered more ground than she'd thought in a short time and a blind panic. She'd just keep going. She looked at the nearly flat stub of lipstick she had left, and at the dark clump of trees ahead of her, and hoped she was closer to that path than it seemed.

Several more minutes of digging into the lipstick holder to get enough lipstick to continue marking trees brought her no closer, though. That pat on the back she was saving for herself was seeming less and less deserved. Then she happened to look up at a tree straight ahead of her, looming out of the darkness. A patch of faint moonlight had escaped the canopy of leaves above and landed squarely on the trunk, and what she saw made her frown in confusion.

The tree had a large wine-colored X, faintly waxy in the pale moonshine. It had been drawn crudely on the trunk, and her first thought was *I didn't do that. That's not one of mine.* Of course, it was a silly thought. She was pretty damned sure she was the only one out there marking trees with lipstick, so who else's could it be?

Still, it was displeasing to see one X ahead of her when she thought they'd have all been behind. She was sure she'd been going in a straight line, so how had she managed to double back to any of the marked trees anyway? The idea resurfaced that it wasn't one of her Xs at all, and that was why—which was silly, wasn't it?

She glanced behind her and around the marked tree, but couldn't tell what was familiar and what wasn't. She took a deep breath and tried to exhale the unease she felt. She'd just check out that X over there and at least see if she could remember when she'd made it and thereby figure out at what point she'd started retracing her steps.

Moving cautiously, as if the tree itself might bite her, she approached the trunk and examined the X. It certainly looked like lipstick. She touched it, smearing the mark, and rubbed the waxy residue between her fingers, then held them up to look at them. It was her lipstick, all right. So it had to be one of her Xs—no entertaining silly thoughts otherwise. But how could she have gone so wildly off course? Was it when she had gone left past the overgrowth of grasses and shrubs?

She took a few steps back and studied the X again. She just couldn't tell in the dark, in unfamiliar woods, where and when she'd made the X. That tree, as far as she was concerned, looked just like every other one—at least every other one she'd marked. She supposed she should have marked distinctly different types of trees—skinny and fat, short and tall, pines, cedars, and oaks. But could she have even remembered what she marked and when, well enough for that to make a difference?

Julia let out a little growl of frustration. Her brain refused to accept that all that walking had been for nothing, and that she was no closer to the car than she'd been before. But there was the X, *her* X, on the tree. Tears welled up in her eyes and she let them blur the X for a moment before wiping them away with the back of her hand. *Damn.*

Well, she couldn't stay there all night staring at a tree. It occurred to her that if she really had doubled back, then there would be another X ten feet ahead of her, and at the very least, she could follow her own trail of Xs to where she'd gone off course. She peered into the dark beyond the tree and wished she had her cell phone for the flashlight app. With a sigh, she plunged forward into the inkiness.

Arms outstretched to help her navigate the lightless woods, she walked for what seemed like a long time. She could barely make out the trunks in what little moonlight filtered through the leaves, but she was pretty sure she'd come across no more Xs. It was useless. She was just about to turn back when there it was—an X on a tree that caught enough moonlight to look glossy. As she got close enough to make out its details, she saw that one of the legs was smeared, and for a second she had a horrible sinking feeling that she had managed to wind up where she started again. However, as she studied it, she noticed that this smear was on the opposite side, and tapered off in an odd, wiggling way around the side of the trunk. Maybe a bear had brushed against it, or a deer. She moved closer for a look.

Up really close, it didn't look like a smear at all. There were marks more deliberate than just squiggles and swirls—actual symbols, it looked to her, and not smears at all. Her stomach tightened as she followed them around the trunk.

"Wait," she murmured out loud. "That can't be right. I didn't . . ." It was difficult to make out details—the moonlight was a little fainter here—but she was sure the trail of markings ended with a pair of crude stick figures. One was running, its hair streaming out behind it. It carried a bag on a strap. The figure behind followed, its legs tented in exaggerated movement. That one held a line from which protruded a triangle on its side—a simple stick-figure version of an ax.

Like the symbols, the figures had been drawn in lipstick. *Her* lipstick.

I can't be seeing that. I can't! No no no no no! her mind screamed. She snapped her head back and forth, frantically searching the Stygian patches between the trees. Could it have been Darren? Was he out there still? Had he seen her Xs and drawn this to scare her? Confuse her? But where would he have gotten the same color lipstick? She glanced down at the tube in her hand, what was left of the lipstick itself clinging to the nearly hollowed-out base. She threw it as hard as she could, disgusted.

A funny thought, an alien idea really, passed through her mind that she had done it herself, that the trauma of the day had somehow played itself out as she marked the trees and she had just blocked it out. But that seemed as crazy to her as Darren lurking around in the shadows, drawing on trees with lipstick to torment her. It was ridiculous. This whole thing was—

Long, bony fingers on her shoulder made her cry out, spinning around. No one was there. A low-hanging limb from a nearby tree had caught a chill breeze and bounced a skeletal branch just enough to tap her on the shoulder. She glared at it, wanting to both laugh and cry in relief and frustration, before turning back to the tree.

The stick figures were gone. So was the X. Julia sucked in a breath. She touched the trunk, felt the cracked, uneven bark beneath her fingertips, then drew back her hand as if bitten. In truth, she would have sworn it had been cool to her touch but the bark itself had moved under her hand.

She was losing her grip, just like in all the urban legends about this place. Maybe that was how it happened to people. Maybe traumas or stress or fugues or whatever made them see, hear, and think crazy things, and those hallucinations kept them wandering around until there just wasn't anything left in them. Or maybe she was overtired, sad, scared, and lonely, and her mind and the flimsy light were playing tricks on her.

Or maybe all that time with Darren and no other support network had done more damage than she thought.

Pull it together, girl, she told herself. *Come on now. Get it together and get out of here. We're fine. Everything's fine.*

Julia turned away from the tree and headed in a different direction entirely. She was very tired suddenly and very confused, but she was most definitely done with X-marked trees for the night. A new direction, any direction other than the insane circles she'd been making, would be a welcome change.

She realized with some frustration as she backtracked that the last X she had come across, the one before her little hiccup of unreality, was nowhere to be seen. She was, if possible, even more lost than she'd been to begin with. She couldn't quite bring to a conscious level of her mind the idea that she might actually have to spend the night out there in the woods, but it was pushing closer to the surface all the same.

As Julia reached a small clearing she didn't recognize at all, she sighed audibly. She wanted to scream, but the frustration stuck in her throat. She looked around helplessly. Which way should she go now? She didn't want to be stuck here, but she doubted she'd ever find her way anywhere at night. Most of her surroundings were swathed in shadows so thick that she could have been buried alive, for all she could see.

Common logic dictated that when people were lost—in the woods or elsewhere—they were supposed to stay put, to make it easier for rescuers to find them. That assumed, of course, that someone—any-one—was out there looking. Even if someone was, it could be hours, maybe even days before anyone found her. The Pine Barrens spread for miles and miles over a few different state forests, and no one knew she was in Nilhollow specifically—not unless by some chance they'd found her car. Even if they had narrowed it down to Nilhollow, even with dogs and helicopters and search teams, it could be . . . well, longer than she thought she could stand being there. Not to mention, what would she do if she ran into a further problem? The heat could dehydrate her. She could starve or break a leg or get cut and develop sepsis. She could fall off a cliff or get attacked by a bear, or . . .

No. No, she wouldn't, and she just couldn't sit there waiting. God, she'd already been out in the dirt and heat and dark longer than she'd have liked on a good day, let alone all that had happened that afternoon. She wanted out of there, and sitting like a lump on a log, figuratively or literally, wasn't going to help her case.

Then she saw the figure.

A silhouette, it emerged from the darkness between the trees and into a patch of moonlight just beyond the far edge of the clearing, about sixty or seventy feet away. She couldn't make out any features or details, but the build was tall and wiry, masculine, and so was its stance. It stood motionless, neither moving toward nor away from her. She felt a surge of hope; maybe whoever it was could help her get out of there.

"Excuse me," she called, taking a hesitant step closer. "Excuse me, I'm lost and—"

She shut her mouth. What if it was Darren? *Oh God . . .* She squinted, trying to make out whether the silhouette held anything like an ax in its hands, but the harder she tried to discern the outline of its shape, the more it seemed to waver and meld with the shadows around it.

"Um, hello?" Her voice sounded odd in her own ears, out of place and tiny.

The figure didn't answer. It didn't move.

"Okay," she said uncomfortably, the hope she'd initially felt draining from her. She hesitated to move away, to turn her back on it, whoever it was, but she didn't think getting any closer to it was a good idea, either. Did it mean to hurt her? It looked like it had rolled around in leaves and twigs, if the silhouetted crown of sticks around its head was any indication. Maybe it was lost, too. Was it as startled to see her as she was to see it?

She tried one more time. "I'm sorry if I surprised you. I've just been wandering around here for a long time and I'm lost and I was wondering if you knew which direction the road was?"

She wished she had a flashlight. *A flashlight and pepper spray*, she thought. *Just in case.* It occurred to her that the figure didn't have a flashlight, either. Timidly, she asked, "Are you lost, too?"

The figure tilted its head to one side as if curious but said nothing.

Julia suspected she wasn't going to get any help; it was best to disengage. "Okay, well, I'm going to keep looking, then. Have a nice night."

She backed up a couple of steps, and was surprised to see the figure move toward her to match the distance. She paused, then took two more steps back. The figure took two steps forward.

She frowned. "Uh . . . Darren? Darren, if that's you—"

A sharp crack to her left made her flinch. It was followed by a few echoing cracks all around her. When her attention returned to the figure, she saw that its hand was raised as if in a frozen wave.

She felt a chill under her skin, and recognized it as the certainty that this figure was the one who had drawn the figures on the tree. Further, she had the crazy but indisputable notion that despite the human outline, the figure watching her wasn't a person at all.

She felt tears welling in her eyes, born of fear, exhaustion, and frustration. She didn't think she had it in her to weather whatever it was that was standing across the clearing from her. Maybe it was easier to just stand there and let whatever was going to happen, just happen.

Then the figure's eyes seemed to burst into twin points of green flame. She cried out. Something deep inside her disagreed with her about standing still, because she found herself running in the opposite direction, her purse banging rhythmically against her hip as she flew through the darkness, heedless of branches and rocks and roots. Behind her, she could hear that crackling, moving from treetop to treetop, keeping pace with her. Occasionally, heavy tree branches fell alongside her, but none came close enough to hit her. She didn't know if it was the thing with the fiery eyes or something else, but whatever it was, it didn't seem to want to hurt her just yet. Rather, she felt helplessly shepherded deeper into the Pine Barrens, deeper into the heart of Nilhollow.

When her leg muscles burned and her lungs felt squeezed empty and she couldn't run anymore, she finally stopped, panting heavily, and listened. The woods were utterly silent—no tree frogs, no crickets, no bats. No sound at all.

She sank against a nearby tree and burst into heaving sobs, shaking as she pulled her knees close to her chest. When she'd cried herself to exhaustion, she put her purse down and laid her head on it, and before her thoughts could drift back to the thing that had been chasing her, she'd fallen into a deep and uneasy sleep.

FOUR

O fficer Pete Grainger found himself repulsed by the man in cell 4 almost immediately.

As a New Jersey state trooper at the Red Lion Station for three years, Pete had seen all different kinds of people brought in from those damned Nilhollow woods with the full spectrum of DSM diagnoses. This man's story was, on the surface, more or less the same as numerous others. He had been picked up in the Nilhollow area of the Pine Barrens with blood all over his shirt. A quick look-over revealed only two major injuries: a sharp stick jutting from his shoulder, and a severe facial wound by his mouth. However, it was impossible to tell without testing the shirt whether the blood was his or someone else's. He didn't seem able to tell them whose it was, either, nor could he tell them much about himself. He had no ID of any kind—no wallet or driver's license, no credit or bank cards, and whenever police or staff asked him for personal information such as his name, what he'd been doing, where he was from, how he was feeling, or even what year it was, he'd laugh wildly until the pain in his cheek caught up with him and he'd turn away. They'd taken him to the closest hospital to get his facial wound stitched, the stick removed from his shoulder, and that wound cleaned and patched up. However, the hospital was a small, privately funded one, and they had no free beds and no psych ward to assure that he wouldn't hurt himself or others. It would be some time before the psychiatric hospital in the area, St. Dymphna Psychiatric Medical Center, could provide facilities for him, so custody of the damaged man fell on the state troopers until people from St. Dymphna could come pick him up. That kind of situation didn't happen often, but it had happened before, and Pete was no stranger to it.

When one looked at the circumstances a little more deeply, though, there were a few unsettling aspects that set it apart from other similar cases. For one thing, when the police saw him staggering along the side of the road, he had vines wrapped tightly enough around his neck to have bruised it. He'd taken off when he'd seen them, and they'd followed him to a small clearing to find him gnawing on a bone of the right size and shape to be a human femur. The sounds had been pretty horrible, between the crunching of the bone and the odd choking sounds his throat made from under the vines . . .

Pete had been disgusted on an almost primal level before he'd even seen the man's face.

The guy was an odd case, to be sure. Under other circumstances, he might have been normal looking. His strawberry-blond hair was strewn with leaves and tiny twigs but it had been cut recently, and his jaw displayed no more than a day or two's worth of stubble. There wasn't much to explain how he'd descended into such wild savagery in what, by Pete's estimation, couldn't have been longer than a week. The man's blood tests and tox screens were still out, but the preliminary medical exam had shown no track marks, no dilated pupils, no outward signs of brain damage or disease. He looked well fed, with an athletic body, but appeared not to have slept in days. His clothes and hair smelled like old leaves and dirt as well as campfire smoke, but that could describe just about any camper a few days into an expedition in those woods. Hell, it could describe a hiker after a few hours on the trails. Still, there was something unwholesome about him, and while it wasn't a smell, exactly, it clung to him all the same, a cloying kind of wrongness hanging on him the way cigarette smoke lingers in people's hair and clothes the day after a party.

A lot of individuals the state police picked up, particularly from near the Nilhollow area, had to some degree a kind of wrongness about them. It was off-putting, but not enough to induce the kind of repulsion Pete felt toward the man in cell 4. No, with him, it was something more than that. That guy was not just another derelict with sunstroke or dehydration or some bad trip; he'd been chewing on someone's *bone*, for God's sake. There was something cruel, something malicious about him. He was *dangerous*. It was a gut reaction Pete couldn't quite explain but found impossible to ignore. The man seemed both restrained and feral, a coiled thing biding its time. The few words he did speak gave him an air of having a much older soul than body. His guttural laughter and smoothly animal mannerisms were cautious, deliberate, nearly silent, like a predator.

A predator. Cunning darkened his eyes.

The Red Lion Station was to keep him for a few hours in a holding cell until Sanchez and Wilkes from St. Dymphna could pick him up, and Pete, being the new guy, had drawn the first half of the night guard shift. Between those beastly eyes watching him and the weird choking noises the man still occasionally made despite being freed from the vines, he had set Pete on edge. In truth, it made Pete want to hit the guy in the face. It took a surprising amount of restraint not to.

He had finally dozed off on the cell's cot at about eight thirty that night, to Pete's relief. He was sure to sleep awhile; he needed it, if the bags under his eyes were any indication. Hearing the light snores from cell 4, Pete finally began to relax. Night shift would be smooth, then. After all, the man was behind bars. Even if he hadn't been sleeping, what was he, really, except wild eyes and weird breathing? Just a nut job. Pete was a trained New Jersey state trooper with a gun. It had been ridiculous of him to have been unnerved by it. It wasn't like the guy could actually cause trouble from inside the cell anyway.

As he made his way to the coffeepot in the back-room kitchenette, he realized with some consternation that all his self-reassurance had done little to dispel the distinct feeling that whatever had happened to the man out in Nilhollow had broken something inside him irreparably. Something had infected him, and was rotting him from the inside out. And when his shell cracked and whatever it was leaked out of him, would it spread to others?

And what the hell kind of thought was that? Pete shook his head. The man in cell 4 wasn't some rotten piece of fruit, overripe and ready to burst from its putrid interior. He was a guy—just some guy. Maybe violent as well as crazy, maybe not. But he was just a guy.

Pete took his coffee back to cell 4 and peered in. A part of him needed to confirm to himself that the man was still in his cell. Of course he was; he was still sleeping, although fitfully, mumbling through an argument with someone named Kenny. Pete shook his head and was about to walk away when the man screamed, bolting up on the cot. Pete flinched, spilling hot coffee on his hand.

"Ow!" he shouted, switching the mug to the other hand to shake off the burning droplets. "Geez, man, you scared the hell out of me! What—what's wrong?"

The man in the cell looked at him as if seeing him for the first time. The feral look was gone now, replaced by one of abject fear.

The man whispered something Pete didn't quite catch, although it sounded a little like, "The trees moved."

"Um . . . sorry?"

"And the vines killed him." His words were a little stilted due to the sewn-up injury to his cheek, as if forming the words hurt, but Pete could understand him that time.

Pete frowned at the man. Was this guy messing with him? "Who? Who was killed?"

"My brother. The vines came out of the hole in the ground and killed him." He held a hand to his cheek as he spoke.

Schizophrenia, then, or dissociative identity disorder, maybe—it would explain the sudden changes in his voice, eyes, and posture. A sad thing for the guy, but it put his weirdness in perspective, and that tight uneasiness in Pete's chest eased a little.

Pete dragged the metal folding chair from the end of the corridor down to the front of cell 4, sat, then took out his notepad and flipped it open. He didn't expect to get anything approaching the complete, undiluted real story, but Pete had found, even after such a short time on the force, that there were sometimes little glittering gems of truth in the rough rock of insane rambling. A statement from a crazy person was often stuffed sideways with useless babble, but that didn't mean it didn't have its own kind of logic, subject to the laws of the speaker's alternate reality. If parsed correctly, sometimes it could provide at least some basic leads or groundwork information.

This crazy man had blood on his shirt—blood that might very well be that of this mysterious brother. If Pete could find answers about that, however roundabout they might be, maybe it would help him fill in the blanks on his report and help the brother, or at least locate him.

Pete clicked his pen and said, "Okay, tell me about it. Tell me what happened to your brother."

"The vines took him."

"So you mentioned. But how did that happen? Tell me from the beginning—whatever you can. Whatever you remember."

"I remember the trees pulling together. Laughing. They laughed a little. So did I. Kenny looked funny, all crumpled up like that." The man's eyes had taken on a faraway look, as if part of him was still back in those woods, seeing whatever had happened all over again.

"Kenny? Is that your brother?" Pete looked at him, his pen hovering above the notepad, ready to take notes.

The man nodded. "The chasm . . . they or it or whatever made the roots move . . . it killed him. Pulled him in."

"So . . . your brother fell into a hole of some sort then?"

The man's gaze shot up to meet Pete's, suddenly clear. "No! You're not listening!" His hand came away from his cheek, and Pete could see blood just beginning to seep through the bandage. "The vines, man—the *vines* came out of the chasm and pulled him back in. Folded him up like a paper airplane." The man giggled a little, but it seemed more a nervous sound than an amused one, and then the hand returned to his damaged cheek.

"Uh, sure. Okay, vines—got it. I think I'm following you." He made some notes in the notepad about what vines might really mean. "Now can you remember where you last saw your brother? Where this chasm is? Is it in the Pine Barrens? In Nilhollow?"

The man didn't answer. His head was bowed, and for a moment, Pete wondered if he'd fallen asleep again, or was shifting back to the predatory personality that had so repulsed him.

"Sir? Sir, can you hear me?"

"Todd," the man muttered.

"All right, Todd, then. Good. Now we're getting somewhere. Todd, can you give me your last name, so I can get the missing person paperwork started for your brother?"

Todd shook his head. "Mackey. But he's not missing, Officer. I'm telling you, he's dead. I saw him die."

"Okay, I believe you. And you're saying you had nothing to do with your brother's death?"

Todd sighed. "I didn't kill him. The vines did. I tried to . . . to pull him out again. Tried to save him. But I couldn't." He looked up again and Pete was reminded once more of an old soul, weary and sad, in a young guy's body. "And they'll take the lady next."

This time, Pete's gaze shot up to meet Todd's. "Lady? What lady?"

Todd shrugged. "I don't know. The ax-wielder's lady. The trees told me. They are whispering about it. I can hear them still . . . even in here." He looked pained by more than just his face and shoulder.

Pete made a note in his pad about a missing woman; he thought it might very well be one of the man's delusions rather than anything meaningful, but he put a question mark next to it all the same. A quick run through the Red Lion missing persons files couldn't hurt.

"I'm tired," Todd said suddenly, and lay down on the cot. He rolled over to his uninjured side and pulled his knees up to his chest. He clutched the pillow as if it would keep him from falling off a tilting Earth, and then closed his eyes. "Good night, Pete," he whispered.

Pete hesitated a second, then rose to his feet.

"Uh, okay, well. Good night then, Mr. Mackey. Sleep well." He made his way back to his desk with his pad and mug, what was left of his coffee cold now and his mind unsettled.

I didn't kill him. The vines did . . .

He detoured to the coffeepot in the kitchenette and topped off his mug.

From time to time, dead bodies turned up in the Pine Barrens—accidents, suicides, guys offing their wives, lost hikers . . . it happened. The Pine Barrens, especially those lost acres known as Nilhollow, had a sordid history in that regard. That this guy Mackey had seen his brother fall into a chasm of some sort, or get tangled up in roots as he fell off a cliff or down a hill, well, that was sad, but not so far out of the norm. But Pete felt that there was more to it, something more akin to the *other* kinds of things that supposedly went on in Nilhollow. He had a nagging feeling that he was missing something important, something that would explain that feral, predatory demeanor that had first gripped Todd Mackey. He wasn't sure what that important something was, but he knew the whole situation was more than just some crazy guy—*You're not listening! The* vines, *man. The vines came out of the chasm and*—witnessing some horrible accident or worse, causing it. Pete glanced around the bull pen at the empty desks of the other officers and then at the clock. Maybe he was overthinking it. Perry, Epps, Alvarez, Carver, and Holland would be checking in soon. Sanchez and Wilkes would be picking Mackey up in an hour and a half. Then he would be someone else's problem.

It wasn't until he'd settled back in at his desk that he realized the man had called him Pete. He looked down at his name plate. It read:

OFCR. GRAINGER. He frowned, glancing back in the direction of the cells.

I'm tired. Good night, Pete.

Had he told Mackey his first name? Not likely. He wasn't in the habit of giving out his first name to people on the wrong side of the cell bars, for any reason.

The trees told me. They are whispering about it. I can hear them still... even in here ...

Pete shook his head and made the decision not to put too much thought into it. There had been other officers around when Mackey was picked up and brought in—any of them could have said Pete's name.

He logged into the missing persons database of police files and began looking around. There was something about seeing the numbers, the cold statistics of people who had gone missing in the Pine Barrens, specifically the Nilhollow area, that made the hairs on the back of his neck stand on end. In the last two years alone, eighteen people had disappeared. Four were later updated as suicides, three as murders, and five of them were accidents.

Accidents. He paused, wondering how many were actual accidents, and how many were—*The trees moved. And the vines killed him*—simply labeled accidents because the coroner couldn't determine otherwise.

To say nothing of the other six, who were still open missing persons cases, people who had vanished without a trace. Four of them were men, none named Kenny. The last two were women, a Holly Evans, twenty-four, and a Carol Siegfried, fifty. He wrote the names down so he could ask Mackey if either was the lady in the woods he had mentioned. He thought it also might be worth checking the reports over the last week or so regarding abandoned vehicles, wellness checks, and the like. There were a bunch of them; he narrowed the search to the area of and immediately surrounding Nilhollow.

The little hourglass on his screen began turning over, turning over, turning over, which meant the intranet was thinking. Impatient, he became so focused on getting the results from that search that at first his brain didn't register the screams coming from cell 4. They grew so loud, though, that alarms went off in Pete's brain. They were not screams of another bad dream. They weren't of frustration or anger, either. They weren't even the kind of random, crazy-person screams that jarred the soul simply because they seemed so out of place and time. The screams coming from cell 4 were expressions of absolute terror and very likely no small amount of pain.

Pete ran.

What he found in the cell made him a little sick around the edges. He'd been a trooper long enough to have seen death, but not so long to have seen . . . *that.*

A tree was growing right out of Todd Mackey.

At first glance, that was exactly what Pete saw—bloody roots, clotted with bits of flesh, protruding from Todd's legs and ribs and extending downward to wrap around the metal legs of the cot in the corner of the cell in which he slumped. Thick vines had evidently climbed their way out of his stomach and up from his throat to reach out toward the cell bars. Great splinters of wood grew out of the skin of his arms and face, tiny sticky buds dripping blood that pattered like tiny raindrops to the floor. His eyes were wide, glazed over from the shock of sudden and unfathomable death. The bandage on his cheek hung by two pieces of surgical tape, and Pete could see the stitches had been torn out by one of Mackey's throat-vines. A jagged branch, the big brother to the one they'd originally found in his shoulder, now grew from the bloody hole there.

Todd Mackey had been choked, ripped through, speared, opened in places from the inside out, a mangled thing run ragged with wood. Pete turned away, trying to squelch that mental image he'd had earlier of Mackey being some overripe fruit rotting from the inside, but he couldn't. The corridor was growing fuzzy around the edges and Pete felt his dinner churning in his stomach. He had to get away.

It burst, he kept thinking without really knowing why. *The thing in him, the thing went rotten, the spores or seeds or whatever got inside him in Nilhollow burst him open and oh GOD, what now?* Bent over and slumped against the cinder-block wall next to the bars, Pete gagged, trying to suck in gulps of air to keep his gorge from rising any further.

Once the world had righted itself, he stood, still clutching his stomach, and staggered back to the cell.

And he frowned in confusion as the world swam a little once again.

The tree roots and branches were gone. There was still blood—a lot of it—but it seemed to stem from the broken cot spring Todd still clutched in his hand. He'd slit his wrists, had pulled free his stitches, and had made several gashes in his throat as well. Long loops of clotted blood had splashed along the length of his arms, across his face, chest, and stomach, and even the wall behind him. There were no branches or vines. Pete didn't quite feel up to opening the cell and stepping inside with Mackey's body to check, but his search of the cell from outside in the corridor yielded no sign of anything treelike. How could he have imagined such a thing?

Dazed, Pete made his way back to his desk and put a call in to his captain before calling Wilkes and Sanchez and then the coroner, Becky Simms. It was Captain Stan Mallon's day off. Likely he was home, probably comfortably into his second or third beer and binge-watching Netflix shows, and a suicide on Pete's watch, especially one that interrupted *Longmire*, was going to go over badly, but screw it. Pete was going to need his input, and frankly, he didn't like the idea of being there alone with . . .

With a dead body? Get it together, man.

He wasn't alone, though. Maggie was downstairs in dispatch, and Ellen was down there, too, in the evidence room, plus the others were due to check back in any minute.

He was alone on this floor, though, with an empty bullpen and empty cells. With the body of Todd Mackey.

But it wasn't that, not just a dead body. He'd been around plenty of those. It was that he was alone with whatever had really killed Todd Mackey. His brain kept coming back to the unshakable idea he'd had earlier that the body was somehow contaminated by whatever had driven Todd Mackey insane in Nilhollow. Whatever it was had burst him open from the inside out, and was now sporing or seeding or floating around like smoke all over the cell, the corridor, the whole Red Lion Station . . .

He got Mallon's voice mail and left a message. He was about to call Wilkes and Sanchez next, followed by the coroner and then his partner, Vince Perry, when he happened to catch the search results that had finally come up on his computer screen. Under the list of abandoned cars registered to known users, he recognized a name that sent the contents of his stomach churning in new directions.

Patrol officers had called in a gray 2008 Nissan Sentra with a flat tire and a smashed driver-side window abandoned on Mt. Misery

Pasadena Road. Behind it, parked half in the road, was a bronze Honda CR-V.

The Honda was registered to that bastard Darren Baumhauer. Fate couldn't catch up to him and kick his ass fast enough for Pete. The other car, the Nissan, belonged to his friend Julia Russo. And so help him, if the scenario that the report was suggesting was anything close to the truth—if Darren had hurt her and left her in the Pine Barrens—Pete would kill him himself.

Pete turned to the area map tacked to the wall behind Fender's and Bryce's desks. Mt. Misery Pasadena Road . . . Mt. Misery Pasadena Road . . .

"Shit," Pete muttered, and hit the redial button on his phone. Mallon would have to get his ass down there right quick.

Mt. Misery Pasadena Road was just outside of Nilhollow. That meant Julia was officially a missing person in Nilhollow, just like Todd Mackey had said.

FIVE

It had already been a long and messy morning, and once again, it was vaguely connected to that damned Nilhollow spot.

Stan Mallon had arrived after midnight the night before, following Pete Grainger's call. It had been difficult to make out everything he was saying—stuff about spores and trees and Nilhollow and the crazy guy in cell 4—but he'd ascertained that the crazy guy was now dead, and that Sanchez and Wilkes had been called and notified, as well as the coroner. The latter had confirmed the manner of death was self-inflicted, apparently by a loose spring from the underside of the cot. The body had been removed after the scene was processed, and as the morning shift of officers filed in and grabbed their coffee, Mallon himself had taken Grainger's statement.

And there, as people say, was the rub. It was not that he doubted Grainger's account in the slightest; Grainger was a good cop and an honest one, which Mallon was finding he appreciated and respected as he inched closer to retirement. Further, the scene as he saw it in cell 4 and the coroner's preliminary findings confirmed Grainger's report. And Grainger knew well how to observe a crime scene. His becoming detective was now only a matter of time; he was observant and detailed and shouldered a lot of grunt work without complaining. Nearly everything he had reported could be counted on as credible information.

Nearly—and that was where Mallon was stuck, because Grainger, in being so honest, was risking ribbing at the least, and a psych evaluation at most, by telling *everything* he had seen and heard.

Grainger reported that the crazy guy, one Todd Mackey, had claimed the trees in Nilhollow had crushed his brother, Kenny Mackey, to death, and thought they were whispering to him in the cell right up until Grainger had left him to look into the wild claims he'd made. In and of itself, that wasn't anything Mallon had a problem with putting in the report. Crazy people said all kinds of things. That Grainger was trying to convince him there might be something to it, that it wasn't just the babbling of a delusional man, was a tougher sell.

So Mallon had asked him why he believed it. Grainger had hemmed and hawed a little, starting with the theory that a woman he knew, Julia Russo, was missing; patrol officers had reported that her car had been found abandoned, and there was no record of her at any of the local hospitals, jails, or shelters. The relevancy of this piece of information was that this Mackey guy mentioned a woman in danger of suffering the same fate as his brother because she was lost in Nilhollow, the same woods where Julia's car had been found. Mackey hadn't given a name for this woman, but Grainger was convinced that it was more than just coincidence. He'd said the woman was the *ax-wielder's lady*, and Julia's car window had been smashed by something that could have conceivably been an ax. Plus, she had a psycho ex-boyfriend whose car was found abandoned just feet away from hers. Grainger hadn't wasted any time; after his phone calls that evening, he'd entered all the info he had on Julia and Darren into the New Jersey Law Enforcement Telecommunications System, the National Center for Missing Adults system, the Red Lion Station's internal database, and the New Jersey State Police website's missing persons section. He was wholly convinced Julia was in danger, and had intimated that it wasn't just from Darren.

Mallon had given him an expectant look—Grainger's face and tone of voice said there was more to it—and Grainger had sighed and told him about the tree growing out of Todd Mackey.

In Mallon's experience, Grainger was a grounded kind of guy. He had a healthy skepticism for all things paranormal, supernatural, religious, or otherwise otherworldly. He was as much at a loss for how to explain what he'd seen—or thought he'd seen—as Mallon was for how to report it. He wasn't pushing a delusion through to pass it as a reality; he had no doubts about exactly what he'd seen, but was trying to understand it. It made him sound credible to Mallon.

There was another reason Mallon was inclined to believe Grainger. Mallon had known a town cop out in Lakehaven, one of those areas up in northern Jersey, who used to refer to what he called "spin" cases. Those were cases where the kind of lunatic rantings of crazy witnesses just maybe had some truth to them—UFOs, cryptids, boogeymen, spirits, monsters, ghosts, all the stuff of nightmares that unexplainable evidence seemed to indicate were walking, flying, slithering, slapping, or swimming around the wilder parts of New Jersey. Mallon had thought the guy was pulling his leg; it was maybe a loathing of extra paperwork or laziness. He personally had never really experienced anything of the sort . . . until he'd been given the captain job at Red Lion Station. Since then, there had been a number of such cases, all related to the Nilhollow area of the Pine Barrens.

The people who lived nearby were uneasy with that place. The Red Lion Station had its fair share of calls out to the area to check on everything from strange animal noises and tracks to bright lights in the woods to ritual chanting. Someone was always having car trouble. Many cars like Grainger's friend Julia's were left abandoned on Mt. Misery Pasadena Road. And old folks had answers, it seemed, or at least speculations. They would point out (but only to the persistent questioner) that the odd prints in the ancient earth were dragging and deep, like the tracks of heavy snakes, but irregular, as if those snakes skipped along the ground. In fact, the old folks would say, the prints were more like the roots of trees, if trees could pick up and walk. They'd mention the cracks and snaps of twigs so often nearly eclipsed by heavy, irregular breathing or a low, dull, keening sound. Even the most oblivious to that which was beyond the norm would complain of a heavy feeling in the chest when they were out there, a sense of being watched, and notions in their head that weren't theirs at all. Getting his officers to patrol the Nilhollow stretch was always a pain in the ass; word got around and scared the new guys.

Most of the surrounding towns had legends passed from old-timer to teenager, generation after generation. People believed there was something out there.

Why the New Jersey Pinelands National Reserve didn't just burn it all to the ground was beyond him. He supposed they thought it was enough to leave it wild, virtually untouched woodland—no hiking trails, no picnic or camping areas, nothing to monetize. That didn't stop thrill seekers and extremist hikers from traipsing into there anyway and getting themselves good and lost, however. Or worse.

Weighing the wisdom of it, Mallon decided to tell Grainger he believed the story, more or less, to gauge his reaction. Mostly because it was Grainger—ex–Boy Scout and genuine idealist—and partially because the area had a history, a reputation that everyone at the station knew about, Mallon told Grainger that he understood why the younger officer believed there was more to Mackey's death than suicide. Grainger looked relieved.

"So . . . you don't think I'm crazy, then?"

"Didn't say that," Mallon replied noncommittally.

Grainger remained un-deflated but antsy, his fingers drumming impatiently on his leg. He wanted to go out searching for his friend. It was more than responsibility to the job that made him want to go, Mallon suspected, and that same responsibility was the only thing keeping him there to give his statement.

Grainger said, "I did some more searching through the missing persons database while I was waiting for you. The numbers have doubled in that area over the last two years. And it's not just missing people. Over the last year, there have been more unexplained deaths, murder-suicides, and violent self-mutilations. More admittances to St. Dymphna. I believe there really is something out there—"

"Gas leaks, maybe. Chemicals in the water. Or maybe an abundance of some kids' marijuana crops growing wild."

Grainger shook his head. "No, sir. It's more than that. You've said so yourself. The guys here know it, too. There's something bad out there. And if Mackey brought it here—"

"Coroner checked for spores and seeds, like you asked. Nothing transmittable, nothing airborne that he could find, remember?"

Grainger shrugged. "Maybe it's not transmitted that way. But it gets to people all the same. It got to Mackey. And if Julia's out there, she might be stuck in the heart of it. I've got to go find her, boss." The last part came across as a statement of intent, not a request.

Mallon replied, "This woman—you worked with her and Colby on, what was it, a domestic abuse charge?"

Grainger nodded.

"If you're right, and something is going on out there in Nilhollow, we need it identified and rectified ASAP. I expect you to be focused, despite your feelings for this woman."

Grainger blushed a little. "Feelings?" For all his good looks and common decency, the guy had no game. With a small smile, he asked, "That obvious?"

Mallon offered him an easy grin in return. "These high-powered perceptions and refined detecting skills are why they pay me the big bucks. That, and your voice gets all soft when you mention her. And the time she was in here, you stared at her like a starving man at a steak house." He sat back. "Go. Find her. But take Perry with you— no one goes to Nilhollow alone until we sort this out. Got it? Report back on the hour."

Grainger brightened. By the time he answered, "Yes, sir," he had snagged Perry, who had been, in his very unsubtle way, waiting to hear what was going on, and they were out the door.

Vince Perry had been Pete's partner for the last seven years. Maggie in dispatch had once described him as not everyone's cup of tea (and at the precinct holiday party after a few wine spritzers, as a crude, loud-mouthed Pac-Man), but for all his quirks, Pete couldn't imagine leaving his back to anyone else.

Still, there were times when his way with words rubbed Pete the wrong way.

"So you think killer trees popped the blood balloon in cell four? Is that what you're tellin' me?"

Pete shifted uncomfortably in the driver's seat as they sped toward Mt. Misery Pasadena Road. "I—I'm just telling you what I saw. What I think I saw. I don't know. Look, it sounds crazy to me, too. But—"

"Say no more, Grainge. If you say it was killer trees, I'll roll with it. I've got you, brother. And besides, I've been itching to pull the Nilhollow patrol for months. See what all these townies are talking about, am I right?" Perry also had a habit of calling Pete "Grainge," which by his estimation was a mere vowel away from "grunge" and made him feel (perhaps ridiculously) unshowered. Still, he knew it was better to let Perry wear a thing out than to explain why he'd prefer something else.

"I guess. I just want to find Julia."

"You really wanna bang this chick, huh?"

Pete felt flustered all over again. "We're friends, Perry. She just got out of a relationship—"

Perry waved his hand. "You been hard over her for like, what? Three, four years now?" He laughed.

Pete refused to meet his gaze. "She's beautiful, yes, but it's not like that."

"Like what? You don't want to bang her?"

"Yes. I mean no. I mean—ah, do we really have to do this now? I'm working on fifteen hours of no sleep, I just saw a guy splattered all over our jail cell, and my friend is missing and very likely in trouble. I—I just don't have it in me to do this with you right now." In his peripheral vision, he saw the uncharacteristically serious sideways look that Perry cast him.

"Just trying to lighten the mood, bro. Look, we'll find her, okay? If it's your girlfriend's asshole ex, we'll get him. If it's some other crazy ax-wielding, mask-wearing lunatic, we'll take him down, too. And if it's killer trees . . . well, fuck, we'll have a hell of a story to tell at the bar next Saturday, eh?" He slapped Pete's shoulder reassuringly. "We'll find her. Like I said, we got this."

Pete nodded, let go of the tight knot of breath he'd been holding in his chest, and said, "Okay. Yeah, okay. We'll find her."

There was a pause in the conversation, and then Perry said, "So I'm gonna need a date to my cousin's wedding."

"That's a sweet offer, but no thank you." Pete smirked.

"I can do better than you anyway," Perry said, grinning back. "Maggie, for instance. She likes me."

Pete snorted. "Like you in what way? If you mean 'like' as in if you were on fire, she might dump her drink on you to put you out, then maybe."

Perry snorted. "Nah, man, she wants me. The vibe is there—the spark, ya know? She wants to ride me like a New York subway."

"No one wants to ride the New York subway."

"You know what I mean," Perry said, not flustered in the slightest. "She wants me to throw one in there. Damn, that ass. The things I could do to her in the backseat of this cruiser in six minutes—"

"I'd advise not leading off your smooth talk with the six minutes thing, if I were you."

Perry grinned. "It would be the best six minutes she ever had, I guarantee it. Change her life."

They traveled the rest of the way in relative silence, Perry occasionally humming a few bars of some song to himself or making some comment about the passing scenery or office gossip. It was hard not to think about Julia and what Darren might be doing to her right then, but Pete sure was glad for Perry's inane distractions. At least it leeched away a little of the tense impatience he felt about the drive and what might be at the end of it.

As Pete turned onto Mt. Misery Pasadena Road from Pasadena Woodmanse, though, even Perry grew quiet. *Keeping a lookout for killer trees*, Pete supposed. But the thickly wooded area to their left was intimidating, tenebrous within, even in the morning sun. Pete kept to the speed limit, but couldn't help feeling like he was sneaking down the road past the trees so as not to draw the attention of whatever was in those woods. They drove awhile; the abandoned vehicle reports for Julia's and Darren's cars said that both were found almost all the way out by Glassworks Road. When they were about a quarter of a mile from the turnoff, Pete slowed and pulled off onto the shoulder, then put the car in Park and cut the engine.

He swept the area with a tight expression; there was broken glass on the opposite shoulder across the street and a tiny trail of shredded rubber leading up to it. The cars had already been towed; there were no other signs that Julia or Darren had ever been there. That was the thing about missing persons cases that had always unnerved Pete: It amazed him how people could just be absent from the world they touched and interacted with and sent their own tiny ripples of influence through every day. Even when police could pinpoint the likely last-seen location, the place from which they'd disappeared, it was almost always a neat, normal scene, a part of the world going on as if the missing person had never been part of its reality at all.

Pete settled on the trees. In there, then . . . maybe. Probably. One or both of them most likely went in there, which he didn't take as a particularly good sign. He hoped Julia was okay.

"So . . . here, then?" Perry's voice seemed both breathlessly excited and hesitant. Perry was an excitable type under normal circumstances, so it was hard to tell.

"Uh, yeah. Yeah, I think so," Pete replied. "Cars went off the road there, where the broken glass is. So, yeah, let's start there."

Perry clicked the safety off his gun. "Ready when you are, partner."

As they crossed the street, Pete noticed bits of plastic and metal just at the edge of the grass. Instinct told him it was another bad sign. As he got close enough to realize what it was, he swore under his breath.

"What?" Perry asked, coming up alongside him.

Pete gestured. "A cell phone. Hers, maybe."

Perry whistled. It was his "looks like trouble" whistle, and probably a more honest indication of Perry's thoughts on the subject than anything he'd be inclined to say. "Could explain why she didn't call anyone for help." That she might not still be alive to call was left unspoken, but hung there between them all the same. Glass windows and cell phones didn't break without something or someone to break them.

Pete looked at the trees, gathered close as if in curiosity, and noticed that beyond a thick carpet of ferns and shrubs, there was a dirt path leading away into the Barrens. Pete was certainly no tracker, but he had been a Boy Scout, and thought at least he might recognize if someone had made tracks along the path.

When he turned to his partner, Perry gestured at the path. "Let's do this, Grainge."

They clomped through the ferns and brush with over-wide steps and finally made it to the pathway. Immediately, Pete was hit with that same revulsion that Todd Mackey had initially triggered in him. It was like walking into a cobweb; sticky strands of unease clung to him all over. He shivered but kept walking. Perry, uncharacteristically silent, walked beside him.

Though there was no immediately accessible reason for it, Pete couldn't quite bring himself to call out to Julia yet; he felt as if he would be disturbing something he ought not to bother. That feeling deepened the farther along the path they went. He supposed it might have been a leftover thought from his experience with Todd Mackey, but Pete had the distinct impression that whatever was in Nilhollow was most definitely spreading outward.

He also noticed that the longer they walked, the less ground they seemed to cover. It reminded him of those nightmares where people try to run but can't gain ground. His legs felt heavy, not quite stuck, but like he was trying to move them through water. His arms felt heavy, too.

The effect abruptly ended, though, when they found themselves in a small clearing Pete recognized as the one they chased Todd Mackey to. Trees hemmed it in on all sides, but those facing the clearing were stripped of bark in some places, the leaves or pine needles brown and dying. The carpet of forest debris covering the ground struck Pete as kind of mangy, more so than it had the first time he'd been there, and as he looked around, he realized many of those bald patches of ground were bleached to a bone color. Their shapes gave the unsettling impression of body parts uncovered from hasty burials. Pete didn't remember the decay or the colorless patches on the ground when they'd picked up Todd Mackey, but then, he and the other officers had been focused just then on subduing a man they believed to be wild, possibly cannibalistic, and likely very dangerous. The odd twists of the branches, though, curling into shapes that tricked the eye into seeing faces—that he did remember. This was the same clearing.

That couldn't be right, though. They hadn't been walking long enough or far enough to have reached that particular clearing. In fact, Pete was pretty sure the clearing was the other way.

"Hey," Perry said, his voice low. "Isn't this where we picked up your crazy guy from cell four?"

"Sure looks like it," Pete said. "Not sure how we managed that, though."

Perry shrugged. "Probably a good thing we did. Maybe it's not a coincidence that we and Cell Four found it. Maybe Julia did, too."

Pete considered that for a moment. Perry had an interesting point. Although Pete didn't see or feel anything that made him think the area was the source of Mackey's trouble, there might very well be something significant about the spot, something there that might give them an idea what had happened to Mackey and his brother, or to Julia and Darren, for that matter.

They searched it in relative silence, each taking a side of the perimeter and cautiously working their way toward the center. There were no footprints that could have been Julia's, nor was there the area of disturbed dirt where they had struggled to subdue Mackey. The dirty clumps that had fallen off the femur as Mackey chewed on it were gone, but that was no surprise; Todd supposed whatever wild animals lived in these woods had finished off any remnants. The leaves and grass were a bit churned up near the far edge of the clearing, but not so much that it would suggest a struggle. The few indications of drag marks were narrow, maybe the width of a tree root, but not nearly wide enough to mean a body or even the heels of feet. Pete examined the surrounding foliage for blood, but there was nothing.

He was just about to suggest to Perry that they move on when he saw the waxy red X on a pine tree. It was facing away from him, away from the center of the clearing, and Pete would have missed it except for a glance in the direction he was considering next.

"Perry, look at that tree." He pointed.

"What? There are a million trees. Which one are you—oh."

The two moved around the pine and closer to the mark. It was a large, crudely drawn X about face-height, in a dark red.

"Well, that's not blood . . . What is it? Lipstick?" Perry reached out and touched the X, smearing a corner. He studied his fingertips before wiping them on his pants. "Yeah, lipstick. Your girl's color?"

Pete nodded. "Smart girl. She was marking a trail." He gestured away from the clearing. "I'll bet there are more, maybe leading right to her. Come on."

There was nothing like a hiking trail in Nilhollow, but the going was easy enough; Pete supposed they were following an animal trail, with slightly tamped-down grass and spaces wide enough between trees to move without a lot of ducking and weaving. It was likely that Julia, who was not an outdoorsy type at all, would try to find the easiest way to traverse the unfamiliar terrain, and in lieu of an actual trail, the path they were on would have seemed safest to her.

Serving as confirmation, another X-marked tree appeared in front of them, and Pete felt both a glimmer of hope and of relief.

"Got another one!" He jogged over to it, with Perry right behind.

Pete frowned as he studied it, though. This one was a little different than the last. For starters, the color was an even darker shade than wine—almost blood-clot black. And it wasn't quite an X, but rather, something closer to a headless stick figure with arms raised. Above it was a table shape that inexplicably reminded Pete of a dolmen, and above that, stacked on top of each other, three words:

NO
ONE
LEFT

"What the fuck is that?" Perry asked, his voice soft with amazement.

"I—I don't think Julia drew this. I don't know what it is, but . . . but that's not hers." Pete reached a hand out to touch it, to see if it was lipstick or something else, thought better of it, and pulled his hand away.

"Is that meant for us? Was it actually left for us? 'Cause if so, that's fucked a hundred ways to Sunday."

"No idea." At that moment, it didn't sound so crazy to think someone knew they were out there—someone who wanted them gone and thought they could be scared into leaving. Maybe that someone was Darren, or maybe there were others. *Maybe*, he thought dryly, *it's a message from the killer trees.*

The wind rustled the trees around them as if in anxious and impatient reply, urging them to leave. Pete looked up to the treetops and the pale patch of cloudless sky above them. He felt swallowed and claustrophobic and helpless, like he was looking up from the pit of a deep throat. To stifle the beginnings of panic, he dropped his gaze back to the waxy symbol and words on the tree. "Maybe we should move on."

"No argument here," Perry said. His hand rested on the handle of his gun.

They moved deeper into the forest, and the wind seemed to blow against them, carrying a vaguely unpleasant scent. The farther in they went, the more frequently they came across a tree with a mark in that same dark, waxy substance: not a sign of Julia, but of someone—*something*—else. None of the subsequent marks were Xs, nor were they anything quite like the odd stick figure. Some were simple arrows pointing up, down, or deeper into the woods, while others were those same headless, cheering stick figures that bothered Pete for reasons just below the place his conscious mind was willing to go. Though no two marks were the same, Pete was inclined to believe that they were all made by the same hand; all had the crude heaviness of one who was not used to writing, and all appeared to be made in that same blood clot–like stuff. He wondered if Julia had seen them and whether it had scared her. He also wondered if whoever made them had Julia already, and if so, what was being done to her. It took effort to banish the possibilities from his mind.

"Let's check the time," Perry said. He held up his cell phone to check. "Aw, it's dead. That's weird. I thought I had at least half a battery left."

Pete, who had fully charged his cell phone that morning, took it from his pocket and tried to turn it on. The screen remained black. He held down the button for a few seconds, but it still wouldn't turn on. He exchanged glances with Perry. "I'm getting nothing. Maybe something's draining the batteries?"

Perry glanced up. "I have a theory. I figure it's what, ten, ten thirty? Midmorning sometime. But it's dark as hell in here. And not just because of the tree cover, Grainge. Look." He pointed up, and they paused to jointly examine the sky.

The patch of sky above them had gone from ashen to a twilit blue. Pete frowned.

"Electromagnetic energy," Perry said.

"Huh?"

"Electromagnetic energy coming up from the ground, man. Read an article on it online. Well, actually, it was a click-through from a porn site. 'Science is sexy,' the ad said. Go figure."

"What about the electromagnetic energy, Perry?"

"Well, apparently it's this natural phenomenon that occurs in some places. This energy, it, like, comes up out of the ground and does all kinds of weird things to your head and body. People used to think certain places were either cursed or holy, depending on how the electromagnetic energy made them feel. Now this stuff would mess up the phones, mess up our heads and stomachs. And I don't mind telling you. I've had rot-gut like a wicked hangover since we got here, and my head is pounding. Feel that? Like something pushing on your chest, breathing on you? It's messing with our sense of direction, our sense of time. Could even cause hallucinations."

"Hallucinations?"

"Sure," Perry replied. "Day looking like night, lipstick hieroglyphics . . . singing."

"Singing? I don't hear—"

But then he did. It sounded like both men's and women's voices, soft and rhythmic, almost chant-like, rising and falling on the wind. He couldn't make out any of the words, but there was an unmistakable sense of sinister intent in the syllables, enough that his chest tightened. There was no musical accompaniment that he could discern, other than what might have been either pipes or just the wind.

"I don't think we're hallucinating that," Pete muttered.

"I think we ought to get out of here," Perry said. "Doesn't much matter whether we are or not; if so, then there's something very unhealthy in the air out here, and I don't want to breathe in any more of it—or have those electromagnetic waves break down my cells and give me cancer or something. And if it's not a hallucination, then by the sounds of those voices, we are way outnumbered. And I'll bet law enforcement isn't particularly welcome at whatever little party they're having."

Pete hesitated. The voices seemed to beckon him, to remind him that Julia was out there, scared and alone, maybe hurt, maybe dying. Perry made a good point, however. They didn't belong out there. They weren't equipped to handle any kind of cult or anything without backup. Maybe a search party, dogs, a SWAT team even, would be the way to go. He remembered Mallon's directive to call and check in on the hour. It hadn't seemed so long before, but now it occurred to him that they had covered a lot of ground, however meandering it might have been. Just how long had they been out there? And what was out there in the woods with them? Pete didn't have a headache or stomachache like Perry, but the constriction in his chest and the heavy fog in his head were making it difficult to think. Had he been feeling them the whole time? He wasn't sure. He'd been so worried about Julia that he hadn't thought much about it.

"Pete," Perry said, "I won't lie. This place has me all messed up. There's something very, very wrong here. Wrong like . . . like the guy in cell four, you know what I mean?"

Pete nodded that he did.

"We aren't equipped for this. This is how cops get killed, dig? Fucked a hundred ways to Sunday—it starts with this kind of Satanist shit." Perry, gesturing in the general direction of the singing, looked genuinely scared, an expression out of place on his face.

"Okay," Pete said with reluctance. He felt horribly guilty at the thought of leaving Julia alone out there, though. If not for her, he would have been the first one back to the car. He glanced toward the direction they had been heading and it vaguely registered in the back of his mind that the singing had stopped.

"Look," Perry said gently. "I know you're worried about her. I am too, given what we've experienced out here. But we're no good to her lost and crazy. Or worse. We need help to help her."

"You're right," Pete finally agreed. "Let's get the hell out of here."

Perry clapped him on the shoulder in relief. "Great. We'll radio in to Mallon when we get to the car. Don't want the mother hen worried about us." He grinned for the first time since entering Nilhollow, and Pete tried to return it, despite his misgivings. They headed back the way they had first come.

Pete still felt a little unsettled by the decision, but knew in his head that Perry was right about needing more help. They weren't doing Julia any good wandering aimlessly around the woods. They needed to up their efforts, bring in assistance. Maybe what was wrong with Nilhollow could be dispelled or dissipated somehow with the presence of more people. Surely—

Pete noticed movement before he actually saw the man.

At least, it appeared to be a man. He wore all black, and most of him was obscured behind the thick trunk of one of the pines. He was only about twenty or thirty feet away, but it was difficult to see any details of his face. Pete momentarily entertained the chilling thought that the man had no real facial features, only rough-hewn impressions, then chalked it up to a face mask of some kind. The effect was unsettling.

"Is that her ex—what's his name, Darrel?" Perry whispered.

"Darren," Pete whispered back. "I don't think so."

The figure placed a hand on the tree. The fingers were unusually long and bony, almost branchlike.

Pete kept his hand close to his gun.

"Police! Stay where you are!" he shouted at the figure, who stood motionless, more curious, it seemed, than alarmed. Pete and Perry moved in closer, acutely attentive to the figure's slightest motion. It seemed to be wearing a crown of twigs, which stuck up from the bushy dark hair on its head. It watched them approach.

Then another figure peered out from around a tree close to the first figure, a twin in its dark, shapeless clothes, twig-crown, and nearly featureless face mask. Pete and Perry stopped, their sense of alarm heightened, almost palpable. From a tree to their left, another figure appeared. The tree was too narrow to obscure as much of the figure's body as it did. Pete had little time to wonder about it, though, before another figure, and another, leaned out from behind trees to their right.

"Fuck me," Perry said under his breath. His gun was already drawn, pointed down but ready to blast apart those pale, bland faces.

It seemed to grow darker in the woods just then, and the fog in Pete's head wavered, diminished, then returned with strength enough to make him dizzy for a moment. He blinked and shook his head. He had trouble telling how close or far away each of the figures was.

Were they behind different trees now? Some looked as if they were growing out of the trees themselves. Next to him, Perry giggled.

It took effort to turn his head, but Pete saw Perry doing an odd hop-skip toward one of the figures, an awkward, clumsy movement for the big man. His arms flailed at his sides, the gun forgotten. He hop-skipped forward again.

" 'Through the woods to Grandmother's house we go,' " he sang, and then laughed again.

Pete forced the clouds from his mind, and for a moment, true fear rushed in to fill the vacuum. "Perry? Perry! Don't go near them!"

Perry stopped and slowly raised his gun to his temple. He turned and offered Pete a broad, knowing smile and for one terrifying moment, Pete was convinced his partner would pull the trigger. Perry laughed again, though, and the gun fell away. Pete, riveted in fear to the spot where he stood, was forgotten as Perry hop-skipped forward again, a weird, wounded bullfrog doing a death-dance ever closer to the first figure they had seen. And those figures were indeed deadly— Pete was certain of that right down to the center of his being, head-clouds or not.

"Don't touch them!" Pete called out, but the urgency was already being leeched from his thoughts as well as his voice. It was hard to concentrate. Something was wrong, very wrong, but not in this little patch of grass and pine needles, not right here. Something was wrong over by Perry, over by the figures emerging now from behind the trees to close ranks around his partner.

The pale skin of the figures' faces and hands fell away to reveal a kind of pale gray bark, like some of the trees behind which they had been hiding. The dusky clothes came apart like clumps of dead leaves, falling away as they strode closer to Perry. They were tree-things composed of branches and wood, only vaguely humanoid and tall as a man—a little taller, even—with pale, greenish lights filling the hollows where their eyes should have been. There were five—no, six—no, five . . . Pete couldn't get a handle on exactly how many there were. They seemed to walk or stand one moment, and be several feet away the next, sometimes reaching for Perry and sometimes watching him curiously with their fire-eyes.

I am not seeing this, Pete told himself, hoping it was true. *This can't possibly be real . . . It's got to be in my head. It's got to be whatever's wrong with me right now.* Was this what Nilhollow did to peo-

ple? Did it make them see things? Hear things? He closed his eyes
again and opened them, but it wasn't like what happened with Todd
Mackey. The tree-creatures were still there. He could hear the creaking of their old wood, and the murmuring noises of the scant foliage
on their heads.

And Perry was heading right for the center of them.

Part of Pete's brain, a part being smothered by the fog in his head,
was screaming for him to do something, to get moving and get Perry
away from those things, the little ones (*That's how It sees them*, he
thought, but didn't know what any of that meant) before they speared
their finger branches through him like they must have done to Todd
Mackey, before they infected him with their seeds or spores or whatever and he had grown from the inside out. His legs wouldn't move,
though, and Perry seemed blithely content to dance among them.

Then, for fun, Perry started firing his gun at the tree-things, and
the cloud in Pete's head evaporated.

The first bullet tore through the wooden shoulder-knot of one of
the creatures closest to Perry in a tiny spray of splinters and bark.
The thing jerked back a moment and screamed, a wind-wail, a keening sound but loud and angry. Then it kept coming. A second bullet
tore into another tree-creature through the lower end of a thick root-
leg which it dragged along as it bellowed in rage. Another thought
that Pete was sure was not his own passed through him like a breeze:
Die like the ax man. It was the tree-creatures' intent he was hearing in
his head. They were angry.

The trees moved . . . Todd had told him. *Oh God. Oh God . . .*
Pete's paralysis was broken and he drew his gun, intending to help
his partner. He only made it three or four steps, though, before something whipped around his wrist and tightened. The pain made him
drop his gun and he swore. He looked down and a tree root or vine
had reached up from the carpet of pine needles and grabbed him. Another snaked around his leg while a third reached for his free arm. He
twisted out of its way, and set to work trying to loosen the first root's
grip.

"Perry!" he called as he kicked at the searching vine. It lashed at
the offending leg, sending pain down the length of it to his knee.
"Perry, run!"

Perry danced and laughed and fired his gun.

One bullet whizzed past Pete's head as he struggled with the vines.

Another bullet fired into the woody meat of a third tree-creature's torso, knocking it to the ground. Two others helped it up, and then the tree-creatures were on top of Perry. Their screams faded and were replaced by his—horrible, high-pitched shouts from beneath the tangle of branches and twigs.

Pete tried to reach for his gun, straining against the vines, but they yanked him back.

"Perry!" he shouted, half in horror and half in dismay.

And the vines killed him . . .

He could see the long, crooked arms of the tree-creatures reaching in to the dog-pile on Perry and pulling out chunks of red stuff, which they flung away into the grass. Perry's screams had softened some, and were punctuated now by wet gurgles. More red, chunky stuff flew upward, a spray of it landing just near Pete's feet. It took a minute to recognize what it was, and when he did, he felt his stomach lurch.

It was Perry's liver.

Another wet plop delivered a loop of his intestine nearby, and Pete bent over and dry-heaved the bile in his stomach onto the grass.

It was a long time after Perry stopped making noises that the tree-creatures stopped tearing at him. When they did finally seem to find him sufficiently dead to back off, there wasn't much left of Perry. Pete felt his stomach churn again and he took several deep breaths to calm it. He could see Perry's head, his wide, glazed eyes, and a hollowed-out cavity where his ribs had once protected his internal organs. He watched in horror as vines from beyond the trees weaved through the remnants and dragged them into the undergrowth.

Suddenly, the attention of the tree-creatures shifted to Pete. He furiously renewed his efforts to free himself, but found to his surprise that as the tree-creatures approached, the vines around his wrist and leg loosened on their own, slithering back through the grass.

The tree-creatures were about ten feet away when Pete thought to reach for his gun. He looked from it to them, his heart pounding throughout his chest cavity (still intact, for the time being). They watched him with those green eye-lights. Their thoughts rustled like leaves. He couldn't understand any individual sentiments, just impressions of wariness and distrust. He was acutely aware of the feral danger they presented, their capacity for predatory violence. They seemed to him a separate but affected element of Nilhollow; it had been theirs before time had noticed them, theirs before whatever had killed Todd Mackey had begun to well up from the ground.

He extended his foot and kicked the gun away, toward them.

"S-see?" His voice in his own ears sounded too loud, too shaky. "N-no threat. No threat." He wondered how fast they were, and if he bolted, whether they would be able to catch him. He suspected they very likely could.

"No gun," he told them. "No ax."

They watched him in silence, but there was the slightest shift in the sentiment they exuded.

"I . . . I just want the girl. She's lost in your woods. I want to bring her home—out of the woods," he told them. He felt a little silly; there was nothing in their wooden faces to indicate they understood anything he was saying, or cared one way or another. "Just want to find the girl, before . . ."

His voice trailed off. He didn't know how to finish the thought. Before what? Before they did? Before their forest or whatever crazy sickness that had infected Todd and then Perry could get to Julia, too? Or him? And what if it had already?

Before the Kèkpëchehëlat, their thoughts finished for him. He didn't know what the word meant, but he understood from the sentiments surrounding the thought that they deferred to whatever it was, and found it threatening. Maybe it was the name for whatever was wrong with Nilhollow, the madness affecting those who spent too much time there. Pete had no clue. But he told them, "Yes. Yes, before that."

The tree-creatures considered his words for a moment, and then other alien thoughts found their way into his head.

Go. Go now. All is unwell. The Turning grows stronger. Much is and will be forgotten here. Swallowed up. Time is short.

He nodded, though he didn't fully understand what they meant by that, either.

The command to go echoed in his mind as the tree-creatures broke into piles of leaves that a sudden chill wind twirled away. Pete closed his eyes a moment, and when he opened them, all trace of the things that had killed Perry, as well as any of Perry himself, were gone. Pete's gun was gone, too. He stood by himself in the woods.

He let out a shuddering breath and sagged a little where he stood, the high-alert tension in his muscles slowly easing.

"Okay," he said to himself, inhaling and exhaling deeply. "Okay. Okay." He looked back toward the woods from which he'd come and thought about heading back in there without backup. Without Perry.

Perry. His partner was dead. Why had they killed him and not Pete? Was it really simply because he'd shot at them? Were they so capricious? So crazy? He nodded grimly to himself. Given what he'd experienced of Nilhollow so far and his experiences with Todd Mackey, it was probable that everything there was to some degree insane, steeped in whatever was wrong with the place. Maybe it was a matter of the length of exposure and whatever immunity a person might naturally have to Nilhollow's effects. Maybe like illnesses or poisons, it affected everyone a little differently. In this case, it had gotten to Perry first, had hit him harder, and he'd poked the tigers, so to speak.

Crazy, unpredictable tigers that had torn Vince Perry apart. Had Pete not been in shock, he probably would have teared up.

He walked over to the spot where the tree-creatures had attacked his partner and was surprised to find most of the blood had already sunk into the ground. A few splatters on the long blades of nearby grass and a tiny pool visibly draining between the pine needles and into the dirt were all that was left of Perry. There were no scraps of clothing, no bits of flesh. It was like Perry had been scrubbed out of existence.

It was hard for Pete to wrap his brain around, even with most of the brain-fog gone now. Todd Mackey, the marked trees, Perry, the blood, the tree-creatures . . . He was going to need backup.

Mallon would no doubt come looking for him soon; the man was sharp and had a good instinct for knowing when there was trouble. When he didn't call to check in, it would raise a red flag. It was just a matter of time. For now, though, he was alone.

Alone . . . but not really. They . . . those things . . . were still watching him. He felt that. They would bide their time for now, but they had told him things in Nilhollow were unpredictable, and unpredictable could be very deadly. He wouldn't have much time. Even if he could find the car, the search would probably be a waste of an hour he didn't have. No, if he were to have any chance of saving Julia, then he couldn't wait for Mallon and backup.

Before he changed his mind, Pete dove back into the forest.

SIX

That morning Julia had woken up to the sound of chirping, which immediately ceased the moment she opened her eyes. She had noticed somewhere in the background of her thoughts that birds seldom if ever chirped there—and ditto any crickets or tree frogs. The sound, she thought, had only been part of a dream. Since entering the woods, she had seen no lightning bugs, no squirrels or chipmunks, no deer or rabbits. She was fairly convinced that most times, she was the only one in those woods.

Most times.

Her first night in Nilhollow had been rough, to say the least. She'd slept fitfully and yet still dreamed, and the dreams were ugly. In the one she remembered best upon waking, the one that had bothered her the most, she had started off in a beautiful clearing surrounded by oaks, cedars, and pines. There was a mountain outcropping that extended upward into the clouds of dream-irrelevance, and she had been sitting on one of the rock outcroppings overlooking a small pool of clear water. The stone beneath her was smooth, warmed by the sun, and her bare feet were dangling in the cool water. She'd heard singing far off beyond the trees, and it had seemed like a good idea to follow that singing to its source. So she'd hopped off the rock and wandered away from the pool along a sun-dappled dirt path that wound among the trees. Quickly, though, the sun faded and the shadows knitted together to blur the details of anything but the closest tree trunks. The wind picked up and she remembered feeling more anxious than cold, as if the trees knew something was coming and shook their branches in prediction.

She supposed her mind had incorporated random dream images then, as well as sounds she heard in the twilight of half sleep, which her brain fleshed out in odd ways. As she followed the path, she passed strange and disquieting beings among the trees. One was an unnaturally flexible contortionist in a moonlight-colored leotard, whose skin had been painted entirely white. Her thin lips were black, as were her nails. Her black hair had been pulled into a tight bun so that it wouldn't obscure the rippling of her lean muscles as she folded herself backward and peered through her legs. She blurred for a second or two and in the next, her body had turned over but her head remained upright. The contortionist turned again and then again, her head never moving, but her neck bulged and strained as it twisted to keep her head in position and her eyes always on Julia. Those eyes were entirely black, like shiny obsidian, and she seemed to always have one too many limbs—an extra arm arcing wide here, an extra leg nimbly navigating the terrain there. The contortionist followed her a few feet in a sort of crab-walk, then stopped and watched with those nothing-eyes.

She passed a man on the right who was naked except for a loincloth of leaves and moss. Large patches of hair had been roughly and unevenly shaved off, leaving nicks and cuts that bled a little. What was left was a washed-out blond, like straw, but heavily dusted with dirt. At first Julia thought he was kneeling in the grass, but as she got closer, she saw he had no legs below the knees. His arms were a tangled, broken mess bound to his back by vines, all forming arabesque shapes she was sure even the contortionist couldn't make. His eye sockets had been hollowed out, and sprigs with budding leaves grew from the blood-ringed holes. That bothered Julia more than his maimed body, more than the black feathers and tiny bones stuffed into his mouth or the blood that ran down his chin onto his bare chest. She was sickened by those eye sockets, reclaimed by an indifferent, wild thing of nature . . . and the secret import of the series of simple and complex lattice-symbols drawn all over his body in dark wine-colored lipstick.

She saw an ax in what she thought was the ripped-up remnants of human flesh. She could see the detail, even in the dream—the pores on the skin, the tiny hairs, the watch Darren wore, an eyebrow with one of Darren's eyes, a finger . . . and wet, squishy things beneath that, red and pooling outward, drawing flies, cooling and stinking and rotting in the gloom of the forest's in-between places.

She saw desiccated bodies hanging from trees, barely twitching, the shrunken gray skin wrinkled and tumorous with odd mushroom growths, like the humus of decaying trees.

Then there was the figure from the night before. In her dream, it didn't speak, but it did move. It approached her on the path, a thing clothed in sheaths of dead leaves, its wooden face devoid of any detailed feature. Branches grew from its head. It regarded her with eyes that glinted, reminding her of the way a cat's or deer's eyes will reflect whatever little light is available in the darkness. It took her arm in its long branch-fingers and led her to a new clearing. This one was nothing like the first: The plants here were dead, twisted into unnatural shapes. Sharp rocks and roots along the ground had been overturned, the earth scratched in long furrows. In the center of the clearing was a chasm. It was not wide, but she knew with dream-certainty that it was infinitely deep. Across it was a large slab of striated rock, about six feet in length and four in width—big enough for a person to lie down on. Carved along either side of its length were grooves about an inch wide.

Standing in front of the slab was a very tall, very gaunt man in tattered robes of faded gold mottled with red. They reminded Julia a little of autumn leaves, an idea emphasized by the leaf-and-twig crown he wore. His long hair and beard were scraggly streaks of storm-cloud gray, and small bits of rock and plant were caught up in them. Although everything else in the dream had until that point been very vivid, Julia couldn't make out the face of the man at all. It was a smear of off-white, a blur. His hands, though, she could see—bony, gnarled things that beckoned her toward the rock.

The King in Yellow fall fashion collection, she remembered thinking, and both giggled and then choked down a cry.

She was aware that she was naked without ever having taken off her clothes. Her own body, usually tanned, was very pale in the light of the moon streaming down on the clearing. The tall man instructed her to lie down on the slab and she did. There seemed no point in resisting his silent command. She could feel a warmth, a *hunger* for her rolling up from the chasm beneath. Its vines, long fingers from those depths, snaked up over the edge of the stone slab and wrapped around her wrists and ankles, spreading her legs and arms out until she felt like one of her lipstick Xs.

Until that point, she had felt disquieted and occasionally disgusted, but she didn't feel real panic until one of the vines wrapped around her neck. Another wedged itself into her mouth and down her throat, and she gagged, on the verge of throwing up or choking but unable to complete either. She wrestled against the vines holding her down, but they constricted, rope-burning her where they rubbed against her skin. Another slithered up along the inside of her thigh and pushed into her, deep enough to startle her, to fill her up down there. Another crisscrossed around her breasts, pressing on her chest, her heart, her lungs.

She was going to die. The tall man and his branch-fingered assistant, the oddities of the woods, the multiple pairs of curious firelight eyes that had gathered at the edges of the clearing to watch—they all wanted her to die. It would make whatever was hungry at the bottom of the chasm go away for a while. All would be satiated.

The tall man leaned over her with a large stone dagger and carved a hand-sized symbol like an X, or more like a headless stick figure, into her stomach. It felt like each place the dagger touched her was seared by contact with it. The blood from the cuts welled up and spilled over the sides of her, running off the slab and into the chasm. From all around, a low keening, growing louder as he cut, filled her ears.

Julia could only gag, tears blinding her then spilling away.

The tall man opened his fist and sprinkled something into her wounds—seeds. He was planting seeds. She blinked away more tears. There was a sudden silence as the woods around her held its breath in anticipation. The vines retracted, first from her inner places and then from around her body, but she could only lie there. She had been something else's, and it took a few minutes to regain that feeling that she belonged to herself again. It didn't last long, though. Something was inside her, growing, draining her of the things it needed to live. The watching, glittering eyes became fireflies and rose up into the sky. The sounds of the forest—all the crickets and frogs and birds she never heard when she was awake—filled the silence.

The thing inside her sprouted up through the wound, but she was awake before she saw what it was.

She cried for a long time, quiet, heaving sobs that were meant only for her. She was a big believer in the idea that crying served a number of healthy purposes—a release of anger, frustration, or sadness, for example, or a means of clearing out all the intense emotion so that she could focus on what to do about the problem at hand.

Her problem, she realized as she sniffled and wiped her nose with the back of her hand, was that she was good and lost in the woods, and she needed to find her way out. Now that a good bit of the emotion had cleared, a small idea had been uncovered that she had not allowed herself to give credence to before. It was the notion that there was something supernatural, something potentially dangerous, out there in the woods with her. It was something that had both the desire and the means to keep her lost there, though she didn't want to speculate why. She couldn't prove in the light of day that it was true, but she felt it deep inside her. Maybe she really was losing it, but the idea felt more real to her than most of what she'd experienced since yesterday. This was Nilhollow, after all, and the place didn't have its reputation for nothing.

She lifted her shirt and looked down at her stomach. There were no marks on her, no headless stick-figure shapes. She supposed the logical side of her had known she wouldn't find anything, but the dream had left a very real impression on her.

Yes . . . there *was* something out there, something predatory that the dream had only alluded to. She knew it on a primal level of her soul. So a subset of her problem, then, might very well be needing to outsmart whatever that something was.

Outsmarting anything in the wilderness, with her limited knowledge of outdoor survival, would be . . . a challenge, to say the least. Still, Julia recognized that if ever there was a time to accept a challenge, this was it. She clutched her purse tighter to her. She was not going to give up on finding a way out. She wouldn't give Darren or anyone (or anything) else the satisfaction.

Thinking of Darren, she felt suddenly angry, but it was a cool, forged kind of anger, justified and steady and absolutely necessary. This was his fault, and she deserved better than a life threaded through with fear of him. She'd been told as much before by well-meaning friends and family, but it was the first time she truly felt it for herself. She deserved better than to die out there because Darren couldn't let go.

Fuck him, and fuck these woods, too, she thought. *I'm going home. I just need to figure out how.*

Her lipstick breadcrumb trail had failed miserably. She needed a method that was more consistent, more reliable.

Well, she'd already ruled out staying in one place, even if it would make her easier to find. As far as she knew, no one but Darren knew she was out there, and she certainly didn't want him to find her. It seemed safer and more productive, more the act of an assertive and capable human being, to keep moving. Further, a little part of her suspected that given her directional troubles the night before, it might very well be that even if she didn't move, Nilhollow would move around her anyway. It didn't seem so crazy a thought as it might have yesterday afternoon.

If people came to look for her, she was sure they must have the means to find her, whether she moved or the forest did. She certainly hoped so.

She figured eventually someone would come look for her. She wasn't sure who, though. If she didn't show up for work that Monday, her boss might send an email or text or maybe even try to call her on the cell that Darren had crushed, but that was it. Her parents lived in Delaware now and wouldn't be expecting a check-in phone call for probably another week or so. Her friend Mandy was in Florida for the week, and Pete . . .

Well, there was Pete. Thank God for him. He was a good friend and a cop. He was the one who had put her in touch with Detective Colby in the first place. Both he and the detective knew about Darren and the escalating threats, and Pete had been calling every other day or so to check on her since she'd applied for the restraining order. Maybe he would find her car and realize there was a problem. Or maybe he would think to come around to check on her at the house, and being unable to get ahold of her, would start a search. The idea of Pete coming for her made her feel better. He was a good guy, a loyal friend. He would most definitely look for her if he knew she was lost.

If. But how long could it possibly take for him to realize she was missing? It wasn't like she could really stay lost for long, could she? Did people even really go missing in New Jersey in this day and age? With all the technology they must have had for locating people, they had to be able to find her, right?

Just because no one had found her yet . . .

The wind blew, indifferent to her thoughts. The trees rustled as if chuckling to themselves.

She sighed. That there were so few people who would even notice if she was missing put her life into a dispiriting perspective. No, her assessment the night before had been right. She couldn't wait around for someone to find her. She'd go crazy just sitting there. She had to find her own way. She was on her own.

She remembered hearing somewhere that if someone was trying to find his or her way out of the woods, the best thing to do was to find a river and follow that, since a river ran down from a high place to a body of water, and bodies of water meant eventual civilization. She wasn't sure what happened if the body of water was a lake in some even more remote part of the woods, but she supposed the idea made sense in theory. Water would mean people, because after all, people were always drawn to places where one could fish or swim, and at the very least, some governing body would want to own, monitor, and monetize such places. She supposed it was worth a shot. Maybe she could find a park ranger at some nearby lake.

She rose to her feet and listened for the sound of running water, but was not surprised when she didn't hear any; she hadn't been able to hear the traffic from the road she suspected was frustratingly close to where she was. She certainly hadn't heard a human voice since she'd hid from Darren. No hikers or bikers, no trail-gazers or trail-blazers. Not even startled animals. Nilhollow only let her hear what it wanted her to hear—the trees talking among themselves, the mournful wail of . . . wind, was it? Or something else? The whisper of the pines. And of course, her own footsteps. Her own breathing and heartbeat.

Still, something was giving life to what did manage to grow in Nilhollow. There had to be a water source somewhere.

She looked at the nearest tree and saw moss growing to the left of the trunk. She was pretty sure she remembered from Girl Scouts that moss always grew on the north side of things. Her sense of geography wasn't great, either, but she knew there was a lake northwest of Nilhollow. Okay then, there was a place to start. She headed off on a diagonal in her best estimation of northwest of the moss.

She looked up through the canopy of trees. She didn't think it was quite noon yet, and so maybe the position of the sun might confirm that she was, in fact, moving in the right direction. The treetops knitted too closely together, though, for her to make out more than a patch of cloudless sky. It was an unusual shade of blue, not quite right for that time of day. She sighed. Nothing about this undertaking was going to be easy, apparently. That was okay. She would do just fine. She told herself that, almost chanted it to the rhythm of her own footsteps. *Just fine, just fine, everything is just fine.* Regardless of the color of the sky, it was still daylight out, and that had to make it at least a little easier to find her way around without going in circles again.

Just fine, just fine, everything is just fine.

As she walked, she thought about her apartment. She had never wanted to be home so badly in her life. She missed her bed and her sheets, her toothbrush, her favorite tea mug. She missed her bathroom, her tub in particular. In her closets, she could barely fit two pairs of shoes side by side, but the apartment could boast one hell of a tub—sleek, cool porcelain, long enough for her to stretch out in. She would have loved a bath just then, to soak in the hot, sudsy water. Some people had comfort foods or glasses of wine, some had a favorite pair of pajama pants, but for Julia, baths made everything and anything better. There was something about the cocooning warmth of the water that made her feel safe and secure. A bath could ease cramps, ease tension, make her feel complete, clean, and whole again in a way that even a shower couldn't quite do. She enjoyed dozing in the tub, and despite the half-joking warnings of well-meaning acquaintances that she could drown like that, she'd never once even slipped under the water. Perhaps it was that she never slept heavily, or maybe it was the occasional lapping of the water against her skin that reminded her, even in the haze of half sleep, that she wasn't really in bed. Whatever it was, she had never been afraid or even anxious about anything once the bathwater was running.

Julia missed her apartment so much that it felt like suffering through a death. Maybe she'd never had much in the way of lasting, deep, and meaningful relationships, but she'd built herself a true home, a sanctuary, a haven of security and peace that was all her own, and if she could just get back to it, she could take a bath and wash all of yesterday and today from her memory.

Just fine, just fine, everything is just fine.

There was no clearly defined path, but she thought she was doing a pretty good job of heading northwest as the crow flies, as much as she was able. It felt like she walked a long time. She had no one to talk to, and rather than talk to herself—she was doing enough of that inside her head—she made occasional comments to her purse. It didn't feel as weird as she thought it would. Mostly, she whistled. She found, though, that the whistling grew labored as the terrain became a little tougher to navigate. There were a lot more roots and upturned rocks, as if something had been digging or kicking up dirt. Her feet were getting tired, as were her shins and calves. It also felt like she was heading uphill . . . but if she was supposedly heading toward a lake, shouldn't the ground be sloping downward? She wasn't sure. Maybe the lake was on a plateau or something. Besides, there would certainly be dips and crests along the way regardless.

There was a crack of wood and some rustling sounds nearby and for a terrible second, she half expected to see one of those mutated creatures from her dream. She turned her head in the direction of the sound just as she stepped down on a few loose stones. They slipped out from under her, and her legs were suddenly moving in two different directions. She managed to keep one foot from sliding out from under her, but her other kept going, bending sideways and twisting painfully at the ankle as she tried to regain control of it. Despite her best efforts, she spilled clumsily into the dirt, swearing as her legs splayed out in an uncomfortable V. Her ankle pulsed pain like a beacon, and a momentary flare of panic engulfed her. She may not have known much about the outdoors, but even she knew an injury like a sprain or a broken bone could mean death for someone alone in the woods.

She stayed put for a while, holding her aching ankle between her hands. She couldn't ice it, and wasn't sure if binding it tightly would help. She opted not to bother, since she couldn't think of anything to bind it with. She breathed deeply, slowly, willing the pain to go away, and by degrees, it eased up a little. She checked beneath her sock for swelling. The skin was red, but not puffy, so far as she could see. She thought that meant her ankle likely wasn't sprained, and that made her feel a little better. She sat for a few more minutes, though, not wanting to take chances, and waited until her ankle was no more than a dull throb above her shoe.

She rolled onto her knees and got up with slow and measured movements, taking care not to lean too heavily on the injured foot. It occurred to her that a walking stick would help to steady her and maybe take some of the weight off that foot. She supposed she could also use it as a weapon if she needed to. Her thoughts briefly flickered to Darren and how she'd wanted to kill him, but she brushed them aside.

Peering around her, she spied a long, fairly thick branch half-covered in pine needles and oak leaves. It had a small Y on the end. She picked it up and was surprised to find it was light. The stick was a little too long to use as a crutch—she'd have to break the far end off to fit the Y under her arm—but it was otherwise perfect.

She set off again with her stick, the *just fine, just fine* mantra renewed but now to a hop-step, hop-step, and had covered maybe a tenth of a mile when she saw the beginnings of a clearing. Her heart felt lighter, and she allowed herself the small hope that this might be all over. A clearing could mean civilization, or at the very least, a ranger station or something. A faint, bilgy smell wafted in from that direction, and Julia thought it just might be the smell of dead fish. Unpleasant as it was, dead fish meant water. Water meant a river or lake. And that meant people.

Oh, please be a lake. Please. For the love of all that's right and good in the world, please be a frigging lake.

She broke through the clearing and the hope in her immediately withered and crumbled. The clearing was disappointingly devoid of a lake, or of water of any kind, for that matter. In fact, it was very dry, with bushes and tree leaves unnaturally curled and brown and unhealthy-looking. *Certainly no oasis, this*, she thought, and tapped her stick against the ground as if punctuating the thought. The smell there was stronger, and she realized it wasn't of dead fish. Of something dead, most certainly—something rotting out of the sight of prying eyes—but not fish. It turned her stomach.

Then her mind finally registered what was in the center of the clearing, and was immediately filled with a revulsion so intense it made her light-headed. The smell no longer mattered, because she couldn't breathe. She dropped her stick and gasped for air in a desperate attempt to hold on to the clarity and detail of consciousness.

Before her, a chasm stretched like a tight, wicked grin across two-thirds of the clearing, small vines twitching upward along the edges like tiny tongues licking lips. It was just like she'd dreamed it, not wide but infinitely deep, and as she stood rooted in horror, willing the world to remain in focus and the air to fill up her lungs again, there was a small tearing sound. The ground at the corner of one end of the chasm fell away in a little spray of rocks and dirt, and just like that, the grin was wider.

From her distance, she couldn't see into its depths, but she was glad; it might very well have broken her mind if she had looked straight down into it. She knew that as surely as she knew her own hands. It made her know, made her understand its nature somehow, just by her being near it. She could feel what radiated up from there and it was terrible, more awful than anything she had dreamed about it. It wanted to pull her in, feed on every part of her, straight through to her soul. It was a sickness, a poison that had damaged Nilhollow and everything that lived in it, everything that came in contact with it. It filled her head with ugly images of what was to come and suicidal thoughts. It stank of rotting blood.

There was another tearing sound, this one louder. More earth fell away. More long tips of vines sprouted into view, whipping and lashing at the foul air.

The chasm was widening.

"No. No no no no no," she whispered. She staggered back into the woods, to the cool shadow between the trees. Everything was most definitely *not* fine. Then, forgetting her ankle, she turned and ran.

SEVEN

Mallon was worried, and so he drank coffee.

A half hour after the appointed check-in time, he'd tried calling both Pete Grainger's and Vince Perry's cell phones several times, and neither had answered. It was possible—no, scratch that, likely—that there was poor-to-no cell reception out in Nilhollow, so he hadn't really expected an answer the first time. By the fourth time with no response, though, Mallon's gut had kicked in.

It had served him well over the years, that gut, that instinct for knowing when trouble was happening or about to happen. It had been a guiding force in both his personal and professional lives, as much a burden as a safety net. It had given him the heads-up that his first wife was gambling away their retirement fund and that his second wife was cheating on him with his old friend Paulie Foreman, and it had kept a bullet from tearing through his chest during a Wawa holdup back when he was a patrolman. It let him know Fred Houston had sucked up a few good lungfuls of carbon monoxide from his Audi in the double garage of his fancy Ocean County beach house, and let him know his niece was pregnant with her first baby.

It was his gut that told him now that Grainger and Perry were in trouble out there in those damned woods.

If one looked at the current situation with that pair of abandoned cars—a lady and her stalker ex-boyfriend possibly lost in the woods—those were bad circumstances, the kind with ugly endings. Mallon was sure the woman, Julia, was a lovely person, particularly if Grainger held so ardent a torch for her, but it didn't look good for her. He knew that, and he supposed Grainger did, too. The thing was, he was concerned that no responses meant circumstances might be just as bad for his guys, too. Grainger and Perry were trained law enforcement officers with guns. Further, Grainger had grown up in the area, and probably knew parts of that state forest as well as his own backyard. Maybe he didn't know Nilhollow so well, but Grainger knew those woods. His officers should not have had any trouble doing a preliminary search of the area, and if circumstances had gotten more complicated than that, even Perry had enough common sense to call for backup.

So where were they? Why weren't they checking in like he'd told them to?

Mallon had had a bad feeling about the whole thing from the moment Grainger and Perry walked out the station door. His gut had told him it was a mistake to let them leave. It wasn't that he couldn't trust them or worried inordinately about them. They were good cops, capable men. But there were the stories about Nilhollow, some more credible than others, and every once in a while, a reason for those kinds of stories reared its leafy head. Something might very well be going on in that forest that was more than just a lover's spat gone wrong, something Grainger and Perry would be unprepared for. It was starting to feel more and more like a stupid move to have let them go out there.

Most of the stories the Red Lion Station had investigated and filed about Nilhollow were little oddities, little unexplained circumstances that gave the responding officer a good story to tell at the bar or at worst, a night of uneasy sleep. Of course, there had been one guy, Joe Franklin, who once had investigated lights in the woods, what Mallon's grandmother used to call will-o'-the-wisps. Joe wouldn't talk about what he'd seen or heard that night, but his resignation was on Mallon's desk the next day. All Mallon could get out of him was some mumbling about the way dead girls whisper.

"What?" Mallon had asked, unsure he'd heard the man correctly.

Joe had grimaced like he'd eaten something sour. "Old, old memories. Old voices from the past. But it's shown me I . . . just can't do this job, boss. I'm done." And he was. He'd turned in his badge and gun and never looked back. Mallon had thought at the time that Joe probably just wasn't cut out for the job. Plenty of people weren't, and that was okay. But then, after a drunken night at a popular cop hangout in town, called O'Malley's, Joe had blathered on about a cold case from when he was a little kid, where a bunch of little girls had gone missing, and how the wind could blow such a way through the trees in Nilhollow that little dead girls told you all their secrets, and Mallon had wondered if Joe maybe would have failed a psych evaluation. When a year and a half later, Mallon was called out to Moorestown to cut down Joe from one of the rafters in his dining room, Mallon wasn't so sure a psych evaluation would have revealed the crux of Joe's problem. He supposed the suicide note did, though. It was only one line, hastily scribbled across a piece of notebook paper:

Can't take the whispering anymore.—Joe

While the crime scene unit finished up inside the house, Mallon had sat a long time in one of the old lawn chairs in Joe's backyard, smoking a cigarette as dusk crept in all around him. Joe was the first officer he'd ever lost, even if he hadn't been an officer at the time. And why? Will-o'-the-wisps and whispers? What had happened to Joe in Nilhollow?

Little green glowing beacons of lightning bugs in Joe's garden had left faint and fading trails, and Mallon shivered in spite of the warm summer air.

He remembered concluding that Nilhollow didn't just take drunk and drugged-up teens, or woefully underprepared hikers and campers. It took smart, capable cops, too. Sometimes it followed them home, and that made it seem somehow more sinister, more calculating, more predatory than the usual indifferent natural world.

Most of the guys working for him today hadn't known Joe Franklin. They knew about Nilhollow, though. They joked about it— *half* joked—but among them was an unspoken, understood unease about the place, which Mallon did little to dissuade. It kept them alert. One had to be alert in Nilhollow, always. He knew that, not just from work-related run-ins but from his own personal experience, as well.

It wasn't anything the other guys at the station knew about. It wasn't in his file, wasn't going to follow him through his career and come back and bite him when he was up for promotions. It was on his own time, off duty, and he'd handled it on his own. It was a big contributor, though, to the fine-tuned sensitivity of his gut when it came to Nilhollow.

When he was a younger man, back before his current position at the Red Lion Station, he'd actually very much enjoyed taking walks in the woods. He'd grown up in northern Jersey, back when there were still acres of woods to walk through, and he'd spent many a sunny Sunday afternoon along the wooded paths of Ramapo Mountain, Stokes, Jenny Jump, and Worthington State Forests. He'd even done little hiking trails in the forested parks of Morris and Sussex Counties. He hadn't really thought of it as hiking, or of himself as a hiker. Those were the folks who did the Appalachian Trail with big rolled-up packs on their backs and bottled water in their hands. He just liked to stroll along the paths and reconnect a little with the beautiful things. His job consisted of a lot of ugliness, a lot of the insides of rooms where angry, tense, or traumatized people, usually unhappy to see him and his ilk, were holed up answering questions they really didn't want to answer or simply couldn't.

So Mallon took any chance that came along to get away from that, to be where things made sense, where if violence had to take place, it served a purpose, and if death happened, it was only to make way for new life. Mallon didn't think about mortgage or alimony payments in the woods, nor did he worry about heart attacks or paperwork or how much it would cost to get his wife at the time the new washing machine and dryer set she wanted for Christmas, while still saving to fix the roof and update the septic system. In the woods, there were no office politics or Facebook politics, no reality TV and internet memes, no late payments or mounting bills. He didn't worry about getting too old or too tired or too fed up with the people he was supposed to be protecting and serving—not out there in the woods, he didn't. Among the trees, there was a sense of vibrancy, immortality, and extraordinary magnificence. There was a feeling for him of a majesty bigger than himself, of life unfazed by the little daily, weekly, or even yearly minutiae that most people worried themselves into early graves over.

Every detective Mallon knew had an escape—fishing, poker, woodworking, car restoration, booze, women, volunteer work, cooking. It was necessary to have a pressure valve in a job like that. For Mallon, getting out to the woods was his escape.

Then he started working for the Red Lion Station.

Mallon had looked forward to the idea of exploring a new state forest, especially one as virtually untouched as Nilhollow. He imagined it was a little like how astronauts must feel, stepping onto land that had never felt the tread of human feet.

The rumors didn't much phase him. If Mallon had ever been inclined to admit to a flaw, it was that he believed too much in his own wits and his senses, and was disinclined to accept that there was a challenge he couldn't meet if he had half a mind to. If anything, the old-timers' warnings to stay out of those woods only spurred that little stubborn aspect of his character to prove to them that their ghosts didn't know who they were messing with.

It had been an early fall day, and Nilhollow was beautiful, a blazing conflagration of reds and yellows and oranges where the oaks and cedars grew, and deep greens and purples bristling along the groves of pines. There were no hiking or biking trails, no signs or paint squares on trunks to indicate human taming, only Mallon and the wild nature all around him, and he loved it. Sure, he had noticed the unearthly stillness of the place, the distinct absence of birds and squirrels and deer. He had noticed the occasional odd scent. But it was autumn, and the smells of earth turning over, of life giving over to death for a while so that new life could start again, were not all bad. There was a powerful sense of that grandness in Nilhollow, the passage of ages right over the heads of men. The fact that Mallon couldn't hear the dull roar of traffic seemed appropriate, even reverent. What was that quote about trees being temples and forests being cathedrals? That was about right. It was the closest he'd ever felt to what other people thought of as God.

And there may very well have been gods in Nilhollow, but not the one his dear old Irish-Catholic grandmother seemed so fond of.

Mallon had made it a half mile or so into Nilhollow when to his delight, he discovered a small grove of trees that seemed clustered in an almost perfect circle. Within the circle was a clearing containing piles of cairn stones, some of them about waist high, forming small angular inward spirals around a deep, narrow ditch in the center. It was an amazingly painstaking work of art, really, the way the stones were placed, like tiny upward-facing solar systems in tiny galaxies all over the universe of the clearing. The tallest stacks occurred at random intervals, or so it seemed to Mallon, and featured wide, flat stones on top, while many of the smaller stacks featured flat stones as bases with smaller ones forming small pyramid-like mounds. Mallon was no expert, but he heard once that many cairn stones, particularly those of the indigenous people of the area, were meant to represent people and animals. He imagined they might represent something more celestial or at least spiritual, though. All of the flat-top stones had dark brown smears of finger-painted markings on them, symbols vaguely reminiscent of eyes or mouths, arrows, stars, and trees.

From the branches surrounding the cairn stones, small lashed-together constructions of twigs and branches hung, mostly somewhat X-shaped. There weren't many of them, and they weren't all the same formations or size, but Mallon found them fascinating—found the whole grove fascinating. It had obviously once been a very sacred, very carefully constructed monument to something, and although Mallon didn't know anything about the ancient people who might have made it, their respect for the place was palpable. He couldn't help but share that respect, too.

The most unusual aspect of it was a small center table (it reminded Mallon of an altar), which stood waist high and was wide enough only to straddle the center of the deep ditch. On it lay a kind of corn-doll thing with a crown of sticks and leaves. It was small, the size of a child, clothed in scant strips of hide and fur. A burlap sack formed its head and hands, and its body was a collection of bound sticks. A crudely painted face consisted of two black-orbed eyes, and a small, jagged mouth had been roughly torn into the fabric beneath a little painted nose so that it appeared to be screaming. That silent scream was choked off by a clump of black feathers and little bones stuffed inside the mouth. On its body sat a little piece of blue checkered flannel.

A discarded scarecrow of some kind? No, there was something about the look of the corn-dolly that suggested it had been made specifically for that grove. It was old and faded but still decades, maybe centuries newer than the stone slab on which it lay; someone had to have put it there recently, a new offering in an old church. While it nettled him a little that someone else had recently been through what he'd come to think of as his private sanctuary, what nagged at him even more was that piece of flannel. There were faded stains on its underside that he thought could be dried blood. Who had put it and the corn-dolly there, and why? Glancing around, Mallon saw no beer cans, no cigarette butts lying around, no wax drippings or graffiti, and no plastic or bits of glass—essentially, no signs of teenagers playing Satanist in the woods.

His gaze traveled back to that piece of flannel. His gut told him it meant something.

It seemed sacrilegious in a way to step among the cairn stone spirals, but he did, carefully picking his way around the rocks so as not to disturb any of them. Instinctively, it seemed important that they remain just as they were.

At the center, standing by that stone altar, his head had begun to ache and his limbs felt heavy. It had felt a little like that point where drunk starts to transition to hangover. The feeling wasn't coming from the doll, it seemed, but from the stones. No . . . *not* the stones, but under them, from the ground itself. From that ditch beneath the altar, which he noticed now was longer than he'd first thought and much deeper, its bottom shrouded in caliginous obscurity. The longer he stood there, the more pervasive that sluggish, queasy feeling got, spreading across his face and down to his chest, his stomach, even his groin. Impulsively, he snatched the flannel, and then as quickly and carefully as he could, navigated out of the stone spiral. Once he had returned to the woods proper, his head cleared immediately, and he felt much better. He looked from the grove to the tiny bound sachet of flannel he had removed from the corn-doll's mouth. Carefully, he untied it, and spread the contents out on his palm.

There was a quartz crystal, some herbs he didn't recognize, tiny bones that crumbled a bit when he touched them, and a small piece of wood about the size and shape of a Scrabble tile. On the piece of wood was a series of minutely painted symbols way more complex than any on the cairn stones or in any of the lattice works. They didn't look at all like the symbols of an indigenous tribe's language to him. In fact, they didn't look like any symbols or language he had ever seen. His gut told him they were meant to counteract ideas from a language and philosophy he probably was better off never knowing.

He had tied everything back up in the little piece of flannel and without really thinking it through, he pocketed it. That night, he had put it on a small shelf in the hallway outside his bedroom, where he kept interesting things he found on his walks, and then he'd mostly forgotten about it.

That was before Hurricane Sandy and all the flooding. Out of curiosity, Mallon had gone back once after the storm to see if the cairn stones had been knocked down, but time and nature had changed the area so much. The spot where the grove was located was now a barren, somewhat unhealthy clearing—no stones, no circle of trees, standing or otherwise. The only thing even remotely familiar to him in that clearing of sparse and strangled vegetation was that deep, narrow ditch in the earth and the dead-things stench it emitted. Once after that, he went back to what he thought was the same spot, and even though he'd always had a pretty good sense of direction, he couldn't even find the clearing, let alone the ditch. If he had been the type given to imagination, he would have thought the woods rearranged themselves between every trip he made to Nilhollow.

He'd lost track of the area somehow, but it hadn't lost track of him. He'd had terrifying nightmares after finding the clearing the first time, the kind that jerked him awake, soaked in sweat. In each of the nocturnal scenes the most heinous acts unfolded and he couldn't stop any of them. In many, he was bound by vines and tree roots while the people he loved most were tortured to death in the most archaic and barbarian ways. All of the atrocities occurred in the heart of Nilhollow and all of them featured that tiny flannel pouch in some way. So he'd gotten rid of it—he'd swiped it off his shelf and burned it in the garbage can outside, in fact, before gathering up the ashes in a bag that he drove to a dumpster the next town over. He wanted it as far away as possible. That had helped with the nightmares a little; they weren't as frequent or intense as they used to be. But they still haunted his sleep from time to time, just to remind him of all the sadistic, depraved things he couldn't stop people from doing to other people, no matter how good a cop he tried to be.

As Mallon sat at his desk drinking coffee, he thought of that little flannel pouch and what he'd found inside. He'd done occasional research on its contents over the years, ever since the nightmares started. Some spiritualists—Wiccans, pagans, and whatnot—believed quartz had purifying properties. They believed the same thing about certain herbs. Practitioners of voodoo often used flannel to make protection sachets. Corn-dollies were a Celtic way of appeasing and offering shelter to corn spirits after harvests. He'd even found something about using bones as a talisman, but the article online was not terribly specific as to what for.

So what did it all mean? In Mallon's mind, absolutely nothing. He had come to understand that it hadn't been the pouch that had given him nightmares, but the force coming up from that chasm, the rotting essence that had made him feel sick, which the little flannel pouch had been marinating in for countless years. Probably, the flannel pouch had been meant to stop that force, and it had miserably failed. It was essentially nothing powerful enough, if one were inclined to believe in the power of those things to begin with, to have caused or prevented what happened—what was still happening, apparently—in Nilhollow. Neither were the cairn-stone galaxies and the little wooden lattice trinkets, however beautiful, or all the other occult odds and ends that his officers had occasionally pulled out of the woods with recovered missing people and dead bodies.

People who knew a little about a number of magical practices in the world but not a whole lot about any one of them had been dabbling. Maybe they were well-meaning sorts who'd had their own run-ins with Nilhollow. Regardless, he was pretty sure that layers of halfhearted beliefs and amateur attempts at magic weren't making things there any better. If anything, he thought they might possibly have made things worse. All that focused energy had done nothing more than scatter whatever was left tying that place down to the laws of reality.

Maybe the power coming out of the ground among the stones had always been there. Maybe at some point it had gone bad. Maybe the earth moved, shifted, cracked open, threw up the bad things that made it sick, or maybe some other universe had sprung a leak under this one, and *its* bad stuff found its way to the surface. Maybe it was acid rain or pollution or global warming. Maybe it was secret government testing. Who the hell knew? It didn't matter, because Grainger had been right about the increasing numbers of missing people, murders, suicides, and even so-called accidental deaths in that area.

Still, it was a conflict between his very rational, proof-seeking brain and his animal-instinct gut. There might still be people, *real* people and not ghosts, monsters, or UFOs, who believed more fervently in all those stories than the average townsperson, the kind of people who would do whatever it took to manifest those things, or give the appearance of their manifestation. They might honestly believe there were creatures to be appeased in the forest, and they might not be above kidnapping the occasional hiker or assaulting the occasional investigating officer to make that happen. Did unexplained things happen out there? Oh, most definitely. But a lot of things could be explained by good old-fashioned human evil.

So which was it, in this case? Where were his officers?

Mallon drank more coffee, picked up his cell, and dialed a number.

If Grainger and Perry didn't check in by the end of that hour, Mallon was going in after them.

By the time the sun had swept past the midday position in the sky, Pete was exhausted—far more exhausted than he should have been. He was also hungry and a little thirsty, with no means to relieve either condition. Those concerns weren't as pressing as his fatigue, though. He knew some of it was shock, trauma, and the gradual dissipation of adrenaline. He thought some of it was the exertion of struggling through the wild growth of the forest. He feared it was also the constant inhalation of the air in Nilhollow, the constant brushes with its ferns and tree branches and pine needles. To keep himself going, he worked a problem over in his head, a disparity he couldn't quite resolve.

When Todd Mackey had been found, he most certainly had been exhibiting weird behaviors. He had appeared crazy enough that the local psychiatric facility was interested in evaluating him. But then while Pete had been asking him questions, he'd seemed normal . . . well, almost normal. Rational, at least. There was clarity in his eyes, an understanding of his words that suggested to Pete that he was okay, at least for a while. Then whatever he had carried with him out of those woods seemed to have doubled down on him, and it killed him.

The first part of the problem was more what Todd implied rather than said: that the woods had gotten to his brother first and killed him outright. If that were true—and those tree-creatures he had seen, whatever they were, seemed to prove that—then why had one brother been killed and the other spared, at least for a time? Was it specifically to promote some kind of . . . seeding? Or was it just that Nilhollow was like rabies, in that once a person was infected, it was only a matter of time?

The notion led to the second part of the problem. Perry had succumbed so quickly to some kind of madness, but Pete was . . . well, more or less okay. He didn't feel great, granted; his mind and body felt hungover and he gladly would have sacrificed a few fingers for a couple hours of sleep. Still, he felt in control of his mind. His thoughts were his, and so far as he could tell, they were sane and rational. But were they? Was he really okay? And would he feel it if—*when*—Nilhollow finally got to him?

After Perry was killed, he'd guessed the crazy-sickness could have been like poison ivy—some people were more allergic than others, and the more he thought about it, the more he felt sure that was the case. Maybe some people could stave off the insanity better or longer than others. Maybe some folks were easier targets.

He chuckled bitterly to himself at that last idea. His old man had told him all his life that he was an easy target. Too quiet, too meek, too easy to fluster. He used to wish he could be more like his old man, with a strong handshake, an alpha-wolf presence, and a voice no one ever ignored. However, in the end, it hadn't gotten Richard Grainger much in life besides Margie Grainger, Pete's mother, and that hadn't evidently been enough for him, so he'd up and left when Pete was eight. Eventually, at some point thereafter, Pete had ceased to find anything to admire about his old man.

Pete shook his head. Thinking about his parents was not only disheartening, but it wouldn't explain what he was up against and it certainly wouldn't provide any clues as to where Julia might be.

No one left.

Those were the words painted on the tree. He chose to interpret that as meaning Julia and Darren, and maybe others, were still there, that no one had yet left the woods. It was more hopeful than the alternative, that there was no point in looking for anyone anymore.

Nilhollow wasn't that big—no more than, what? A mile square? He'd find her. He couldn't *not* find her.

He hoped she was okay, wherever she was. She had to be terrified. Julia had many strengths, but she would have been the first to admit that self-sufficiency was not high on that list. One of the things he found so attractive about her, though, was the fact that she actually was very capable, even though she didn't always see that. She had amazing reserves of strength. She was smarter than people thought, more resourceful than people noticed, and a hell of a lot braver than anyone ever gave her credit for. She was so beautiful on the outside, but she glowed on the inside; she was vulnerably, endearingly honest with her heart, a heart so full of love and understanding and appreciation, even if those things were wasted on assholes like Darren. She was complex and fascinating and fun and spontaneous and in some ways, utterly fearless.

And because of all that, Pete knew she was still alive. She had to be. He hated to think of her being scared, because he had no doubt she was, but he knew that she could make it through anyway.

If she didn't run into those tree-creatures, that is. Or worse. He thought again about Perry and shivered. Pete was starting to believe that those tree things might actually be the least of his problems in these woods. The idea of a driving force behind the crazy-sickness, something that had even corrupted those tree-creatures, made sense when he thought about what happened to Perry. He didn't think the tree-creatures had driven his partner to attack them just so they could kill him. They had seemed as surprised by his behavior as Pete had. And what had they told him?

All is unwell. Much is and will be forgotten here. Swallowed up. Time is short.

Maybe they hadn't only been talking about him and Julia forgetting things, or being forgotten or swallowed up. It had sounded to him like maybe they knew they were susceptible to the craziness in Nilhollow, too. That could be what their warning meant, that next time he encountered them, they might not remember why they had let him go—or remember him at all. They might not remember that there was a good reason not to tear him apart, too.

Further, the tree-creatures had indicated something worse, something even they seemed afraid of. He couldn't remember the word they had used, but they thought of it as something Pete would want to protect Julia from. The sense he got from them was of something big either in size or importance or both. How did that thing fit in with Todd Mackey's story, or what happened to Perry? How did it fit in with what might be happening to Julia? Was it the cause of people going crazy or going missing in the woods? He didn't get that vibe from the tree-creatures; rather, he felt they thought of it as a worst-case example of what happened when that crazy-sickness ran rampant inside. Maybe it was the thing that thought of the tree-creatures as the "little ones." Geez, what in God's name would he do if he came across *that*? As Perry would have said, he'd be fucked a hundred ways to Sunday.

The tree-creatures had said something else of interest, too: *The*

Turning grows stronger. He couldn't have said why just then, but he thought the Turning, whatever it was, might be how the tree-creatures thought of the origin of the crazy-sickness. If it was growing stronger, his time was running out.

As he trudged along, he happened to glance up and notice that the trees in front of him rippled a little, as if he was viewing them through a wave of heat.

Uh-oh. That couldn't be good. He slowed his pace. Trying to focus on the trees hurt his eyes and head. He turned away until the feeling eased up a little. That brain-fog was coming back, though, and Pete didn't know how to stop it. He had to get out of there. He shifted his attention back on the trees.

There stood Perry.

Pete blinked. The breath in his chest tightened. He could feel a pulse of pain in his head with each beat of his heart. What he was seeing, that couldn't be right. That couldn't be Perry . . . could it?

"Vince?" Pete's voice was small. The word hung between them.

To say Perry looked off would have been an understatement. He looked like he'd been buried, dug up, and slapped back to life, as Pete's grandmother used to say. Perry smiled as if his face was a little rusty just beneath the pale skin. There was something wrong with his eyes, too. They looked . . . flat, somehow, the way a painted doll's eyes looked flat, and they didn't seem to fit quite right in his head. Also, there was a faint, coppery light behind them that seeped out around them from the sockets. When he waved, his movements seemed stiff and uneasy, like he wasn't used to using his body. Some part of Pete knew it couldn't be Perry. It was a marionette version, a Perry-puppet, that stood there grinning at him. Part of the Nilhollow crazy-sickness. But which had been the hallucination—Perry's death, or Perry's apparent resurrection? It was hard for Pete to make that determination with his head pounding like it was.

"Perry? Perry, man, are . . . are you okay?" The question sounded lame even to Pete. Of course Perry wasn't okay. He'd been ripped limb from limb by tree monsters and tossed like confetti. How could he possibly be okay?

He looked in one piece now, though, not that it was a particularly comforting improvement. His hair was sticking up in little cowlicks, and there was a crust of dried blood following his hairline from his temple to just above his right eye. His uniform was a mess, too, torn in places and smeared with mud—or dried blood; it was hard to tell against the dark material—and kind of cardboard-looking, molded along his body like a shell rather than fabric. His pockets were torn open, and he was missing a shoe. Overall, he looked faded, the way some of the plants growing around the trees looked faded, as if whatever tied them—and Perry—to this world was being drained away.

Pete's eyes narrowed. He watched Perry cautiously, although Perry's slow advancement toward him wasn't overtly threatening.

"Hey, buddy," Pete said, holding up a placating hand. "Maybe, uh, maybe you should just stay there. Just hold on a minute."

Perry shook his head. He was close enough now that Pete could see that a faint blue pattern beneath his skin, not like veins but more like wood-grain, had given him that unwholesome grayish appearance. The trees around him rippled, and Pete felt suddenly light-headed. He thought he heard faint singing again, coming from somewhere far behind Perry. Every part of him screamed in silence that something was wrong, that Perry was dead and that he would be, too, if he let that abomination come any closer to him, but he couldn't quite figure out how to run.

Pete went to grab for his gun instead, then remembered he didn't have it anymore. In front of him, Perry laughed, made a shooting gesture against his own head with two fingers and a thumb, then laughed again. It was a very hollow sound, not like Perry's laugh at all. The light behind his eyes glowed a little brighter, and for one awful moment, Pete thought the brightness might have just enough power behind it to pop those eyes right out of their sockets.

Of course, it wasn't Perry. Not Perry at all. He'd known that deep down, but . . . he had to admit, he was having some trouble that day with what was real and what wasn't. If it wasn't Perry moving toward him, what was it?

Pete backed up. A weapon . . . he needed a weapon. He searched the ground for something he could use.

The Perry-thing stopped a few feet in front of him and its parched, rough lips pulled back. Pete felt sick. All of the Perry-thing's teeth were tiny, sharp shards of bone and wood—rows of them, packed tightly together in a dirty, predatory grin.

"Gonna kill ya, Grainge," it said. The voice echoed with the same hollow timbre as its laugh. "Gonna feed ya to the Chasm."

"I don't think you want to do that," Pete said, buying time. His glance fell on a large stick at the base of a nearby tree. He thought he might be able to snatch it up before the Perry-thing was on him.

"Oh, but I think I do. The best part of living things is their dying."

"What are you?" Pete didn't really expect an answer, but he felt compelled to ask, anyway.

The Perry-thing laughed. "Don't you know?"

"I know you're not Perry."

It shook its head. "No, I certainly am not."

"Are you one of those tree-things?"

The Perry-thing looked impatiently to the sky, then back to Pete. "Oh, Grainge. I'm not one of the little ones. I am the Turning! I am the Willfulness Beneath the Woods—much older than the trees, older than your little tree spirits, the *manëtuwàk*, older even than their mad forest king, the Kèkpëchehëlat. I am the clay of destruction, the echo of all things buried and waiting. Come to the grove and see. See the Chasm."

Pete nodded slowly as he took a step toward the stick. "So . . . you're the madness in this forest. You're the one who's making everyone sick. Crazy."

The Perry-thing clapped its hands in delight. "I am the madness and the clarity, the lies and the truth. The voice that issues from the throat of the Chasm. I'm not a someone, but an everything."

Pete took another step toward the stick. "You're batshit insane, is what you are."

"These little names and titles are fun. Your kind puts so much stock in words and titles. And I enjoy them. I do. But in the end, what to call me really shouldn't matter to you. You're going to die regardless, to feed the Chasm. Your bones will be ground to dust."

Pete dove for the stick. His hands closed around it and he swung it up and toward the Perry-thing. It grinned at him briefly and then the stick connected with its face . . . and passed through a haze of spores. Pete coughed and quickly turned away from them.

When he turned back, an arm thrown up over his nose and throat to keep the spores out, he saw that all traces of the Perry-thing were gone.

He stood panting a moment, his body sore, his lungs feeling as if he'd inhaled the unsatisfying cold air of deep winter, and he knew that he'd been close—too close—to the heart of what had destroyed Mackey and Perry. Why it hadn't destroyed him yet, too, was still a mystery, but he suspected it might have had something to do with a unique goal in mind that kept at least some of his thoughts clear.

"Julia!" he called out, desperate in that moment to hear her voice, to know she was okay. "Julia!"

All thoughts of staying quiet and under the radar of whatever ruled the woods had left him. The craziness, the Turning, knew he was here, just as the tree-creatures knew he was here. There was no sense hiding.

"Julia!"

He listened for several long seconds, but there was no answer. He did his best to suppress that panic in his chest. She was okay. She had to be. And he would find her. He started walking again, his body tensely on guard. Maybe she was hiding somewhere. He hoped she was.

There was an awful lot to hide from, though.

The little ones, the tree-creatures, the *manëtuwàk*—they were some kind of elemental spirits, it seemed, at least according to the Perry-thing. Pete wasn't sure it was such a reliable source, but the idea of elemental tree spirits made a lot of sense. Pete could vaguely remember from grammar school a history chapter on the Lenape tribes that had settled the Nilhollow area ten thousand years ago, and *manëtuwàk* sounded like it could be a Lenape word. In fact, the concept of tree-spirits sounded very much like a belief ancient tribes would have had. The other word, the Kèkpëchehëlat... that was the powerful thing the tree-creatures had referred to; Pete was sure of it. The Perry-thing had intimated that it was some kind of bigger, badder version of the *manëtuwàk*, their forest king, which was in keeping with the mental impressions the tree-creatures had given him. It was perhaps why they were afraid of it, and afraid of how much of a hold the Turning had over it.

What worried him most, though, was the Perry-thing itself. It had rambled and pontificated a lot, but what, exactly, was it? Pete suspected it wasn't so much an entity as simply a force gone insane itself, a manifestation of the powerful insanity that infested Nilhollow. Pete thought maybe the Perry-form was meant specifically for him, a means of this sentient craziness beneath the earth to communicate with its victims. It appeared as Perry to him because guilt could be a significant driving force in the direction of madness, and maybe madness and death, the deterioration of body and mind, were what sustained it. It didn't matter if it was human or inhuman deterioration; apparently it affected both equally.

If it was a thinking force, then Pete guessed it wanted to survive, to grow by spreading itself through its environment . . . and to feed. To lure prey, it got into the mind and tried to trick it, confuse it, and wear it down. That suggested to Pete that if there was a way to shield one's mind, one might be able to avoid going insane long enough to get out of there.

Pete rubbed his head, which was not completely clear of the brain-fog seemingly caused by close contact with the madness-infected denizens of Nilhollow. All of these theories about tree spirits and thinking forces from underground sounded outlandish, but seemed to fit. Of course, he'd always known that there was an internal, personal logic in a madman's hallucinations. How could he possibly tell if it made any true sense, or was just his own crazy-sickness taking root and already spiraling out of control? How could he be sure of anything he'd experienced since he'd set foot in the woods?

A frightening thought occurred to him. What if he was somehow responsible for killing Perry, and didn't even know it? Could he have imagined creatures tearing him apart as he murdered his partner himself?

No. He took a deep breath and exhaled shakily. The idea was too inconceivable to entertain. Even crazy, it just wasn't in Pete to have hurt his partner and friend. This was the insidiousness of Nilhollow, he decided—the confusion, the self-doubt. It was meant to distract him and break him down.

Well, that wasn't going to happen. He was going to find Julia and get them both out of there.

And that was when he heard the scream.

EIGHT

Julia flopped down against a tree trunk, breathing hard, aware of each and every little discomfort in her body: the roughness of the tree bark against her back through the thin material of her T-shirt, the cold dampness of the leaves she sat on, sinking into her jeans. The chilly air that brushed across her bare arms promised only to get colder. She was getting hungry. Her head hurt. Her ankle ached and her feet had blistered in at least two places. She had to go to the bathroom.

And she was helplessly, profoundly, overwhelmingly lost, in an area of the Pine Barrens with the shadowed reputation of swallowing people whole. She was alone.

She didn't really think she was alone in Nilhollow, did she? She was pretty sure she was not. Maybe Darren was still somewhere out there tracking her, hunting her down, creeping closer through that unearthly stillness that blanketed everything, clutching his ax.

Although it wasn't Darren that she kept feeling was watching her. Her intuition told her that. Her dreams told her he'd never watch her again. But something *was* watching her. Sometimes she thought she even saw its hands in the curves of branches and its face in different clumps of leaves. It was stalking her. Maybe the figure she'd seen was a manifestation of it, possibly trying to gauge her reaction, and even as a featureless shadow, it had scared the hell out of her.

There was also that chasm, and the dreadful implications surrounding it, which she couldn't quite convince herself were just dream-remnants. This forest was bad right down to its essence. A maliciousness permeated the air, the ground, the strange growing things. "Murderous woods," indeed. And she couldn't find her way out of it.

Tears of frustration welled up in her eyes. They felt cold as they spilled down her cheeks, as if this place had stolen her inner warmth like it had already stolen her sense of safety and her confidence. Maybe those three things were one and the same.

Julia took a deep and shuddering breath. *No.* Now was not the time for helplessness or panic. She thought about Darren again, couldn't help it—thought about how often he had called her useless, crippled, and weak. She wasn't. She *wasn't.*

She couldn't argue the fact that people had done things for her all her life, from her parents, friends, roommates, and coworkers to a string of boys and men who had been eager to impress her. She had always been willing to believe those people's stated or implied intentions of genuine affection or helpfulness, and to accept their gestures as the signs of caring they were presented to be. It had taken her awhile to spot the often passive-aggressive resentment beneath their words and actions; it had simply never occurred to her that any of these people might have had ulterior motives in paying for things or offering to drive her places or fixing things for her. Frustration with her or others' successful fulfillment of those ulterior motives changed things, but Julia hadn't realized that at first, so it had often left her dumbfounded when people around her inexplicably gave up or turned on her. In fact, it ironically had taken Darren to make it painfully clear, Darren with his distance and impatience followed by possessiveness, his hostility and his explanations, curt and cruel as they were, and finally, his threats.

Maybe through inexperience she had, for most of her time on the earth, been largely helpless when it came to the finer points of day-to-day adult life. Maybe she had needed Darren early on. He often had told her that the only thing she brought to the relationship was sex, and it had made her try all the harder to prove she could be more. She'd begged for second chances, for the room to learn and grow as partners. She always managed to say or do something to set off that disapproval, building to rage, but she certainly tried to make things right. Her capacity to love earnestly and vulnerably, her depth of understanding and patience—perhaps they didn't matter to Darren, serving only to reinforce in his mind his picture of her as a naïve damsel in distress, a fairy-tale child in a woman's body. But she'd come to realize those qualities were good things, even lovable things. Things Darren didn't appreciate, and so would have to live without now.

The first time he left her, she should have recognized it as the cruel and manipulative method of control it was, but she hadn't—not then. He wasn't violent or threatening then, just disapproving, just chipping away at her self-esteem so he could pour himself through the cracks in her. She was crushed, of course. She believed he was right, that she'd be nothing without him. She couldn't have imagined feeling more lost than those first few days after the breakup. But then he'd taken her back, and in doing so, consumed her sense of self again, sealing off her complaints, her fears, her protests. Even now, surrounded by the silence and the trees and the sun arcing toward an early dusk, she was not nearly as lost or alone as she'd been under Darren's renewed efforts to hold on to her.

When she left him, she'd sworn that no one and nothing would ever make her feel that way again.

She was not helpless, not anymore. She'd found strength in herself once, and would do it again.

Julia ground the tears from her eyes with the dirt-streaked heel of her palm and sniffled. She'd triage her discomforts, get back to herself so she could think clearly. She could do this. She was not useless.

She rose on shaky legs and made her way to a small dirt patch that an underground root had caused to slant down and away from her. She pulled off her sneakers and set them aside, then tucked her socks into them. The cool earth beneath her feet sent a shiver through her. She glanced around again for those spying eyes she couldn't seem to find before realizing the ironic ridiculousness of that, and then, with a small, self-conscious smile, she unbuttoned and unzipped her jeans. As she pulled them down, goose bumps stippled her legs. She felt exposed and vulnerable. She had to fight against years of behavioral training and the urge to cover herself as she slid down her underwear. She squatted, and although she could feel urgent pressure in her bladder, it took a long time for the urine stream to flow. She closed her eyes and tried thinking of waterfalls while she flexed the tiny muscles down there, then tried imagining she was in a real bathroom, safe and alone. Finally, when she tried thinking about nothing at all, the dam broke. She giggled, relieved, at the soft patter in the dirt. Tiny splashes against her ankles struck her as distasteful, but that was a minor thing compared to the triumph of completing the act, as well as the small but real victory of having found a spot that minimized the potential messiness.

She wiped with a clean but wadded-up tissue she found in her jeans pocket, then pulled up her underwear and jeans. She washed her hands with a little bit of water from her water bottle. *There*, she thought, satisfied. *One problem solved.*

A growling insistence in her stomach presented the next issue to tackle. She had that half-squashed granola bar at the bottom of her purse. It wouldn't be much, probably wouldn't do for long, but it was something. After that, she'd probably have to rely on the forest for food. She frowned. She remembered reading somewhere that a lot of weeds and wild berries were edible, but she had no idea how to tell which ones. Could she eat pinecones or acorns? She thought so. What about moss? She made a face. She was almost certain the strange red, brown, and white fungal growths peeking up from the brush or clinging to tree trunks were poisonous, but what about leaves or tree bark?

She rummaged through her bag for the granola bar, and was relieved when her hand closed around the rectangular shape. She tore into the wrapper, devouring the bar faster than she probably should have and washing it down with a conservative gulp of her water. She probably should have saved some of the bar for later. Who knew when, or what, she'd get to eat again? She supposed if she broke her compact's mirror, she could somehow wedge those glass shards into a stick and use it like a knife, but she didn't think she'd be fast enough to hunt something. Even if she could hunt, she didn't much relish the thought of killing something to eat. She thought she might very well starve before she ate a bug, in fact. So she was back to taking her chance on plants when the time came. But she'd have to worry about that later. For now, the granola bar had taken the bite out of her hunger, and for that, she was grateful.

Before putting her socks and shoes back on, she examined her feet. It was a relief to find she hadn't collected any more blisters, though the old ones oozed a little, and the souls of her feet were red and sweaty. The cool ground beneath them felt good, and she dug her toes in and wiggled them. She inspected her ankle and thought it was starting to look a little swollen. She had no idea how to tell if it was sprained; she didn't think it was, but the ache was starting to match the one in her head. She leaned some weight on it and it responded with a flare of pain. She thought maybe she was supposed to wrap it tightly, but nothing in her purse was going to accomplish *that*. She sighed.

She dug around in her purse until she found the small bottle of ibuprofen and shook two pills out into her hand. She considered the pain for a moment, and dumped out another one. Then she took all three with water from her bottle—she'd never been able to swallow pills dry—and tucked both the water and pain reliever bottles back into her purse.

Julia took a deep breath and exhaled slowly. *Okay, so far so good.* She was managing. She was okay.

She pushed thoughts of that chasm and of the dream from the night before from her mind. She *was* okay. She was just fine. Everything was fine.

Above her, the sky was growing dark, even though it was too early for that. Time apparently moved differently in Nilhollow, though, just like distance seemed to be laid out arbitrarily. She'd heard that rumor, among others, but her time in the woods had proved it true for her. Maybe it should have bothered her more that so much evidence around her confirmed that Nilhollow was haunted, but just then, she was more concerned with the immediate and concrete dangers of being lost in a forest in general. It occurred to her that it was likely a way for her brain to cope with a situation that would otherwise have overwhelmed her, and that was okay. If she ever made it out of Nilhollow, she was sure she'd have plenty of long nights to catch up on all the layers of trauma, naturally or supernaturally caused, that her experiences had provided.

If she made it out? She caught herself. Thinking like that wasn't going to help. She wondered if the other people who had gone missing in the woods had gone through the same trains of thought. Had their plans to navigate their way out failed, one after another, as hers had? Had they been hungry, thirsty, dirty, and bug-bitten? Had they been scared?

And worst of all, had they known they were never going to make it out? At what point did it finally sink in that things weren't going to be okay?

She shivered.

Days, maybe. Weeks. Those people wouldn't have given up after only a day or so, and neither would she.

She looked down and noticed a small, horizontal hole in the thin material of her T-shirt, maybe an inch or two above her belly button.

If she tore it straight around, she could use the fabric to support her ankle.

"I think I found a bandage, purse," she said to the little bag beside her.

She tugged the T-shirt over her head and methodically ripped at the hole until she had a somewhat uneven but essentially usable strip of fabric. She replaced the T-shirt, then wound it like a bandage as tightly as she could around her ankle and was surprised to find it felt better. She tied it off, satisfied with her work. Just let Darren and her parents and her friends see her now. That idea made her laugh out loud, and the sound echoed loudly around her. She didn't care.

Now, she needed a plan. First, she'd find a weapon, just . . . well, just in case. Whether she came across a bear or Darren or . . . or something else, she wanted to be prepared. Then what? She could keep walking, but she didn't imagine that would do much more good than it had already. Nilhollow wasn't that big and she knew she should have come upon at least one of its borders already, but it didn't seem to matter. She was pretty certain that Nilhollow wanted to keep her there, confused and wandering indefinitely. So did she finally stay put? That didn't seem like a good idea, either.

You could go back to the Chasm . . .

Julia frowned. That wasn't her thought. It was an invasive, alien idea and she disagreed wholeheartedly. Why would she ever want to go back to that chasm?

It's the only thing that doesn't move, the alien thought-voice told her. *It's a fixed point in these woods. A starting point.* She shook her head. She was starting to lose it, really and truly. Voices in her head were not indicative of a survivalist mentality in good working order.

"I'm not going back there," she said aloud. It felt good to say it, even though she wasn't sure who she was saying it to. She spoke aloud again, repeating the sentiment to her purse. "I'm not going back there, no way. I'm getting out of here."

What she was thinking while she was talking was that she really wanted to rest. She felt very drained, and someplace safe to sleep appealed to her more just then than blazing yet another useless trail through Nilhollow.

A low rumbling in the sky made her look up. Was that thunder? The idea of safe shelter seemed even better. If only . . .

When she looked back at the way ahead, she jerked back in surprise, her heart picking up its pace a little. The woods in front of her had changed. Instead of a span of trees, there was a small cabin, tucked away between some tall pines. She blinked, but it was still there. It definitely hadn't been there before, but there it was now. She was dumbfounded. Where had it come from?

It was a small structure more the size of a large shed than even a small house, only one floor capped off with a gray shingled roof. The wood boards of the cabin itself, the front door, and the small, flat porch and steps leading up to it were once gray or green, but faded and peeling now, the wood grain cracked and splintering. Some of the window shutter slats were missing, and one of the wooden posts flanking the steps and holding up the porch's overhang had large gouges in it like claw marks. The glass in the two front windows was intact, but dusted with pollen or cobwebs or something, so she couldn't see inside.

It was quiet, that little cabin. Even in the insistent breeze that always seemed to be blowing in Nilhollow, the cabin didn't creak. It didn't settle on its foundation, as old as it looked. It just stood there as if waiting to see what she would do.

Above, the sky rumbled again. The leaves of the oaks and cedars behind her rustled in excitement. The pine trees around the cabin offered their own low, dry titters as well. She took a hesitant step toward the cabin and paused. She'd seen enough scary movies to know that cabins in the woods were seldom ever safe shelters. Lord only knew what she would find in there.

That feeling of being watched settled on her shoulders and she glanced around, but there was no one that she could see. Her gaze shifted back to the cabin.

She wanted a place to sleep.

A *safe* place. *That* place wasn't safe. There was no way it could be. What if she fell asleep there and the whole cabin went back to wherever it had come from, with her still inside it?

She was so tired, though. Her ankle ached. "What do you think, purse? Should we go in?" The purse was leaving the decision up to her.

This time, when the thunder rumbled, it brought with it a light rain that found her even through the tree cover. It also brought a flash of lightning. She remembered hearing somewhere as a child that being in a forest during a thunderstorm with lightning was bad. Lightning went for the tallest things it could find, things like trees, and sometimes it knocked branches or whole trees down on people. Sometimes it hit the ground between trees and singed everything nearby. Sometimes it sparked forest fires. *Oh God*, she thought, a sudden panic welling up in her. *What if these woods catch on fire and I'm still lost in the middle of it all?* She felt a little sick.

And as she stood there debating the dangers of lightning and forests versus entering that cabin, the rain picked up. Fatter, heavier drops plastered down her hair and made her T-shirt stick to her skin. Her jeans grew waterlogged and heavy.

In the gloom of the impending storm, the trees around the cabin reminded her of thick, bristly hairs on the back of some great beast. It was no safer outside in these woods, she reasoned; the last twenty hours or so had obviously proven that. She had felt constantly exposed and hunted. It almost seemed silly, really, to stay outside in a storm, especially when a building offering an *in*side was so close. The cabin was likely to be dry, at least, and she was exhausted. She wanted to be wrong about it being a trick of the forest.

Another flash of light and a sharp crack behind her made her jump; that decided her. She limped toward the cabin.

She was surprised to find the steps and the floor boards of the porch didn't creak when she walked on them. She even paused, shifting her weight to her good foot to make some sound. The boards should have creaked—it would have been a sign of normalcy—but they didn't.

She braced herself as she opened the door. It swept open on silent hinges. Inside, it was dark. She stepped through the doorway.

It took a few minutes for her eyes to adjust and make out shadowy shapes of furniture. To her right was an old couch and a small, rustic coffee table. Beyond the coffee table were two closed doors, possibly a bedroom and bathroom. To the left was a wooden table surrounded by matching chairs. Beyond that was a doorway that she thought probably led to the kitchen. She couldn't see much in the way of detail, but everything looked normal.

The door eased closed behind her, cutting off the little bit of light and the sound of rain. Inside was a tomb of cool, black silence. She dripped rainwater on the floor, but even that made no sound.

For several minutes, she just stood there, waiting for something, anything to indicate the cabin was part of the living, breathing world around it. In her mind, she thought she might be able to relax if she could hear the sound of rain on the roof or windows or smell damp wood. With frustration, she realized no sounds, no smells, nothing of even the weird outside world of Nilhollow was accessible to her. She whistled. That, at least, she could hear, but it was a very solitary sound, so isolated as to be unwelcome. She didn't try it again.

At least in here, she was pretty sure she was genuinely alone. Nothing was watching her, so far as she could tell. Julia already felt so far removed from her old life, like she'd been put on a high shelf and could see glimpses of the normal world but was too far away to get back to it. The disconnect made her think of Pete. God, how she hoped he'd find her.

Her hands outstretched, she felt for the couch in the darkness and found it. It felt flimsy and dusty, as if the fabric would disintegrate beneath her fingers. Grimacing, she pulled her hand away. She certainly wouldn't be able to sleep on *that*, no sir. The thought of touching the couch, of sinking into its decomposing cushions, curled the edges of her stomach.

Then she heard a thump. It was instinct to look around, but she saw nothing. Her heart thudded in her chest. She wasn't alone after all. A growl from somewhere in the shadows several feet away made her jump. In her head, she whispered a little prayer. *Please please please don't let it find me please don't let it hurt me please please please make it go away . . .*

Another thump and a dragging sound made her back away from the couch. It sounded like someone was moving the furniture in the darkness . . . or maybe dragging heavy limbs along the floor.

Very close to her ear came a whisper: "Julia." She flinched away from it, crying out, then clapped her hand over her mouth. There was a wet slapping sound somewhere close to her foot, and more dragging. *Slap, draaag. Slap, draaag.*

It had been a mistake to come inside—she saw that now. She felt flushed and light-headed. A mistake to limp right into the forest's version of a Venus flytrap. She couldn't see and it was hard to breathe. The interior gloom felt slippery and unwholesome as it slid down her throat, filled up her lungs, flooded her ears and eyes and nose.

She had to get out of there.

She backed toward where she thought the door was, and bumped into a low corner of something. Confused, she eased herself down into a crouch and felt around. A diagonal of perpendicular wooden surfaces led upward into the gloom. Stairs? She frowned. The cabin was only one floor. Where could steps possibly lead? Up to daylight, maybe? Could the cabin somehow be underground now? It would explain why she couldn't hear the rain outside and why it was so dark inside. Was she in a shed-sized coffin, then, deep in the earth? The thought of being buried alive in that horrifying place sent flares of panic through her stomach. She felt as far up along the stairs as she could reach from the bottom step, her fingers grazing over the wood until it wasn't wood anymore but something soft, wet, and vaguely sticky. It moaned when she touched it, and she yanked her hand back, hastily rubbing it against her jeans to get all remnants of whatever it was off her fingers.

She limped quickly away from the stairs, stretching out a hand to guide her. She had to find the door, and hope to hell she wouldn't open it to a wall of dirt.

Suddenly, the sounds around her stopped. No thumping and dragging, no moaning. Again, she was enveloped in the deafening silence. She glanced around blindly, every tiny hair on her body standing on end. The sounds had stopped, but she sensed the things that had been making them were still there, surrounding her in the pitch black, waiting. She braced herself for contact from any direction. She tried to breathe quietly, to somehow shrink herself to as small a spot as possible, to be just a little harder to find. She doubted, though, that the things in the cabin with her were as sightless as she was. They had probably found her already.

Then there was a rapping sound, like someone knocking on the door. The sound came from in front of her. She didn't move. She didn't think she wanted to know what was on the other side. Maybe it was what the things in the cabin had been waiting for. She held her breath and waited, too.

After a few seconds, the knock came again, louder, and she jumped, her nerves tingling. Goose bumps rippled across her skin. That knock had sounded somehow more real than anything else she'd experienced since getting lost, and the hopeful thought gradually began to take hold in her mind that maybe it was Pete—Pete, or someone else come to rescue her. This might be her chance to finally get out of Nilhollow. When a third knock parted the silence, she edged toward the door in its wake but made no move to open it. What if it wasn't someone come to rescue her? Her heart pounded in her chest.

"Julia?" The voice wasn't one she recognized, and it was somewhat muffled by the closed door. However, the voice sounded as real, as promising as the knock.

Her hand found the doorknob. She hesitated for a second, then turned and pulled the knob. Dim light, but above-ground light nevertheless, fell on the hallway floor as the door eased open.

What she saw on the porch dragged a scream out of her, and the air in her lungs with it. The world swam away from her before she could get it back, and she collapsed in a small heap in the doorway.

The tall, skeletal thing on the porch, the thing with just enough flesh over the skull to still cling to one of Darren's eyes, screamed, too. It was the high peal of wind, the roar of pounding surf, and it shook the crude furniture of the cabin with its force. The costumed surface of bone material crumbled away to reveal a skeleton of vines and sticks which swung the ax it was holding and buried it in the door frame. Its eyes glinted coppery, triumphant light. Then, satisfied for the time being, it crumbled to a pile of kindling on the porch across the doorway from Julia.

NINE

Mallon had already put a call in to the missing persons division to discuss organizing a ground search for his missing officers and the girl, Julia, and her ex, Darren. He'd also phoned the Brendan T. Byrne ranger station to solicit their help, as well. Mallon believed the circumstances of the four disappearances could easily be categorized as suspicious, and further, it was a wilderness situation, which meant risks to the safety of the missing were naturally higher. He didn't have much to go on in reference to Julia and Darren beyond what Grainger had filed in the system; neither seemed to have family locally, he didn't know what either was last wearing, and he wasn't sure beyond a guess based on the abandoned car report how long either had been missing. As far as Grainger and Perry, he at least knew where they had been headed, when they'd left the station, how they were dressed, and what they were driving. He thought he'd start with finding his own officers first. With any luck, all four were already together, and he could bring them all home at once.

On a grid-lined map of Nilhollow spread out on his desk, he started making notes regarding which of his remaining officers and which park rangers would search which sections. Nilhollow itself was about a square mile, a manageable size provided they hadn't moved beyond that area. He suspected they hadn't; beyond Nilhollow was a lake and a river, as well as numerous hiking and biking trails. If they had managed to wander into the state forest proper, it was likely someone would have found them already.

He'd send the cops and rangers out in groups of four. He'd have them sweep Nilhollow top to bottom until his officers and the two civilians were found. If there were cultists in there or drugged-up crazies or rabid bears or even some kind of government experiment in biological warfare with plants, he'd be ready for it.

On his laptop, he had a .pdf file sent by email from an old friend, Kathy Ryan. She was an expert in the most obscure aspects of the occult and a freelance consultant to police forces on matters that had . . . extenuating circumstances, he supposed one might call them. It was his gut that had made him contact her in the first place, because his gut, with each passing hour, seemed more and more certain that he was going to need the kind of information she could provide. He suspected Kathy had been surprised to hear from him, but she didn't ask questions. She was good like that. And fortunately, she was familiar with the legends of Nilhollow and of its sordid history. Although she was away on a case, at his request she had sent some information he might be able to use. The document contained a thorough history of what her sect of elite paranormal experts believed was *really* happening in Nilhollow, plus the words and procedures for binding and healing rites and clearing negative energy, just in case cultists, crazies, bears, or genetically enhanced plants were not the problem.

And the problem, as suggested by the document Kathy had sent, was two-fold. The first issue was nature spirits—elementals—and some pretty powerful ones, from the sound of it. He didn't know if he believed that nature spirits had killed a man in his jail cell or abducted two civilians right out of their cars. But then, he wasn't sure what to believe was happening out in those woods. Regarding the second issue, there was far less information on it. The ancient tribes of Lenni-Lenape in the area had called it the Turning of the Earth, and from what he could gather, it had something to do with a widespread change that seemed to negatively affect everything, including, Kathy's researcher friends believed, the elemental spirits. Kathy's notes seemed to indicate that the Turning of the Earth, according to Lenape folklore, had a maddening effect on those exposed to it for too long. It drove people to murder and suicide, among other things that closely and uncomfortably echoed his old nightmares.

The idea of a kind of force that infected people did serve to back up what Grainger had said about spores or seeds or something that got into the heads and hearts of people like Todd Mackey and made them crazy. What this force, this Turning of the Earth really was, though, Mallon could only hazard a guess.

Was the document more of the same mumbo jumbo that he'd found over the years, suggesting useless tactics like those stacked up in that clearing in Nilhollow? It was hard for him to say, but he didn't think so. He'd known Kathy a long time, and although he knew little about her experiences in relation to her job, he knew people trusted her abilities, and she made a pretty damn good living from helping cops with circumstances outside the normal human experience. He wasn't sure if humans were able to affect the super- or preternatural, or if they were even meant to, but he believed Kathy knew her stuff. If anything could transcend the piss-poor attempts at magic he'd already seen, then Kathy's recommendations would be solid examples.

At the moment, despite what his gut and Kathy's notes were suggesting, Mallon was more interested in the document for educational purposes. If the problem was a human one, he needed to understand the kinds of humans he was up against. If he could glean from the document the means to either reason with or scare off any delusional deep-woods nut jobs with elements from their own belief systems, all the better. If they truly believed they were summoning spirits, perhaps he could arm himself with the right thing to say or do to make them think their efforts would fail.

And if the problem was not a human one . . . ? Well, he would educate and arm himself for that possibility as well, he supposed. His gut demanded that.

He figured he was going to feel silly, but he knew of a shop a few towns over where he could pick up white sage and some other items mentioned in Kathy's document, if it came to that. His gut told him it would. His gut, at least, was one thing he always believed. And there was also a hardware store where he could pick up a few more items that would give his head some satisfaction as well.

He clicked the print button on his laptop and the printer near his desk whirred to life. He wasn't ready to tell his officers just yet about Kathy's group's research involving Nilhollow, but he wanted it with his paperwork for reference. The printer dropped several papers into the tray and Mallon picked them up, leafing through them as he made his way back to his desk.

The first six pages had printed correctly, and he gave a little satisfied grunt as he shuffled each page behind the last. Then he came to the seventh page, and nearly dropped the whole stack. On his laptop, he scrolled down to the end of the document. It was only the six pages; that last message wasn't there on-screen. He put the other pages down and stared at the words on that seventh piece of paper as if he could make the illusion go away beneath his gaze. Those words were there, though, and the slightest trembling in his hand made them bounce across the white surface.

It read:

Can't take the whispering anymore.—Joe

Mallon peered through his office window into the bullpen where his officers sat, scanning their faces and body language for tells that one of them had played some weird, sick joke on him. It wasn't likely. Most of these young officers didn't even know Joe Franklin, and none of them was the kind of guy to do something so tasteless, not even Perry. So where had the note come from?

Spores and seeds, old man. Spores and seeds, he thought, and then brushed the thought away.

He crumpled up the paper and threw it in the wastebasket. Then he gathered up the papers and was about to head out to the bullpen to brief his officers on how the search would go, when his phone rang. He paused, deciding to answer it only on the off chance that it might be Grainger or Perry. He put down the papers and snatched up the phone with a hurried, "Captain Stan Mallon."

"Hiya, Captain Mallon."

The voice sounded familiar, but he couldn't place it. It wasn't Grainger or Perry, though. "Hi. Can I help you?"

The voice gave a dry, papery chuckle. "I doubt that. You couldn't before. But maybe I can help you."

Mallon frowned. He was in no mood for games. "Look, I'm in the middle of something right now. Wanna tell me what this is about?"

"Don't tell me you don't remember me, Captain."

"Should I?" Mallon sank back into his chair and switched the phone to the crook between ear and shoulder. He did remember the voice . . . or thought he did. But the owner of that voice wasn't around to use it anymore. He clicked on the phone's recorder.

"Did you get my note? You did, I think. You told me I was welcome back if I changed my mind about quittin'. 'Member that, Captain?"

Mallon leaned forward. "I remember telling someone that, but you're not him."

"How've you been, Captain?" the voice asked in a pleasantly conversational way. "How's the station? Ooh, how's O'Malleys? Gee, I miss that place."

"Fine. All fine. Who is this?"

"I'm fine, too. No more dead girls whispering. Guess they ain't got nothing to say to a guy who's dead, too."

"I'm going to ask one more time. Who is this?"

That dry chuckle came across the line again. "I think you know. After all, you helped cut me down from my dining room rafters, 'member, Captain?"

"You're not Joe Franklin. He's dead." Mallon was surprised by the vehemence in his own voice. He considered hanging up the phone but didn't.

"Awww, Captain. Say it again."

"What?"

"What you just said," the voice responded, fraught with unspilled laughter. "Say it again."

"I said that you're not Joe Franklin, because he's dead."

"You're right," the voice agreed. "Couldn't pull the wool over *your* eyes."

"You're just some sick asshole disrespecting the memory of a good man."

"Was Joe a good man? Maybe, but he was weak. It didn't take long to ruin him beyond all hope of helping him."

Mallon was silent, contemplating the possible meanings of those words. *It didn't take long to ruin him*. What the hell did that mean?

"Tell me," the voice went on. "How are Grainger and Perry?"

"It sounds like you might know better than I would," Mallon said evenly. His heart rate sped up a little. What did this guy know about Grainger and Perry? If only the trace on his phone were working, dammit.

"Seems to me they'd be easy to ruin, too. Time is running out. Doors are opening and closing at the same time."

"Are you threatening officers of the law? Because if you are, I will personally bring hell down on your head."

"Your law doesn't matter. Nor do its officers. And neither do you."

"And who the hell are you again? I didn't catch that."

"I am the voice from beneath the woods, the will of chaos. I am the true divinity over those who speak for the trees because they have no tongues."

"So you're a crazy person? Out in Nilhollow, maybe?" This was the guy; everything in Mallon was screaming that this guy, whoever he was, knew all about his officers' disappearances, and maybe those of Julia Russo, her ex-boyfriend, and others, too.

"Perry has no tongue either. Not anymore," the voice said, and then did the hanging up for him.

Mallon sat with the receiver in his hand for a long time, staring dumbly at it. When he finally replaced it in its cradle, he noticed the tremble in his hand was a full-on shake.

He rewound the recorder and played it back. He heard his own voice answering the phone, but the reply came through only as a low whistle, like wind over an opening. The entire recorded conversation went that way—his voice, and the wind-whistle in response. It unnerved him, hearing what sounded like the unraveling of a man's mind, his own mind, as he grew increasingly more and more upset with nobody.

When the conversation ended, he played it back again, listening for anything remotely like Joe Franklin's voice, or any voice. Again, all that had recorded was his voice and the whistling of . . . what? Bad phone lines? The great beyond?

He played it back a third time, turning it up to listen intently. And there . . . there it was, beneath the interference. It was faint, but it was there . . . a whispering of words. He couldn't quite make out all of them, but he caught a few, and scribbled them on a nearby notepad:

ANCIENT
TREES
CHASM
SPIRITS
TURNING

Mallon frowned. The guy on the phone hadn't said any of those things, to the best of his recollection. Frustrated, he pinched the bridge of his nose. He could feel a headache coming on. Maybe he hadn't heard those words. Maybe he was losing his marbles. Maybe stress had finally caught up to him . . . or Grainger's spores and seeds.

He scanned the pages of the printed document again, comparing it to his notepad. One by one, he found the words in the document, all except "chasm." He wondered if that was significant. Was there a chasm in Nilhollow? A chasm . . . a chasm . . .

He looked at the sectioned map, scanning the topographical features for a chasm. He'd never seen anything like that in those woods, unless a person could count that ditch under the altar, which gave Mallon the idea that what he'd talked to on the phone was not so much a who as a what. He wasn't sure how the pieces fit together yet, but he was pretty sure that the Turning, the force behind the horrors in Nilhollow, had been communicating with him through suicide notes and phone calls. And if it could reach him all the way out here . . .

He grabbed the stack of papers and stormed out of the office.

TEN

One of the frustrating things about forests as big as the Pine Barrens, Pete had noticed growing up, was that sound bounced. It was difficult to tell which direction a sound came from, and he figured that was often why people got disoriented. They listened for sounds of running water to find rivers, or of traffic to find roads, and often, they ended up heading in the wrong direction. The scream he'd heard could have come from anywhere. In fact, it seemed to come from everywhere. It was his instinct to run toward the source to help; he supposed that instinct was why he'd become a police officer in the first place. However, he wasn't so sure where to go—or if he should even go at all. His sense of duty quickly won out over his mistrust of the forest's illusions. It could have been Julia screaming, after all. He thought the scream originated from somewhere behind him, so he turned and headed that way.

Most days, he felt like a pretty good cop, confident that in his own quiet, awkward way, he was making the right decisions. What authority he did wield came precisely from the assumption by other cops and civilians alike that he was the kind but dim-witted deputy of a backwoods New Jersey town, so when he stood up for himself, he was personally gratified to find they paid attention and did what he told them. But this situation was so beyond the pale that he would have welcomed leadership and instruction, particularly from Mallon. He had great respect for the man, who had given him chances and trusted his judgment well before Pete believed he'd earned it.

He also once again wished for his firearm. Few things made a guy feel safer than a Sig Sauer P228. More so, he wished Perry was there, too, cracking jokes or making blatantly obvious observations or just humming to himself, as usual. There was something about being alone in the wilderness, this particular wilderness, that made him feel just on the verge of panic, as though at any second, something would rush at him from the woods and overwhelm him. The silence was part of it; he didn't even want to chance talking out loud to himself, for fear that he might draw the wrong attention. He also thought talking to himself might just be the first slide on the slippery slope to the pit of Nilhollow's madness.

He had to keep moving. He focused his thoughts on finding Julia. He'd investigate the scream, see if it had been hers. If it was, he hoped it was only a scream of fear and not pain. He thought of Perry, and how his screams had dwindled down to gurgling, and his breath caught in his chest. He couldn't save Perry but he would save Julia. He wouldn't let anything bad happen to her if he could help it. She was another one who'd seemed to trust in his abilities early on, to trust him by some intuition or instinct, and that meant so much to him. She was good like that. It was yet another thing about her that he lo—

Whoa. Love? Was he thinking that he loved her? The notion had come so easily to him. Was that at the heart of his obsession with finding her? Was it more than just needing something for his brain to focus on, a problem to solve to keep from panicking?

Of course it was, he realized. His brain wasn't working so hard on Darren's rescue plan. In fact, if he were to be brutally honest with himself, wasn't there just the tiniest little part of him that hoped the forest had already taken care of the asshole?

He shook his head and almost voiced the denial out loud to make it seem more real. He wouldn't wish what he saw happen to Perry on anyone, not even Darren.

Darren, who was competition. He felt a sudden and encompassing rage flash-flood his system. He hated the guy. Darren, who had gotten the honor of being able to touch Julia all over and then had actually made her feel bad about it! Darren, who had looked so smugly superior even in the presence of the restraining order he and Perry delivered. God, how he'd wanted to punch that smirk, cave it in along with the rest of that face. Darren, who had tormented the woman he—

Pete clawed at the collar of his uniform. The green all around was suffocating him, drowning him. These weren't his thoughts . . . were they?

He had to keep going. He had to get himself and Julia out of there. Maybe he had never been made of the tough stuff like his father, and even now, his father might not see him as much of a man, but he wanted Julia to. God, did he ever want her to.

As he was walking, his boot kicked something heavy. Expecting to see yet another tree root or rock, he looked down. There was a glint in the grass. He bent down and was surprised to find an ax. He hauled it up by the handle. It was heavier than he expected.

An ax? He glanced around, half expecting to see the owner of the ax nearby. There was, of course, no one. Was it a real ax, then? Who would just leave an ax out in the middle of the woods?

In Nilhollow, he supposed, it might be any number of murderous crazy people.

There were specks of blood on the side of the ax head, but not the blade. Someone had been hurt near this ax, but not likely *with* it. He wiped the blood off on the grass. He hoped to God it wasn't Julia's.

He gripped the handle in both hands. It wasn't a gun, but it was a weapon. A weapon tree-creatures just might be afraid of, unlike a gun. He hoped . . . He kept going.

It was disorientation or wishful thinking or both, but for a few perfect seconds before total consciousness, Julia thought she was home in bed, warm and safe. When she awoke, it took another second or two before everything—the rain, the cabin, the things in the interior dark, Darren's corpse with an ax—came flooding back to her. She sat up and fought the urge to cry. She was still in those god-forsaken woods. She hadn't escaped. She hadn't gotten anywhere. She was still trapped. How long had it been? She didn't think more than two days had passed, but it felt like such a long two days. *Damn it. Damn this place.*

Her stomach growled. She had nothing left in her purse to eat, and even if she could identify what berries or plants were edible, she doubted she'd be able to find them before it got too dark to see. Besides, she wasn't so sure now that it was a good idea to ingest anything that grew here.

Maybe that was part of how Nilhollow got to people—weakening them with starvation. Then it finished them off with silhouetted figures in the woods.

Her head and ankle ached, so she popped three more ibuprofen from her purse, finishing off the last of her bottled water. She unwrapped her ankle and winced at the swollen red flesh, then wrapped it up again. She didn't know if it was good for her ankle or not, but it felt better tightly bound that way.

Then she checked herself, felt her face, checked her arms and legs and stomach. She didn't know whether something she'd dreamed about but couldn't remember was weighing on her subconscious, or those things in the dark had touched her while she slept, but she felt an overwhelming need to make sure she was still all there, still a solid part of the real world.

For a long time after, she sat on the floorboards, holding her purse in her lap. That little purse. Thank God for that. She'd come to think of it as almost a companion now. She petted the fabric with soft, affectionate strokes. It was there for her, offering her its contents when she needed something, hanging on no matter how far she ran or what the forest threw at her.

"Thanks," she said to it. "Thanks for being here. Thanks for staying."

She flinched as the wind creaked through the pines looming above her. It drew her out of her daze, and when she finally glanced around, she almost laughed. She didn't, though. It would have sounded crazy, too loud and too desperate, even to her.

Most of the cabin was gone—but not all of it. The front porch remained, though the overhang was gone, as well as the posts to hold it up. The cabin's door frame still stood, though most of the front wall of the house was also gone. The few remaining boards surrounding the doorway were jagged and splintered, like something very large had bitten through them. Perhaps strangest of all were the interior floor boards. Enough of them remained to support her body, jutting outward like diving boards from the door frame, but the rest of the interior, including the furniture, the somewhat-stairs, and whatever unimaginable structures might have been under the floor, were gone. It looked to her like a tornado had touched down right on the cabin and ripped away everything but her and what she had touched.

She was glad most of the cabin was gone. If she had to spend another night in the woods, she thought she'd actually prefer sleeping under the trees again. An old song popped into her head, one she remembered her grandpa singing when she was little, and only the one part:

Where did you stay last night?
I stayed in the pines where the sun never shines
And shivered when the cold wind blows

This time she did giggle out loud, and then was wracked with a trembling that took a minute or two to go away. Sure, she'd stay in the pines and shiver when the cold wind blew. She'd stay there tonight, and maybe the next night, and the next night . . .

Around her, little sounds of movement like crackling, creaking, and muffled thumps made her head dart in different directions. *They* were everywhere, all around her. *They* were watching, waiting, the eyes from the in-between places and the faces in the trees. And she giggled again, louder, because even she knew that sounded like the delusion of some paranoid person. It wasn't though . . . oh no. They *were* coming to take her away, ha ha, hee hee, ho ho, like the other song said.

But not if she could get away from them first.

Julia breathed deeply, inhaling the scent of pine and old wood. She slung her purse strap over her shoulder and got unsteadily to her feet. It would be getting dark soon. It was Nilhollow; it could be dark any minute, on a whim. She had to be ready.

She glanced out toward the endless span of pines, cedars, and oaks, spindly sentinels already gathering darkness to them like cloaks. Between them, she could already see glinting pairs of eyes igniting in the dark, just like in her dream. It was more than feeling them watching her. Now, she could see them. She turned back to the doorway.

Then she spied the ax. It was still stuck in the door frame, a tooth caught in the muscle of the cabin's old carcass.

"Well, look at that, purse," she said to the little bag hanging by her side. "I think we've found ourselves a weapon." She limped over to it and after a couple of tries, managed to wrench it free. *Her* ax now. Let something just try to fuck with her when the darkness came.

By degrees, the shadows deepened around the trees. The *manë-tuwàk* felt the Turning seeping with renewed vigor from the Chasm. They thought they knew how the Kèkpëchehëlat felt. The Turning engulfed them in waves that ignited directionless rage. It caught them up on its currents and blew them through the forest. The leaves rustled in aggressive expectation and the tall grasses, ferns, and bushes, shook in their passing. They felt nothing, thought nothing but the

Turning. It was more binding, more compelling than the far-moving ones' ritual words and gestures had ever been.

The far-moving ones had called it Mahtantu, the spirit of death. The ax-wielding ones had called it the Devil. Some of the *manëtuwàk* believed the Turning was a force of nature, just as they were, but one from a void where creation and destruction were no longer held in balance. Some of them believed it was a force of *un*-nature, from a place beyond the access of even nature spirits. Either way, the *manëtuwàk* agreed on one thing: The moving and wielding ones, who thought the Turning was part of an ultimate evil, had no idea how right they were.

Deeper in the forest, at the source of the Turning, the Kèkpëchehëlat waited. The *manëtuwàk* hadn't seen the forest god since it had torn up the ax-wielding one, but they could feel it. They knew the Kèkpëchehëlat fed solely on the Turning now, and had swallowed as much as it had been swallowed. They could feel its rage-sickness like a heat that singed the trees. It was becoming something else, something more powerful and deadly with the help of the Turning.

They wondered what it was waiting for. What did it know that they didn't? What was coming? They supposed soon enough, once the Turning swallowed them, too, they would understand. There was some Plan, and the Kèkpëchehëlat was an instrument of that Plan. Soon, they would be, as well. And they were just at the point where they had begun not to care.

It was then that they sensed that the two moving ones, who they had given indifferent passage through their woods, were now armed with axes. Their howls of rage shook needles from the pines. Twigs snapped and smacked. The tidal wave of rage crashed over them again, wiping away thought, and they sped through the forest, bent on destroying.

A bruise-colored dusk had settled on Nilhollow by the time Pete stumbled into a clearing. He blinked several times, believing the wooden structure he was seeing was a trick of his eyes. It looked like a cabin that had been mostly torn down. A door frame and the platform of part of a floor still remained, as did most of a porch. It was hard to tell in the fading light, but he thought he saw movement beyond the door frame.

His heart sped up.

He took a few steps closer, clutching the ax more tightly. There was most definitely someone, some*thing* there. It leaned against the door frame, rocking a little. He was tempted to call out to it, to ask it if it was okay. It was possible the figure was the source of the scream, and might be hurt. Hell, in that forest, it was *probable* that anyone he came across, any *real* person, of course, was hurt in some way.

He opened his mouth to say something, then closed it again, remembering the thing that had pretended to be Perry. He didn't think he could trust his eyes. Maybe not even his thoughts. The forest could use both against him.

He moved a little closer.

The figure swung around the edge of the door frame and into the feeble light, and Pete's heart leaped in his chest. It was Julia! The ax dropped to his side and he ran to the porch in spite of his misgivings. He stopped short, though, when he saw a similar weapon in her hands.

"Julia?" he asked softly. Had the woods already gotten inside of her? He thought of Todd Mackey with the bloody vines and branches snaking out of him and shivered. "Julia? Are . . . are you okay?"

She was glaring at him from beneath a lock of leaf-and-twig-strewn hair. Her clothes and hair were soggy, as if she'd been caught in the rain, though it hadn't washed off the dirt that smudged her face and arms. He also noticed that her T-shirt was torn. The strip of fabric, he saw, was wrapped around her ankle. In both hands, she clutched an ax so tightly that her knuckles were colorless; for a moment, Pete thought the bones were actually protruding through the skin. Then saw it as a trick of the light.

"Julia, it's me. It's Pete."

Her posture softened a little at his voice, and recognition dawned in her eyes. "Pete? Is that really you, or are you a . . . another part of the forest?"

"It's me, hon. It's really me, I swear." He climbed the stairs and extended a hand to her, approaching her like a wild animal. The ax in her hands trembled, but didn't lower. As he got closer to her, he could smell faint traces of her perfume. He touched her shoulder, and her whole body relaxed. Tears rolled down her cheeks and he pulled her into a hug. He could feel the edge of the ax digging into his ribs; her grip remained tight on the handle.

After a moment she looked up at him. "Thank God you're you. And you're here. How'd you find me?"

"I honestly don't know," he admitted. "I saw the report about your abandoned cars and came looking. I just had a feeling you might need help."

She laughed, but it was an uncharacteristically harsh, bitter sound. "You were sure right about that."

"You're tough, though. A survivor. I knew you'd be okay." He squeezed her hand, and she looked grateful.

"I've been looking all day. I'm lucky I did find you. I'm just glad I got to you before . . . uh, well, you know . . . before dark. But, um, I have to ask . . . are you here alone? Is Darren with you?" He glanced around the remains of the cabin but saw no sign of anyone else. Part of him was secretly glad for that.

Her expression darkened, but there were no fresh tears, he was glad to see. When she spoke, her voice was flat and soft. "He attacked me. Out on the road. He . . . he wanted to kill me, Pete. He tried, but I ran. I just kept running and I lost him. I don't know where he is now. He had an ax." She eyed his suspiciously, and he set it down for the time being against the door frame.

"Okay . . . okay," he replied, glancing around. "First things first—let's get ourselves out of here, and then we can figure out where he went."

"Pete," she said, and loosed one hand's grip on the ax to grab his arm, "there's something out here. Something evil. I . . . I don't think it'll let us leave. It's not a person, not exactly, but . . . something. I know it sounds crazy, and I know I've been under some stress, but you have to believe me."

Under some stress? He wanted to hug her again. He had no doubt she'd been through hell and survived more than many better-prepared people who'd gone into these woods. He was damned proud of her. "Hon, I know. I believe you. I do. I've seen things, too. Spirits . . . tree-creatures. The souls of these woods and, I think, maybe the thing that has been poisoning them. Perry and I . . . ." His voice trailed off. "It's not safe out here. We have to try to get out."

She nodded, clutching the ax again. "Whatever it is, I'm going to kill it if it comes near us." Then, seeming to think of something, she said, "Pete, where *is* your partner? Is he with a search party or backup or something?"

He hesitated in answering, not sure how to tell her about what happened to Perry or that Pete himself wasn't in any better a situation than she was. He didn't have to; she read it on his face. She deflated a little, and so did he. He hated to disappoint her.

"Okay," she said, more to herself than to him. "Okay, let's do this. We can do this."

He picked up the ax again and noticed that she flinched slightly.

"Right. Uh, can you walk?" he asked, glancing at her ankle. "Do you need to lean on me?"

"No, I'm okay. But thanks." She took the hand he offered, though, and followed him with a little limping shuffle through the doorway and down the porch steps.

Pete got out his flashlight and shined it into the gloom ahead. It offered a bright beam of light that cast odd moving shadows along the tree trunks from leaves and branches. For a moment Pete thought he saw faces in the shadow-shapes, but then the flashlight flickered and went out. Pete smacked the end of it against his palm, trying to jar it to life again, but it remained dark. Behind him, he heard Julia giggle.

"Sorry," he said, heat flushing his cheeks.

Her hand wrapped around the crook of his elbow. "No, don't be. It's okay. If we were stuck in a regular forest, rescuing me would be easier."

He wanted to say something witty or at least reassuring, but didn't have the words. He squeezed her hand and felt her smile at him.

They walked awhile in the darkness. Pete couldn't quite remember when the sun had set, but he thought they were heading east, in the opposite direction from where he'd last seen it. East was where the road was. They just needed to find the road.

Both of them jumped when the little flashlight in Pete's belt suddenly came on, and they giggled nervously to each other.

"Well," Pete said with a grin, "maybe that's a sign that things are going to go our way, huh?" He unclipped the flashlight and shined the light on the woods in front of them.

Julia screamed as they took in the sight. Hanging from ropes among the trees ahead were several bodies, which looked flayed of all skin. Actually, they were more than just skinned, but turned inside out. Inexplicably, loops of intestine and brownish or reddish lumps of organs hung from exposed bone or muscle. Eyes hung low from stringy messes above what Pete thought might be lumps of tongues. In many cases, the brains sat freely on top of the bowed heads while hair wove indiscriminately around them. Many of the atrocities had lungs plastered to their chest. The worst thing to Pete was that on the few chests where his trembling hand could focus the light, those lungs were still weakly expanding and contracting.

"Oh my God," Pete said. "What the . . . what happened to them?" He considered for a moment trying to help them, to cut them down.

Julia limped forward, seeming to read his thoughts. "We can't help them. We can't touch them. We just have to go past them."

Pete looked at her, surprised. "Uh . . . okay. Are you sure?"

"Yes. I think they're a trick of the woods. Or a trap. It doesn't want us to go this way, so it's trying to scare us into backtracking. Or if we don't—if we try to cut them down, they become something else and attack us." She clutched his arm tighter.

"Okay, then. Can we go around them?"

The bodies, hanging like grotesque lanterns, swung slightly in the breeze. Pete turned the flashlight in different directions, searching possible alternate routes, but the bodies were everywhere, skinned and glistening with blood, surrounding them, closing them in.

"Guess, not," he muttered.

"Let's just go through them," Julia whispered. She was pale, but there was resoluteness in her eyes. By instinct, she pulled the ax closer to her.

As he and Julia crept close to them, the bodies collectively made a kind of muffled wheezing, rasping noise, though how they could was beyond Pete. A sickening smell crawled up his nose and down his throat, and he gagged. It was not a meat-rotting smell, not an animal death smell like he expected of eviscerated men and women, but rather that of some rotting plant material, like grass or vegetables.

They passed under the bodies. Looking up at them, Pete could see them trembling slightly, as if cold. He supposed it probably was cold without skin. He wondered if any of them were the people who had gone missing in Nilhollow. He shivered, too.

The shuddering chests and slight movements of the limbs seemed to indicate the bodies were in pain. Some oozed greenish-yellow fluids. By the coppery light that emanated from beneath them, the inverted faces looked like masks pasted on. He felt Julia recoil against him. He looked back to check on her. She looked disgusted but determined to go forward.

Just as Pete and Julia reached the midst of the hanging bodies, they heard a series of groans. The bodies began jerking the ropes from which they were hanging as their limbs flailed wildly. The groans became whines that built quickly in volume and pitch.

"What are they doing?" Julia's voice was little more than a breath strangled by her terror.

"I don't know." Pete put up a protective arm to move her behind him, and she limped obligingly.

One by one, the bodies dropped to the ground all around Pete and Julia.

"This is bad," Julia muttered, leaning into Pete to keep moving.

The jumbled heaps of inverted meat began to rise to unsteady, bone-and-muscle feet.

"That's worse," Pete said.

"Run," Julia told him.

"But your ankle—"

The corpses began moving forward, closing them in.

"Run!" Julia shouted, and the two bolted into the woods.

Mallon knew a Nanticote-Lenape woman who he'd met, ironically enough, through Joe Franklin. Her name was Olivia Standing Deer, and Mallon used any excuse he could to visit her coffee shop. She was beautiful; she had sharp cheekbones and pouting lips that never quite found their way into a full smile, a face both proud and graceful. She was thin but not too thin, not anorexic like some millennial model but healthy, curvy the way Mallon liked. She had long, shining black hair that she either braided or, more often, left to fly free, and the darkest, richest, most captivating brown eyes. She often wore a T-shirt with some writing or other on it and blue jeans with boots. She was proud of her heritage, but at the same time, she refused, as she put it, "to be the token dime-store Indian for people to gawk at." She was feisty and complicated, sharp-witted and sharp-tongued, and Mallon thought that if he wasn't ten years too old for her, he'd have already tried to make her wife number three.

That evening's visit was more for business than pleasure, though. She knew a little of her people's old language and more of their old stories and legends, and he thought she might be able to shed some light on some of the contents of Kathy's occult file.

He walked into the warmly lit café and brightened when he saw her at the counter. It was evidently a slow night; a thirty-something sat sipping from a mug and reading a paper in a booth by the corner, and an old man at the far end of the counter was absently munching on a Danish while reading a newspaper. *Good*, Mallon thought. *Fewer ears and fewer distractions.*

Olivia gave him a warm and genuine smile when she saw him, and waved him over to a seat by the counter. He sat, putting the file down next to a clean and empty coffee mug.

"Hey, Stan. What can I get for ya tonight?" she asked, her hand already reaching for the mug.

"Nothing tonight, I'm afraid," he said with a note of apology in his voice. "I'm working a case. And actually, I thought you might be able to help."

"Me?" She looked surprised. "How?"

"I was wondering if you could tell me what the Lenape know about Nilhollow."

She gave him an odd look. "Are you serious? That's going to help you with a case?"

"A missing persons case, and yeah, I really think it might. More than you might think."

She resumed wiping the counter, obviously hesitant to answer him. "Well," she finally said, "I know my people don't like it. Don't like to talk about it. Never have. My grandmother used to say it was Nilhollow and not the white men that chased our people up to Canada."

"What do they think is wrong with it?"

Olivia tilted her head and looked up at him. "*Manëtuwàk*—spirits. You know, elemental spirits of the trees, rocks, water, wind. That sort of thing."

"But I thought your people used to be all in touch with nature and stuff. Worshipped nature gods and whatnot."

Olivia rolled her eyes. "Yes, we hold a very healthy reverence for all of nature, particularly for the *manëtuwàk*. But the ones in Nilhollow are believed to be crazy. You know, dangerous. But it's not their fault. Something in Nilhollow poisoned everything. Drove the *manëtuwàk* crazy, or drove them away. It made Nilhollow soulless and filled that void with corruption. I think my grandma once said it was a kind of power that came up from the ground. Not a being, not a spirit like the *manëtuwàk*, but an intelligent force of some kind. Something older than the spirits, older than the world as we know it—older than the tribes of ten thousand years ago, certainly. They called it the Turning of the Earth. Apparently, at some point, this force, this Turning, grew strong enough and spread far enough that Nilhollow was no longer safe. It chased away the animals, the insects, and birds. But it caught up the *manëtuwàk* and hurt them. It scared the people. Supposedly, my ancestors, the healers of the Lenni-Lenape tribe, couldn't get rid of it or reverse it, but they could limit it. They performed a ritual to bind the poison to the area of Nilhollow and keep it from spreading."

Mallon nodded, glad to hear the information in the file verified by another source. "And the—what did you call them?"

"*Manëtuwàk.*"

"Right. Is it the *manëtuwàk* they believe to be hurting human beings, or the Turning?"

"Both."

Mallon nodded. "But if your ancestors bound this force, this Turning, then what is there to be afraid of?"

Olivia shrugged. "The bonds don't last forever. They've been weakening for decades, maybe centuries. Without the binding rituals, the Turning will just pick up where it left off. Keep spreading."

"And is there a way to, you know, restrengthen them? Re-bind the Turning, I mean?

Olivia narrowed her eyes. "What is this about, Stan? What do old Lenape stories have to do with your case?"

Mallon shifted on his seat. "Afraid I can't get into specifics, Liv. But I can tell you that two of my cops, guys I feel responsible for, are missing in Nilhollow. And what I'm dealing with, what I think is responsible for their disappearance, may involve people who believe very much in everything you're telling me, so the more you can tell me, the better."

"I'm sorry to hear that, Stan." She looked genuinely concerned, and it warmed him. "But, honestly, I don't know much else." She turned and began fixing him his usual—coffee, black—in a to-go cup. "I'm not an expert. In my family, they were just bedtime stories, urban legends, not much different than what the old white folks around here tell of the place."

"So you can't tell me anything about the ritual your ancestors performed? What they said?"

Olivia turned and slid his coffee to him. "Are you kidding? Do you know the words to rituals your Irish ancestors performed ten thousand years ago?" She smiled. "Honey, I get that in movies, magical Indians always offer great ancient wisdom to help save the day, but this isn't the movies, and you're talking to the wrong Indian if you want that kind of help."

Mallon conceded her point with a shrug. "Okay, but ... but if I showed you some words, would you at least be able to tell me how to pronounce them?"

"Uh, sure, I guess. If you think it will help your case."

Mallon offered her his most charming smile. "I certainly think so."

Softening, she smiled back, that coy turn of her lips he loved so much. "Okay, cowboy. Show me what you've got."

ELEVEN

The *manëtuwàk* were distracted, even in their rage, by a presence more alarming than the two with axes. They slowed their pursuit, some of their blind anger dissipating. They rustled and whispered to themselves, blowing like a breeze toward the edge of the woods. Something was happening just outside of Nilhollow, where the roaring, wheeled beasts vomited and swallowed the moving ones. There were red, blue, and white lights, and mumbled language. There were dogs sniffing and barking from the ends of long ropes. It was a gathering of the moving ones. They were planning on entering Nilhollow. There were many of them—twenty-five, maybe thirty. They were coming.

What the *manëtuwàk* found distressing were the moving ones' barking tools; there were many of them, sitting in skins on the hips of the moving ones. They spit bugs which split bark and wood and burned through the flesh of animals and killed them. The moving one they had torn apart had attacked them with such a barking tool, and they decidedly hated it almost as much as the ax. Their rage flared.

There was more, though. One of the moving ones had brought other kinds of tools which they thought might be worse than the axes or the barking tools. The *manëtuwàk* weren't sure what those new tools might be, because the thoughts of that moving one were . . . shielded somehow. It made them uneasy.

To add to their unease, the Kèkpëchehëlat sensed the moving ones assembled just outside Nilhollow, as well. The *manëtuwàk* could feel its rage-sickness progressing from a heat to a storm-cloud. It was tearing through the woods like a high and howling wind, swirling the darkness around it and feeding on it as it fed on the power of the chasm.

The moving ones! It was heading toward the moving ones. It had known they would come. They were what the Kèkpëchehëlat—and the chasm—were waiting for. The trees quivered.

By the time Mallon made it to Nilhollow, it was dark. Five state park rangers, fifteen state troopers, four guys from the Missing Persons Unit, two with dogs, and four local guys had already gathered into little groups, talking, smoking, and drinking coffee. A team of CSIs in white scrubs were all over Grainger's and Perry's patrol car, collecting fingerprints and fibers. One shook his head at Mallon as he passed by; there was nothing, no clue as to where the missing officers went.

The local police had taped off the area, and the press had already begun to congregate beyond, craning their necks and buzzing like flies every time an officer came within fifty feet of them. They tried swarming Mallon as he got out of his car. They seemed to see something in his expression and his steely refusal to even acknowledge their presence, so they backed off, waiting for easier prey.

Detectives Colby and Sarinelli, along with two rangers and some of the other officers, were gathered over the hood of a black sedan, consulting the map of Nilhollow he had given them. They were pointing and conferring, speaking in hushed voices more for the purpose of appearing in charge than because they had anything to say that the other officers couldn't hear. He didn't dislike Colby and Sarinelli, but would not have handed out any promotions to them, either. They could often be dull and unimaginative, but they worked like horses. As long as they put their time and effort in now, Mallon had no problem with them.

They looked up as Mallon joined them. He nodded and responded to their greetings.

"Captain," Colby said with a grim smile and a handshake. "We've got seven groups of four waiting for your go-ahead, plus Sarinelli and I and Ranger Perkins here, coordinating. They're your men, so as far as jurisdiction, everyone's in agreement that the lead on this should be you." He smiled in a way that made Mallon think his being given lead had less to do about respect and his capabilities and more to do with humoring the old captain who had let two of his officers get lost in the big, scary woods.

Mallon chose to work with their veneer for now. "Right. Let's get this going. Full sweep—place is no more than a mile square. We should be able to cover that pretty easily."

The other men nodded.

"Okay, listen up," he shouted, and was vaguely pleased that his voice still commanded authority, old captain or not. The crowd of officers gathered closer. The media strained to hear, but he dropped his voice to a no-nonsense rumble. "Four people are missing—two civilians and two cops. We're going to search every tree, every blade of grass until we find them. We bring in the lights, the dogs, all of it. Tag whatever you find, document it, and report to the command post immediately if you have a lead. I want those people found.

"One more thing. It's important, and frankly, I don't give a damn whether you think it sounds crazy or not. I can't impress upon you strongly enough to be ready for anything in those woods. I mean anything. You know the stories about Nilhollow. We all do. I have reason to believe these disappearances may be connected somehow to those stories—or to people who believe wholeheartedly in them, which would make those people dangerous to cops. Be careful out there tonight. Be on guard and stay with your unit. Nothing is too weird to believe tonight, got it?"

The assembled men and women were silent, their expressions mixed: He saw respect for his position and his directives masking confusion, surprise, and impatience. He hated being looked at that way. He supposed Colby and Sarinelli were silently questioning the wisdom in handing over the lead to a superstitious old man. He suppressed a defensive grunt.

Waving it off, he said, "Just be ready. For your sake, and my peace of mind, okay? Now go." He turned back to his car and went to the trunk. The detectives had begun to follow him, but slowed their advance when he got out the battery-powered chainsaw and a blow torch he'd bought at the Home Depot, which he dropped into a large backpack. He thought he even saw them frown a little when he added the printed pages of Kathy's document on Nilhollow, a small hatchet, and a sandwich from Olivia's shop. Then he turned back to Colby and Sarinelli, who were staring at him like he'd finally pitched the rest of his marbles into the woods. He smiled to himself.

"You, uh, going to explain those, Captain?" Colby asked.

"Nope," Mallon said and kept walking.

The detectives hurried to catch up.

"Sir, where are you going?" Sarinelli asked.

Mallon stopped and turned, his impatience escaping in an audible huff. "In there." He gestured toward the woods.

"What—what about the command station?"

"What about it?"

Colby and Sarinelli exchanged uncertain glances. "Aren't you going to . . . you know, coordinate everything?"

"Why? You two can't handle fielding radio reports and shuffling the map around without me?"

The two detectives stared dumbly at him.

"Look, you handed me lead on this investigation, and I'm leading. My people are in there. I'm going in after them." Mallon turned, and before either could express another asinine thought, he plunged into the forest.

So this was the famously haunted Nilhollow. State trooper Brent Carver was largely unimpressed.

Unit six of the search party was the first to enter the woods, and not to be out-heroed by anybody, Brent had taken lead. They'd followed the path until it petered out to rocks and dirt, and then found themselves almost knee-deep in thick brush in some places. In others, the ground had its own kind of mange, its little patches of dirt exposing an overturned graveyard of bleached and half-buried rocks. As a whole, Nilhollow was, for the most part, both wilder and unhealthier than the rest of the Pine Barrens around it, but otherwise, to Brent Carver it was just like any other forest in New Jersey.

Just a bunch of overgrown weeds and old trees, Brent thought. *Waste of space. Waste of time, too. What does Mallon think we're gonna find in the dark?*

Brent and fellow state trooper Helen "Hell-on-wheels" Cadmonson had been paired up with a thirty-something townie, Carl Witherspoon, and a painfully awkward but totally hot ranger and Russian transplant, Oksana Volkova. They'd made it in as far as a tree with a dark X on it, probably a hiking marker of some sort, and so far, their search had been uneventful. Their flashlights swept back and forth, back and forth over tangled shrubs, pine needles, and squat little mushrooms, but they saw nothing by way of clues that might explain the disappearance of those troopers or the civilians. No torn cloth, no orphaned shoe, nothing. In a way, it was laughable to Carver that they would. Nope, no Perry there, in that tangle of ferns. No Grainger under that downed trunk there. Not that he expected to find anyone in the dark.

Being in Nilhollow at night didn't bother him. He wasn't afraid of the place like some of the other guys. He wasn't afraid of much of anything, but certainly not of a bunch of trees. He thought most of the stories people told about the place were grade-A bullshit. No, it was just that he could think of a hundred better ways to spend an evening. Was he concerned about his fellow officers? Well, sure he was, a little. But they'd been gone less than twenty-four hours, and he didn't really see any reason for the captain to panic just yet. For all anyone knew, they could be out drinking at a bar somewhere in the next town over, or shacking up with chicks on the company dime, or hell, shacking up with each other, even. Who knew? And even if they were in the woods . . . well, he didn't know those guys well, but he thought they had at least enough of a brain between them to hole up for the night, get some sleep, and wait until daylight to try to navigate their way out again.

To Brent, this was a prime example of why he had to have administrative aspirations. Where were the high-risk factors in these cases? What made the bosses suspect an immediate threat to their safety? It was a waste of taxpayer dollars to pay cops to uselessly tramp through the darkness when nothing he'd been briefed on proved they were even missing. As for the civilians . . . well, the guy probably offed the woman and then himself. That's how those things usually went. He and his team were looking for bodies, not living people— bodies they could find more easily in daylight. The whole thing was a waste of time.

Brent knew that with his personality and his training as a state trooper, he was exactly what the public needed and exactly what the media said was wrong with cops. He was okay with that. The general public wasn't that bright. They needed people like him to put things in perspective. It was a different world than when Mallon was starting out. It was an ugly, dishonest, thieving, lying, murdering world out there, even in small towns, and the fucked-up things people did made no sense unless a person accepted that humans tended toward moral entropy. A society like that couldn't be policed by the idealists of the world, like Mallon—the people who assumed lost cops couldn't possibly be lost because they wanted to be. They had to be policed by the realists of the world. And he was such a realist.

This job, and its constant call to interpret how to uphold the law, had made him a realist practically before he was out of the academy. He had been disillusioned early on to find his job was more paperwork and speeding tickets than shoot-outs and car chases. Still, Brent liked being a cop. The occasions on which he could exercise his authoritative common sense—his sister called them power trips—made it bearable. This wasn't one of those times, but there were enough to keep him going. Breaking up bar fights, arresting meth-heads—he loved that shit. He also loved that he got to carry a gun. Plus, chicks dug the uniform . . . and the handcuffs. They went wild for the handcuffs. In fact, he'd had a date to show them off to a chick named Barbara before he'd been pulled in for rescue duty.

Eyeing up the ranger chick, though, he thought he might be able to salvage something from the night after all. She looked nervous as hell to be out there, which Brent thought kind of funny, given that she probably knew Nilhollow better than any of the cops did. From what he could see, there wasn't anything to be afraid of. Sure, it was unusually quiet in those woods, except for the occasional joke or snippet of conversation from one of the units, and even those were uncharacteristically restrained, like in a library or church. And yeah, in the dark, the trees looked a little like long spines jutting from the earth, with bristling hairs growing down their lengths. Many had lost their leaves already, probably to something like Dutch elm disease or whatever affected the trees out here. And there was a faint smell that reminded him of the time he had to rake out rotting leaves from under his grandmother's porch. Still, it wasn't nearly as creepy as all the old-timers made it out to be. Listening to them, Nilhollow was a fairy-tale death trap.

"Hey," he said, repositioning himself in the search line to walk alongside her. "Oksana, right?"

She blushed and nodded, tucking a long strand of brown hair behind her ear.

"I'm Brent," he said, offering her a winning smile. "Nice night for a search party, huh? These woods are something else."

She nodded again. Evidently, she wasn't much of a talker. Brent was not deterred. "So tell me, why so tense, huh? You being a ranger and all, you must know these woods like the back of your pretty little hand."

Oksana looked distinctly uncomfortable. "Da. I know these woods. In Russia, I grow up near the forest—beautiful, peaceful, loving forest. My whole childhood I spend there. I love it. Except when I come to work here. This place . . ." She made a face and shook her head. "This forest is no good."

"Really?" Brent continued, feigning interest. "What's so bad about it? I mean, really, besides an apparent tree fungus and whatever that smell is . . . you guys smell that?"

"You know," Oksana said. "You heard about this place, da? The woods are not safe."

Brent chuckled. "You're talking about the spooky campfire tales the old people tell? It's just a forest, and those are just stories."

She shook her head. "No, not just stories. When you spend time here, you feel it. The *leshiye* are all around here."

"*Leshiye*?"

"I don't know word for it in English . . . I think, woods-spirits? Ghosts of trees. Not dead but not alive as we know it. And I think there are . . . other things." She blushed deeply in the faint flashlight glow.

Brent glanced over her head at the other two, who were listening to the exchange with small smiles. He tried to hide any trace of mockery in his expression as he turned back to Oksana. "Other things? Like what?"

"I don't know what they are. Bad thoughts. These woods are bad. Always I don't take night shift, only day shift. I leave gift, and the *leshiye* leave me alone."

"You, uh, leave gifts for tree ghosts?"

She nodded, blushing again.

"What kind of gifts?" Brent pressed her.

She glanced back at the others, aware that all three pairs of eyes were on her, listening with scoffing amusement, and shook her head. "No more. We talk about this no more. We have a job to do."

"Aw, come on, I'm sorry if I offended you," Brent said, giving her a warm smile. "Seriously, I'm genuinely interested. What kind of gifts do you leave?"

She hesitated. Her expression was one of mistrust. She seemed to consider it for a moment, then reached into a pocket of her uniform and pulled out a small lattice-type construction of sticks, vaguely pyramidal. Tiny colored strings bound the sticks together.

The other two moved closer to her, shining their flashlights on the lattice so they could see.

"That's pretty cool, actually," Helen said. "Did you make that? What is it?"

"Is it Russian?" Carl asked.

"No, not Russian. Older than that. Much older. I learn about it here from other rangers. I don't know word for this. Don't know what they think it means. It works, though."

"And that," Brent asked, "keeps them from . . . what?"

Oksana looked him in the eye for the first time since she met him. "From tearing us apart."

The others were silent. There was something about the earnestness in her words that made Brent uneasy. This wasn't some cutesy old-world folklore to her. She believed it.

It was then that they heard a crashing in the woods to their right, and Oksana flinched. Brent squeezed her shoulder. "No worries. Probably just another unit overlapping our search area."

It wasn't anyone from another unit that came out of the woods, though. It was a pair of silhouettes, crouched low and creeping between the massive trunks about thirty feet away. They were big and they moved like animals but were vaguely shaped like people. Brent couldn't make out any details other than that their eyes glowed bright green in the dark, like an animal's.

Brent clicked the safety off his gun. "Hey! Hey you! Hold it right there!"

The figures stopped, their heads snapping up. The glowing eyes focused on him and he felt a sharp pain in his head.

"Damn it, man, what are you doing?" Helen whispered, drawing her gun. "You gonna invite those bears to come over here and eat us?"

The silhouettes stood. Brent didn't think they were bears, and he told Helen so. For one thing, the shape wasn't right. These were tall and bone skinny. It looked to him like they had long, sharp sticks growing out of their heads and shoulders.

"What the fuck are they?" Carl asked. "Are they people?"

"Bears," Helen whispered.

Brent drew his gun, his wary gaze fixed on the silhouettes. Those glinting eyes glowed now, tiny lantern-lights of green.

"I, uh . . . I really don't think those are bears," Carl muttered.

"*Leshiye*," Oksana breathed.

"We need to radio this in, guys." Carl tilted his head to speak into his walkie's shoulder mic.

"We need to run," Oksana said, clutching the stick pyramid. She turned to Carver and grabbed his arm. "Now."

"Guys, come on. Get it together. Those are not bears and they're not ghosts, okay? Act professional here." Brent pinched the bridge of his nose, hoping to stave off the pain that had moved to just behind his eye, like a splinter in his skull. It made it hard to think, let alone be patient with these people. Not only was he on a wild-goose chase, but apparently, he was also on babysitting duty.

He strode with purpose a few feet ahead of the others toward the silhouettes. When his flashlight caught them in its beam, though, he stopped. The two figures were not people at all, and certainly not like any animal Brent had ever seen. They were a little like Oksana's stick-thing, composed of interwoven branches, bits of vine, and bark to form heads, powerful-looking bodies, arms, and legs. The eyes, he could see now, were sparks of green fire burning in twin pits in their faces. A horizontal crack appeared like a fault line in one of the faces, slightly crooked, and the thing let out a growl so loud that it seemed to fill his ears and the air all around him and so deep that he could feel it in his chest.

From somewhere behind him, he faintly heard Helen's scream. He was annoyed to find the screaming increased the throbbing in his head.

"The fuck are you?" Brent muttered.

The second one's eyes flashed their fire. It looked like they were studying him, burning through him, igniting him. He felt a sudden, intense anger—anger at the idiots in charge for putting them in the path of these tree-things and anger at the useless pieces of waste behind him who were taking up time and space. The latter irritated him immensely, because they were near and they were helpless, and their stupidity radiated from them like heat and light, hurting his eyes, hurting his head.

He turned and fired a bullet right through Carl's left eye, and the vise grip which held his skull loosened slightly.

One less to babysit. One less beacon of incompetence.

"Oh my God!" Helen screamed in a high, hysterical voice. "Oh my God! What are you doing, Brent? What the fuck, man?" Helen pointed her gun at Brent; it seemed funny to him. Funny little thing, a gun. So much damage, without even trying at all, really. He bowed his head and looked at his feet. Just a little squeeze of his finger. He pointed the gun down and then shot himself in the foot. A little hole exploded in the boot and quickly filled with his blood. He smiled. Then he shot himself in the other foot.

Behind him, the creatures made sounds like rustling leaves. Maybe they found it funny, too.

"Brent, stop it! What the fuck are you doing?" The sound of Helen's voice seemed to come from far away, a sound heard underwater, muffled and strange. His ears were already stopped up with wind-sounds, and his head with thoughts he considered maybe weren't all his.

When he looked up, he could see mouths moving—Helen's and Oksana's, at least—but the muted sounds were gibberish. He laughed. They looked ridiculous, with their mouths flapping and their nonsense syllables spilling out of them. He held up his left hand to wave at them, and then shot straight through the back of it. It left a round hole the size of a quarter. He held it up to his eye and peered at them through it. Oksana was clutching her stick-thing and saying something over and over again in Russian. Helen, shaking a little, had her gun pointed at him. Without ever dropping her aim, she grabbed Oksana's arm and they started backing away. Carl just lay on the ground, bleeding from the hole where his eye had been. Funny. Damn right hilarious, actually.

Then the fog in his head suddenly cleared, taking the humor of the situation with it, and pain rushed to fill its place. This time, he was the one that screamed. What had happened? God, he was shot! What had he done? He tried to take a step forward and the agony that flashed up from his feet dropped him to the ground.

The women had paused, hovering uncertainly between running away and coming to his rescue. He was a fellow cop, for God's sake! They had to get him out of there. He needed a doctor. What the hell were they waiting for?

"Help me!" he cried. "Helen! God, it hurts. Don't leave me here. Help me!"

Helen's eyes, though, were focused on the things behind him, the things looming over him.

He tried to crawl toward the women. "Helen, for fuck's sake, don't just stand there. Call in for an ambulance. Officer down! You know how to fucking do it. Helen—"

That pressure behind his left eye was building again, and he winced, then choked out a cry as it got so unbearable that his vision went black on that side. Then he felt movement *behind* the eye. He didn't know how that was even possible, but he could feel something moving around in his skull like a bull in a china shop, tearing through tendons and delicate tissue. The pressure built to an excruciating degree and then there was a pop as the thing behind his eye pushed it out of the socket. He felt it plop, warm and wet, against his cheek, and he began to whimper. What was happening? Good God, what was happening to him? The moving thing had poked through the now-open space in his head and was meandering upward. He could feel it tugging against his skull. He reached up to touch it with his damaged hand. It felt rough, like a tree root.

With his remaining eye, he looked up at Helen and Oksana. Their eyes were big, ridiculously big, and their mouths were hanging open. That anger welled up inside him again. Stupid chicks with their big dumb eyes and mouths gaping like idiot fish. No way chicks ought to be cops, ever. Too stupid and weak and—

He felt the same pressure building down where one of his kidneys was, and he whimpered again.

"Helen, you bitch! Help me!"

Another tree root burst out of his back. Then his body was a fireworks display of explosions, like the gunshots, except these were from the inside out, one bloody root after another shooting out of him.

Finally Helen, that useless bitch, was spurred to action. She fired at the creatures behind him. A bullet tore through one's shoulder, and the thing roared in anger and pain. Within seconds it was in front of her like a leaf in a strong wind. One branch-like hand wrapped around her throat and the other around her wrist. The tree thing tore her arm off, tossing it and the gun aside. Helen screamed again . . . bitch was always screaming, screaming . . . and then the creature clawed open her abdomen. Swaths of ribs dripped blood and little shreds of skin. Finally, it twisted the hand around her throat and snapped her neck like a twig. Her eyes still wide, her mouth still gaping like a stupid fish, she sank to the ground next to Carl.

If he could have by then, Brent would have laughed at how funny she looked.

Oksana, who had jumped when Helen's blood splattered her uniform, otherwise seemed too stunned to move. She closed her eyes, still muttering in Russian . . . was it Russian? He couldn't tell anymore—and held her stick-pyramid to her chest. The creature loomed over her, its face so close to hers that the fire of its eyes could have singed her eyebrows. It seemed to be taking her in, the sight and smell of her. It reached toward the stick-thing she held, seeming to feel the air around it, then blew back to where the other creature stood.

Brent's vision in his one eye grew fuzzy for a moment. His head felt heavy and his throat felt stuffed with cotton. He was bleeding everywhere; every root was slick with it. He was losing too much of it, dying right there on Nilhollow's forest floor. He turned as best he could to face the creatures behind him and raised his gun. *Fuck it*, he thought. *If I'm gonna die, I'm taking one of them with me.*

He emptied his clip into the one in front of him, each bullet jerking the creature back a step in tiny sprays of splinters. He kept firing long after the clip was emptied, just a series of pathetic little clicks as the angered thing stalked back to where he lay.

"No," he croaked. "No."

Their eyes blazed, but they stopped their advance.

"Please," he said, tears streaming out of his remaining eye. "Please don't."

The root that had grown out of his rib cage snaked into his ear in a sharp drill of pain. The ones in his wrists yanked him down as they dug into the ground.

One of the creatures reached down with long branch-fingers toward his ruined eye. He couldn't see what it was doing, but he felt the sharp ends of those fingers dig into the skin along the side of his cheek and jaw. There was a wet tearing sound and then his face felt like it was on fire. He saw something red and floppy hanging from the stick-fingers. It took several seconds in his haze, but he realized with horror that it was the skin of his face.

He didn't see the creature's other hand until a second before it came down on his skull. Somewhere far off, he heard something crack and felt an odd change of pressure in his head. Then, everything went dark, and Brent Carver, roots and all, sank half into the ground.

Oksana ran blindly through the dark, her feet barely touching the ground, dodging trees only by some instinct. All she was aware of was darkness and the keening of the wind, if it really was the wind, and the strangled screams of that obnoxious state trooper behind her. She had to find other people.

Around her, the wind raced to keep up, wailing in her ears. That terrified her most of all, the sound of that wind, the speed and power and the awful cry of it. It was the voice of those things, the voice of the *leshiye*. Of that, she had no doubt; in Western Europe as well as Eastern Europe, people had names for wind like that, names for the *leshiye*, both good and bad, and a healthy fear of their power. Once, on a trip to Ireland, she'd visited a little pub in rural farm country so remote that most still spoke the old language rather than English. Still, she had found one little old man in a wool cap and sweater, willing to exchange stories of homelands in English by the warmth of the pub fireplace. He had once traveled broadly to experience the cultural flavor of other nations, too, and since he didn't know Russian and she didn't know Irish Gaelic, English seemed a pleasant common ground. He'd told her stories about Irish fairies and elves and wood sprites, and he'd told her stories of the banshees, and how they howled. The latter were omens of death, he'd said, and went on to tell her that over time, popular culture dictated that if one heard the wail of the banshee, it meant he or she was next to die. And that was what the sound of the wind made her think of, the death-wail of the banshee. The breath of an approaching and inevitable death. It drove her speed.

They had let her live, as the rangers suggested they would, because of the sticks. She didn't know how that could be, but it was. She had held her breath, convinced they were going to dismember her where she stood, but they seemed to read the latticework as a kind of friendly message. The sticks meant something to them, passed on some understanding. They were words made solid objects, and the *leshiye* apparently read or felt them as a reason to let her live. She saw now that even in America, so jaded and scientific, so convinced of their sophistication over superstition, even here, some people still remembered and understood. And thank God that they did, because they had essentially saved her life. She remembered how earlier that night, when the search teams were originally assembled, the troopers and local officers had rejected the three or four stick configurations that the rangers had offered. The ranger station only had those few and there hadn't been time to make more, but it wouldn't have mattered anyway, it seemed. One team leader had broken a stick configuration, while the others shoved theirs back in the hands of the rangers giving them. Oksana hoped those few remaining sticks had kept at least the rangers safe.

The *leshiye* were angry at the guns, angry at the invasion. She could feel their sense of having been disrespected and their desire to kill. She suspected that now that they had seen men with guns, it wouldn't take an officer firing at them to anger them. They'd just attack on sight. No one in any of the search party units would be safe until everyone left the woods. And it was up to her to let them know, to make them believe. She had to tell them. She had to—

She didn't see the state trooper in her path until she had nearly toppled him over. He caught her up in his arms and she began struggling against him. He was slowing her down, and they were coming . . .

"Whoa, whoa, hold up, Ranger. What's going on?"

Oksana stopped fighting him; he was stronger, and had no intention of letting her go until she calmed down. She was still on high alert, though. Her chest heaved as she tried to catch her breath, and her darting glances behind her, searching the dark for movement or glowing eyes, betrayed her urgency.

As he looked her over with the flashlight, he saw the blood on her uniform and his voice softened a little. "Are you okay?" he asked. "What happened? Are you hurt?"

Oksana tried to open her mouth to speak, but the words wouldn't come. How could she make them understand? Even in Russian, she didn't think she could find an adequate way to describe what she had seen. She had so little time, and only words they wouldn't believe anyway. The wind was coming. The trees were coming. How could she begin to explain to them how very real and deadly those things were in Nilhollow?

The state trooper stood there with a gentle but firm grip on her arm, waiting for an answer. The four men behind him, one of them

Clark Cohen from the ranger station, watched her expectantly as well. They deserved to know what they were up against. She couldn't let them head blindly in the direction she'd just come from.

She thought about what to say for a minute, and then replied, "Not my blood. My unit was attacked. They are all dead."

"Dead? Fuck, what happened? Who attacked them? Are you sure they're all dead?"

"Yes. There are things in the woods . . ."

"What kind of things? Bears or something?"

"No, not bears. And not people. It take too long to explain now, and time is short. We need to leave this forest."

"We need to secure that area and see for sure if those officers are dead first," the trooper said.

The policemen moved forward but Oksana grabbed at their arms. "No no no, wait. Wait. You can't go back that way. You do not understand—"

"If we have officers down, we need to assist. And whatever you think you saw, if it killed our men, we have to stop it." The state trooper turned to his unit. "Gibbons, call it in to the command post, and call for backup."

A tall, gawky-looking dark-haired man in a state police uniform nodded and turned to his shoulder-mic.

"Greer, you and Gibbons bring up the rear. Cohen, stay here. Keep an eye on her."

"Trooper, listen to me. You cannot fight what killed those police. They are strong. You need to tell your fellow police to leave this place. Please wait. Just listen."

The state trooper turned around, impatience molding his features into a stiff expression.

"Your guns will not help. Your strength will not help. You need to warn the others that whatever slept in these woods is awake now, and it wants blood."

The trooper shook his head. "I don't know what you're talking about, with sleepers being awake or whatever, but let me see if I can make *you* understand. If there have been casualties, we need to secure the scene and neutralize the threat. Get it? We don't run. We're the ones the running people come to for help." He started off again with Gibbons and Greer in tow.

"Officer, please!" She sounded desperate, frantic, and even she realized her words came across as those of a hysterical woman. "Officer, you're in danger. At least wait for the backup."

"Unit three is on its way," Greer told the trooper. "Should be here in five."

Oksana turned to Clark. "The woods-spirits are real—and deadly strong! Like tree-people. I saw them. Felt them. I had the sticks. Was only thing that save me. But I drop it." Tears welled up in her eyes. "I drop it. Tell them, Clark. Make them understand."

She wiped the tears away and could see by Clark's face that he understood. She thought he would. It wasn't just ranger tradition and superstition that passed between them; all the rangers had known on some level that there was more to what they felt in those woods than that. They had stories of their own of tree-haunts, and deadly serious precautions that even the newest trainee was taught, long before that trainee had reason to believe he or she needed them. One couldn't spend nights and days and even more nights in the state parks of the Pine Barrens and not know deep in the soul that those who guarded the forest were always present—and that, unfortunately, those guardians specifically residing in Nilhollow were very damaged in some way. The rangers had suspected the time would come when just avoiding the woods-spirits or leaving them pacifying gifts would no longer be enough.

"Alvarez, wait. Just wait a sec."

Again, the state trooper turned back to them, and this time, he did little to mask his impatience. "What?"

"The rangers," Clark said, "have a . . . a belief. An old tradition—"

"I don't have time for this, Cohen."

"Make time. Hear me out," Clark said. His tone was such that the police stood there, waiting to hear what the ranger had to say.

Clark continued. "We've been keepers, in a sense, of this state park for a long time. As such, we hear stories. Then we see things that bear those stories out. If what Oksana is saying is true, and I strongly believe it is, then heading in like cowboys to secure the scene and take down the threat with guns drawn will only get you killed. You . . . you should have been more careful with the stick configuration I gave you."

"What are we talking about here, huh? What's with all the vague bullshit? You're telling me I should be afraid of ranger superstition. Is that what you're saying?"

"Elementals. They're like guardians of natural things—in this case, trees, specifically. But the ones in Nilhollow—there's something very wrong with them. According to legend, they've been going insane for centuries."

Alvarez crossed his arms. "Still sounds like a bunch of hippy-dippy superstitious bullshit to me."

"Call it what you want, Alvarez. I don't care. Just don't dismiss it."

There was a brief uncomfortable silence that followed, and Clark looked like he was about to break it when they heard some crashing through the bushes nearby. Oksana cried out. Even the police officers jumped.

The members of unit three came stomping through the overgrowth. There were two men in trooper uniforms, a woman with a state Missing Persons Unit badge on hers, and a woman in the uniform of the local police. Oksana noticed that none of their rangers had been assigned to unit three, so there would be no one there to back up her and Clark's assertions.

"Alvarez. You unit five?" one of the men in a state trooper uniform asked. He appeared to be in charge of unit three.

Alvarez nodded. Thanks for the backup, Hoss."

"Don't mention it," the man replied. "What have we got here?"

Alvarez turned to look at Clark and Oksana again. "Rangers here think some of our officers from unit six were killed by . . . what is it, Clark? Forest ghosts? Tree-monsters? That about right?"

Clark and Oksana exchanged glances. When Clark spoke, it was clear he was choosing his words carefully. "In a way, they're both. And neither. Like I said, they're called elementals. They're spirits in the sense that they don't always have physical forms, but they are not the souls of dead people, like ghosts are. They were never human. And before you scoff and dismiss all this out of hand, just listen to me. You don't spend every workday out here—we do. Any ranger will tell you the same thing I am. This is real. They are real. And if Oksana is telling you she saw your fellow officers die and that guns will make the situation worse, they will."

Alvarez sauntered back to them, squaring off with Oksana. "Just what, exactly, did you see?"

His gaze made her uncomfortable. Behind him, the other officers looked annoyed.

"Well, Ranger? What little ghosties did you see in the dark, scary forest, huh?" Alvarez's mocking eyes and his garlic breath steeled her to look him square in the eye.

"I saw two of them. Two creatures, they come out of woods. They have crazy inside them. Pass it on to others. I saw it with my own eyes. They make Officer Carver crazy to shoot one policeman, then himself in the feet and hand. The other trooper, Helen, she shoot at the creatures and it make them very angry. Off comes her arm, and they open her gut. Then they kill Officer Carver. Make things grow out of him. Tear off his flesh."

The other policemen standing behind Alvarez shifted uncomfortably. Alvarez himself hesitated, backing off of her a little.

"Well, how did you escape, then?" the state trooper asked.

"I have sticks," she told him, searching for a way in English to explain it. "These sticks made into figure when I tie with colored string. The *leshiye* see and I do not know what they think, but they leave me alone, so I ran. I drop it, though. It was only thing to keep me alive. We have no defense. So, we will all die if we do not leave this forest."

"You know that sounds crazy, right? I know your English isn't great, but tell me you understand how crazy that sounds," Alvarez said. "For all we know, *you* killed the officers. You've got blood all over you. Maybe I should arrest you right now for murder."

"Yes," she said, somewhat exasperated by his stubbornness. "Arrest me, if that is what you want. Take us out of these woods to your jail."

Alvarez's eyes narrowed. Then he turned to Clark. "You stay with her. We're going to check out the situation. You don't leave until we get back. I mean that. No one leaves until we know what's going on, got it?"

Clark didn't respond. He just stared at Alvarez until the state trooper turned away. Unit three followed unit five into the woods.

For a long time, Clark and Oksana didn't move. They felt the *leshiye* all around them, chattering in the leaves and breathing in the wind. They were nakedly, utterly vulnerable, alone with angry, vengeful guardians watching them like lions watch gazelles. And while it was true the rangers had no guns and no axes to incur the spirits' wrath, they had no stick lattices, either.

They didn't speak. Clark didn't ask her any more about what she saw, and she didn't volunteer any further information. They didn't know each other well outside of work, so little comfort was to be had from familiarity or trust. More so, they didn't speak for the same reason they didn't move; speech would single them out and bring the notice of the elementals. Nilhollow was capricious. It was wiser not to draw anything's attention when the two of them were alone. They didn't want that.

But Clark understood. He could help make the others understand. Alvarez might be a lost cause, but when they reached the rest of the search party, the other rangers would back them up. Oksana thought staying there was just wasting time, but Clark held her arm.

"Just a few minutes more," he whispered. She thought she understood; he wanted to see if Alvarez came back. Though she felt impatient, she supposed there were a couple of different reasons it would be good to wait. Besides the old adage about there being safety in numbers, units three and five would see for themselves, and that would mean more people in their corner, people who would help convince their own to abandon the search.

Those two cops and those two civilians, Oksana thought, were probably dead. If they had come across the *leshiye*, they were almost surely dead.

While they waited, their breaths shallow and quiet, Clark held her. They kept their silence and their stillness. In fact, one could very well have mistaken them for just two lonely trees in the forest until they heard the roaring. It was then, and only then, that they ran.

TWELVE

Julia and Pete ran, oblivious to the sharp hanging branches that nicked their skin and the uneven ground that threatened to trip them up. It was only when the pain in her ankle became unbearable and threatened to bring her down that she tugged on Pete's arm to stop.

"I—I can't anymore. My ankle. I can't."

She figured she had done some irreparable damage to it by that point; adrenaline could only carry her so far. She glanced down and could see that her ankle now bulged beneath her makeshift bandage and sock. The pain came in hot, throbbing waves that blacked out the world for a few seconds with each pulse. It took supreme effort on her part to force everything back into focus. If it hadn't been sprained before, it certainly must be by now.

Pete scanned the gloom behind them as he caught his breath. "Want me to carry you?"

She giggled, aware of how high and thin it sounded in between pants. "It's a sweet thought, Pete, but I don't think that'll work. Just—can I lean on you? I can limp, sort of, if we go slow."

He nodded, looping a surprisingly strong arm under hers and around her back. It took her weight off the bad ankle and the pain relented a little. That close to him, she wondered briefly what she smelled like—dreams and dirt and fear and sweat, probably. He smelled good, though, despite a dirty and dangerous day in the woods. The scent of him made her feel a little safer.

He moved at her pace, but she could tell from his face that he was nervous that those horrors, freed of their nooses, were closing the distance between them. She followed his occasional glances to the inkiness that seemed to be consuming more and more of the woods they'd left only moments before. She couldn't see any sign of the flayed corpses or even any movement in the shadows, nor could she hear their labored breathing anymore. The corpses were, she was pretty sure, an illusion of sorts to get into her and Pete's heads and crack them open, and the forest had evidently grown tired of using them.

There would be other things to terrorize her and Pete, though—she was sure of that. Nilhollow wanted to exhaust them, cause them to despair. It wanted to break them and goad them into acts of depravity and desperation like murder and suicide and God only knew what else. *Things crawling, snaking, and slithering up from that god-awful chasm*, she thought. *That's what else.* She didn't think she could bear that. She'd weathered a lot the last couple of days, but she couldn't stomach having to confront that chasm again. It would push her right over the edge, figuratively if not literally. She guessed that was the intent of that chasm. It wanted to drive them crazy so it could have them forever.

Maybe it already had, and it knew so.

Were they crazy yet, either one of them? How long did it take to go insane? She didn't know. She only knew that as far as Pete was concerned, his possession of the ax made her uncomfortable. He didn't seem so much different to her otherwise, but then, Darren never seemed "off" until suddenly he was, and she was blindsided. Was Pete leading her out of the woods, or was he really leading her deeper into them? Would he turn on her, seemingly out of nowhere, for some wrong word or action, and bury that ax of his in her skull?

As for her . . . well, she thought that Pete probably wished she'd drop her ax as well. She wouldn't blame him if he was keeping an eye on her, assessing all the quirky, nervous little things she said and did. However, dropping the ax wasn't likely to happen. It made her feel safe and in possession of at least a modicum of control. Although they weren't quite on speaking terms yet, she was beginning to appreciate her ax as much as her little purse. Both were providing for her and keeping her going, and so her purse and her ax weren't going anywhere so long as she was alive. She didn't think he'd deny her that little bit of safety and security, anyway, even if he was a little worried about her sanity. He'd seen things, too. Being without a weapon here would feel like being naked—naked and decorated with steaks and thrown in a lion's cage.

She fought the urge to laugh at the mental image of the two of them strung up with cartoon slabs of meat. It would have sounded nuts, even to her. Was she nuts? Did she feel crazy? She didn't think so . . . but she wasn't sure what crazy felt like, if it felt like anything at all.

It occurred to her that if either of them really were insane, the forest probably wouldn't have been trying so hard to mess with them. It wouldn't need to break what was already broken. So maybe they were still okay, both of them. Or . . . were the things they were seeing just misfires of broken minds? Her headache was starting to return.

Julia took a deep breath to clear the thoughts from her head. It was getting hard to think things through; she supposed that was a result of having been in Nilhollow so long. The forest wanted her confused, preoccupied with a frustrating loop of doubt and paranoia, but she wasn't going to let go like that. If she had learned anything since getting lost, it was that any chance for survival involved keeping whatever wits she happened to have, just like her little purse. She had to remain focused. She had to prioritize, just like she had before— take things step by step, solve one obstacle at a time. She wanted to believe Pete was on her side, and right now, he had given her no real reason to be afraid of him. So she'd just watch him, the way he was probably watching her. She'd be ready. And whatever crazy *she* had been exposed to, whatever crazy might be inside her like a germ, she was going to do her best to fight it. She was going to get out of here with Pete. She found, to her surprise, that imagining doing things with Pete, once free of the forest, things like going out to dinner, maybe, or catching a movie, gave her a warm, happy feeling. She wondered if it served as a reason for Pete, too—if he ever thought about taking her out. Spending time with him, like on a real date and not just a car ride to the police station to file another report or grabbing a cup of coffee at that little coffee shop near the police station, seemed to her a damned good reason to keep going.

Other reasons to make it out of there began to take shape as the two trudged along in silence. The reasons surprised her in the intensity with which she felt them. For instance, just then she really wanted it to matter to somebody that she made it out of those woods. More than that, though, she found that it really did matter to *her*. It was a kind of revelation to her that the woman she was trying to save was someone she could like and admire and *want* to save. She supposed with Darren, it had been a long time since she'd felt any sense of pride in her own abilities. She certainly recognized that she both wanted and needed Pete's help, but she also felt a certain sense of pride in having kept herself alive for as long as she had, given the woods she'd been lost in. She wanted to feel she had a part in her own escape from the woods, as well. Now more than ever, she needed to know for her own sense of being that she could trust and rely on herself—not just to prove Darren and her parents wrong, but to prove her old inner critic wrong, too. She was worth saving, whether by her own hand or someone else's. And realizing that felt pretty damned good, despite everything else going on. She just wanted the chance to explore that new philosophy, to utilize it, and build a better life around it than she had lived so far.

"Uh, Julia," Pete said, clearing his throat, "I, uh, I know this is, like, a weird time to bring this up . . . like a really weird time. But, um, I just wanted . . . well, just wanted to ask if you—" He stopped midsentence. His flashlight was flickering along the way in front of them, and she saw it a moment after he did. It was little more than a long smear of dirt devoid of grass, pine needles, and leaves, something deliberate but crude in its layout. Still, it was there all right, snaking around trees and only disappearing once it crested a small hill up ahead.

"A path," Julia whispered. "Oh my God. I haven't seen a path since I first got lost. Maybe it goes back to the road?" She wanted to be excited, but the feeling caught in her chest. If it was another trick of the forest, she didn't think she'd be able to find the strength to start over again.

"Maybe," he said, and she could hear the same guarded hope in his voice. "I sure as hell hope so."

"Pete . . . what are those?" She pointed at the marks that the flashlight beam caught and defined. They looked like gouges and furrows, but ran in all different directions, as if something put up a hell of a kicking fuss but only in the dirt of the path.

"Uh . . ." Pete steered them closer to take a look. He shined the flashlight down on the marks. "Marks of a struggle, maybe," he replied. He shined the light around them, ostensibly looking for some indication as to what might have made those marks. "Or maybe they mean a search party. Looks like a lot of scuff marks for just one pair of shoes."

"So ... that's a good sign, right? It means people are coming to look for us?"

"It would appear that way. If that's what those marks are, I mean. They could be animal tracks, too, but I doubt that. They look more like something was uprooted and just . . ." He didn't finish the thought. He didn't have to.

"Should we follow the path?" Julia wasn't quite ready to let go of the hope the path suggested. Maybe they were near the road. Maybe all this was so close to being over.

He looked up at her. "I don't know. What do you think?"

She thought about it a moment, then said, "I think we should give it a try. I mean, we can't get any more lost than we are right now, right?"

"Good point," he agreed.

He steadied her, looping his arm around her to support her as she hobbled along. Her jittering movements made the little flashlight beam jump. Together, they made slow progress. Even with Pete's flashlight, it was hard to see anything beyond a few feet in front of them. Pockets of shadows loomed, swelled, and burst, casting jagged, sinister shapes against the tree trunks, which made it hard to determine where to walk and where to duck or dodge. Stranger still was that to Julia, it looked like the darkness in the part of the forest ahead of them was lighter somehow, but thicker and harder to wade through and breathe in. It was a kind of chalky gray-black, a simple absence of light mixed with substance to somehow make it tangible.

All around them, the forest was breathing, moving, stretching, reshaping itself. She couldn't see it, but she knew it. The more time she spent in Nilhollow, the more she felt she understood how very much alive it was, and how its feelings manifested. As they moved along the path, she had to force the muscles in her shoulders to relax a little. Every sound, however small, sent her head turning. She was waiting for what the forest was going to throw at them next. It was gearing up for something, maybe like what she had dreamed about. The illusions were getting worse—meaner, scarier, more monstrous. Maybe it wasn't going to be another illusion at all; maybe the trees themselves would spear them with sharp branches, or open up warrens and dens and release flesh-eating beasts. Or maybe her mind and body would simply collapse from exhaustion in her anticipation.

Deep down, she believed that what she was feeling were actually the tree-creatures Pete had mentioned. Maybe just as they seemed able to sense her and know her thoughts and feelings, she could feel them, too. At the very least, she thought she could feel whatever force was driving their behavior.

She was about to voice some of her thoughts to Pete to get his opinion when she realized why the dark looked so thick and gray. A misty, whitish fog had begun to roll toward them from between and beyond the trees. It moved quickly, its fingers grazing their skin all over with a chill dampness as it surrounded them. She watched it swirl and dance with its own surreal kind of grace, adding to the impression of movement throughout the spaces between the trees.

Sometimes a wispy bit of fog would obscure everything, and then a moment later, it would shift and a tree trunk would be inches, even feet closer than it had before. It broke the mesmerizing spell of the fog's movement and set her on edge again.

"Dammit," Pete whispered. "Can't see the path too well. Wait— I think we're off course, somehow, if that tree is the same one I think it is."

"It's okay," she whispered back. "Let's keep going."

There was a pause in which she could hear him breathing, then, "Really? Do . . . do you—"

"I don't think we have much of a choice," she said. "It's spreading everywhere. We can't go back. I can't go back."

"Um, okay. Okay then. Just make sure you hold on to my arm. I don't want to lose you in this."

She nodded even though he couldn't see her, and clutched his arm tighter. They moved even more slowly now, feeling the way with their feet. That was fine with her as far as her ankle went, as it was getting difficult to put anything but the slightest pressure on that foot.

However, she couldn't quite shake the feeling that the trees were creeping up on her in the fog. It reminded her of an old game from her childhood, where one person closed his or her eyes, and in the space of time it took to turn around and face the others, they would have to get as close as possible without their movement being seen. She felt like she and Pete were closing their eyes and counting—*red light, green light, one, two, three!* She fought the urge to turn around and see what had gained ground behind her.

A swath of fog curled away and a low branch swung out in front of her face. She flinched, ducking under it, and wondered how Pete, who was walking almost in front of her, had managed to avoid it. The trees, apparently, were gaining ground all around her.

"Are we still on the path?" she asked.

"I think so," Pete answered. "Sometimes when the fog clears, the flashlight catches the grooves in the path and they kind of shine a little. I don't know why that is, but it helps. I think we're still heading in the right direction. Well, we're heading in the same direction, at least. I think." He flinched just slightly and glanced behind him. Maybe he felt the trees closing ranks, too.

Red light green light one two three. She could just about feel their branch-fingers skimming her shoulder.

He shined his flashlight up ahead, but it only bounced off the fog, making it harder to see.

Swaths of white drifted across their path, sometimes thin enough to grasp the basic shapes of the tall grasses, trees, and bushes, and sometimes so thick that all she could see were moving outlines.

It was one of those moving outlines, developing details as the fog thinned again, that made her gasp. It was coming toward them out of the fog, moving slowly but steadily. It had only one light rather than two glinting animal eyes, and was the same color as Pete's flashlight.

"Pete!" She tugged his arm.

"I see it," he whispered.

As the figure got closer, they could see it was tall and somewhat grizzled, carrying a large backpack and a small police-issued flashlight. He looked solid to her, more real than the encompassing trees. She didn't know if that should be a relief, or a reason to panic. She chose to take it as the former.

"Who is it?"

"Not sure," he answered. "If he was a search party member, he wouldn't be alone."

Pete's body tensed and his arm slipped away so that he could position himself in front of her to protect her as he studied the figure. "Wait," he said. "Holy shit, I think that's—"

"Grainger?" the figure shouted. "Thank God. Are you okay? Is that Ms. Russo with you?"

The speaker moved into the flashlight glow, and Pete gave a relieved little laugh. The figure who had emerged from the fog was an older man, graying a little in his otherwise brown hair and along his unshaven jaw. He was somewhat stocky, the kind of body used to rough activities at one time, with a hard but handsome face and kind but sharply alert eyes.

"Oh my God. Is that really you?" Pete's body relaxed a little, and he led her closer.

It took a moment, but then Julia recognized the man as well. It was Captain Stan Mallon, Pete's boss. When the captain reached out to clap Pete on the shoulder, she saw Pete flinch; he was probably wondering if Captain Mallon was real or another trick of the forest. Julia knew better, though. She knew he was real the same way Pete had been real. For one thing, she had noticed that the illusions never touched them. She believed they very well could, but they didn't, and she thought that was because if they did, their masks would slip and she'd be able to see what was really underneath. There was always something inhuman about them, slightly less tangible than the rest of reality. There was always an earthy smell about them and stiff, wooden movements that set them apart from what they tried to pretend to be. They might have been pretty good at mimicking, but she didn't think they could pretend too long or too well up close.

Apparently Pete didn't, either, because the physical gesture put him at ease, and he shook Mallon's free hand.

"Wow, how did you find us?"

Mallon shrugged. "I think you found me, actually. Are either of you hurt? Debrief me."

"Julia has a sprained ankle and is hungry and a little dehydrated," Pete replied, "but otherwise, we're holding up okay, I'd say."

"Okay. We'll get her to a hospital when we get out of here. What about Perry?"

Pete's expression fell. "He's . . . gone."

"Gone as in lost?"

With great effort, Pete shook his head. "Gone as in killed."

Mallon studied him with an expression that wasn't quite skeptical, but rather, curious. "Killed how?" he asked.

Even in the dim glow of the flashlight, Julia could see Pete choke up. "The stories about this place are true. There are . . . things here in this forest. Deadly things. They move fast and they're strong. Too strong. Several of them jumped Perry. I tried to help, but I couldn't. And yeah, I know it sounds crazy, but I swear to you, it's true. You have to believe me."

"I do," Mallon said, unzipping the backpack. He opened it just enough for them to see a battery-powered chainsaw and a blowtorch, as well as some papers, a few lighters, and other odds and ends. "Now look. I don't know what all you two have seen out here, and frankly, I don't think we have time now for you to explain. I don't claim to have the foggiest idea what you've been through. But I now this place is deadly. And a little research as well as a little personal experience has led me to be a damn sight open-minded about whatever people tell me is out here. I suspect we've only just experienced the tip of the iceberg, in fact."

Pete brightened a little. "So . . . you believe me about the things out here?"

Captain Mallon offered a tight smile as he zipped up the backpack. "They're elementals, I'm told. Nature spirits connected to the trees. But they're only part of the problem. Something called the Turning of the Earth, some sentient force of destruction and chaos, is driving those spirits, as well as anyone caught up in these woods for too long, pretty much bat-shit crazy. How'm I doing?"

Pete looked as if he could hug Captain Mallon. Julia felt so relieved that the tension in her face dissipated and condensed to form tears.

"Couldn't have explained it better myself," Pete said. "But how did you know? And how did you know we were in trouble?"

This time, Captain Mallon's grin was a little less grim. "These high-powered perceptions and refined detecting skills are why they pay me the big bucks."

Pete laughed. It was good, Julia thought, to hear him laugh. "So, what's the plan, Captain? We've been wandering around here for hours. We can't find the way out."

"No," Captain Mallon said. "That seems to be by deliberate design. If my research—or, to be more accurate, an old friend's research—is accurate, then I doubt we'll be able to, until we kill it."

"Kill what?" Julia asked.

"Possibly those tree spirits. More effective, though, would be the killing of whatever this Turning is. To do that, we'll burn this whole forest down to the ground if we have to. But we might not. I think if we can just find the heart of this place and cut it out, a good portion of the madness infecting these woods and everyone in them will run its course, like a fever."

"The heart," Julia murmured. "You mean the chasm?"

"The what now? You—you know about the chasm?"

"Oh, uh . . . not really. I mean, I've seen it, yes," she said, gesturing. "I've been there. It's the most awful thing I've ever experienced. The things it shows you in your head . . ." She shivered.

"You've seen it?" Captain Mallon studied her intently. "The actual chasm?"

She nodded. "Yes, sir, I have. It's in a clearing full of dead plants. Well, not dead, but not really alive, either. It makes so much sense now that the chasm is where all this is coming from. It's just oozing madness and hatred and violence. It floods your whole body when you're nearby. It was terrible."

Captain Mallon's voice softened. "I can tell that this place affected you profoundly. But it is very important that we get to this chasm. I think I can close it or at least plug it up permanently, but I need to know where it is. Do you think you could find it again?"

She thought about it a moment, then shook her head. "I'm sorry. Even if I could face the idea of going back, which I don't think I can, I'd never be able to find it again. One of the things I've noticed about this forest is that every time you're sure you're heading in the right direction, it rearranges itself so that you're lost again. The way that I found it the last time would be impossible to retrace. I'm sorry, Captain."

Captain Mallon nodded. "That's okay. It's possible it'll find us soon enough. I think the key now is to stay together. We can backtrack the way I just came. If the research is wrong and luck holds, we can get you safely out of these woods and take care of the chasm ourselves. But if what I think is going to happen actually does, we'll end up yellow-brick-roading it right to the chasm itself. Either way, we will be moving toward some satisfying conclusion. We *will* get out of here, okay? One way or another, we will."

Julia nodded. She could see why Pete looked up to this man. He looked a person right in the eye as if nothing else mattered but the two of them and that moment, and he spoke with such conviction and authority that she couldn't help but believe him. If he said it would be okay, it would.

Captain Mallon hitched the backpack strap over one shoulder and looped his free arm around Julia's back to help hoist her up. Pete resumed his support on her other side. With the officers flanking her, she found she was able to take more weight off her bad ankle, and the throbbing eased up a little. It was the first time since getting lost in Nilhollow that Julia actually felt safe. *It's fine, it's fine, everything is just fine.*

She thought it really might be okay, this time.

The fog around them was swirling faster now. The trees in front of them were almost obscured completely, and the path was a smear of gray beneath their feet, but still she felt they were making progress in some direction. Julia couldn't tell which direction, but like Captain Mallon had said, it probably didn't matter. She felt better just knowing there was a plan, however loosely formed and indefinite, to take care of the situation one way or another.

Some of her confidence flagged a little, though, as the minutes passed. It felt like they walked a long time without actually getting anywhere new. The scenery around them didn't change, and for all she knew, the forest could have had them treading the same ten feet over and over again. That, to her, was worse than the miles of ground she had covered only to end up either an impossible proximity to or distance from where she'd started. The idea of being unable to make any headway at all, like in one of those nightmares where a person's feet were stuck in quicksand, made her feel a little sick.

"How much farther, do you think?" she asked.

Captain Mallon grunted. "Should have been out already," he said.

"Story of my life, at least for the last two days or so," Julia said with a small laugh.

The older cop gave her an odd look. "Four days."

"Excuse me?"

"You mean four days, don't you?"

"I—I don't . . . I'm not . . ." Her voice trailed off.

The officers exchanged glances. "According to our police records, Ms. Russo," Captain Mallon said gently, "your car was logged in as having gone missing four days ago. Pete only found out about it last night. Our best guess is that you've been missing at least four days. Maybe five."

The world swam in front of her. She'd been out there four days, on only a PowerBar and a bottle of water? How was that possible? How could she have spent four days alone in the woods already? She wilted a little where she stood, her legs suddenly too heavy to keep moving.

"Whoa. Whoa there, ma'am. Everything's okay," Captain Mallon said. "Everything's okay now. We've got you. We'll get you out of here, okay? Just stay with us. Hang in there."

But it wasn't okay. She'd somehow blundered through two completely unremembered days. She'd felt that time had moved differently in Nilhollow, sure, but *two days*? What had happened to her? How could she have lost two days? It made her feel a little sick.

She was still processing the information when they heard the roars.

THIRTEEN

By the time units three and five reached the spot where Ranger Volkova said that Brent Carver, Helen Cadmonson, and Carl Witherspoon were killed, little was left to see except some dragged-through areas of mud where the grass looked like it had been kicked up in clumps. There were no blood splatters or body parts, no dead officers, no weapons or badges. There were no signs that unit six had been there at all.

And there were no tree-creatures, either, Alvarez noted. Who knew where *that* had come from? Maybe the rangers smoked up before heading into Nilhollow. Or maybe it was some weird ranger version of hazing newbies in the forest; maybe they got off on the idea of pulling one over on the cops who were stuck out there in the big scary woods. *Ha ha, very funny, now everyone back to the ranger shack to smoke a bowl.* Alvarez shook his head. It was in poor taste, he thought, to work dead cops into their joke. Carver, Cadmonson, and Witherspoon had probably just left her behind and she wanted to get back at them. It hadn't escaped his notice that Cohen had jumped so quickly to Volkova's defense. Maybe the rangers had some kind of jealousy/disdain thing for police officers. It struck Alvarez as really unprofessional, whatever their motives.

Despite the reasons he could come up with for finding the rangers' story ridiculous, he couldn't quite dismiss the intensity in their voices. There were no tells to indicate they were lying, either, in their expressions or their body language. But so what? Even if they believed what they were saying, it didn't make it real. People could be mistaken, deluded, or nuts. Frankly, the scene didn't bear out their story. How could it? There were no monsters here. There was nothing here at all.

What *was* there in that clearing was a dirt path leading away from the scene of the struggle, if that was what it was, and into the darkness beyond their flashlights' glare.

"Maybe all that voodoo shit Volkova and Cohen were talking about is farther up ahead," Gibbons suggested.

"Maybe," Alvarez replied. The evidence certainly seemed to suggest it, if the path was any indication. There were odd furrows and gouges along its length, like something had trampled through.

The seven of them stuck close together, safeties off on their weapons, senses on high alert. Only Jack Hoss seemed unfazed by the forest. From the muted snippets of the others' conversation, Alvarez got the impression that they were all in agreement about the rangers' story; the idea of gun-hating tree-spirits was too ridiculous to take seriously, at least out loud. It was more of the same kind of superstitious claptrap that nearly all cops had heard regarding Nilhollow at one time or another. Still, the feeling behind the rangers' words and the look of horror on Volkova's face had gotten to them, just a little. Alvarez could feel their anxious energy, how they recoiled from the various snapping and popping sounds around them as though they were being slapped. He just hoped none of them was trigger-happy, or a possible bad situation was going to get a whole lot worse.

As they walked, a soft and silent fog rolled across their path. It did nothing to soothe the nerves of the officers behind Alvarez. Their mumbling to each other had taken on a thin, hushed quality, but Alvarez couldn't make out the specifics of the conversation. Were he more paranoid and less confident, like he thought Carver was beneath the bravado, he might have thought they were grumbling about him or possibly believed that he was leading them deeper into danger. Alvarez refused to entertain such thoughts, though. He was doing his job. They were tasked with finding two state troopers and two civilians, and that was what they were going to do.

Alvarez focused on the navigational task at hand. The way the fog moved, it distorted the oaks and cedars, casting them as predatory shapes with the suggestion of faces and fingers. The pines were even worse; the fog formed gums around their needle-teeth that growled with malice. He didn't like the way the tall grasses and ferns seemed to ebb and flow through the forest, either. At times, they were closer than he thought they should be, ready to tangle around his feet and trip him up, and at other times, he made ready to duck beneath some slanting vine that turned out to be several feet farther away.

And he could hear the trees talking. His *abuela,* his grandmother on his mother's side, had often told him when he was a child that if one listened, one could hear the trees speak through the wind. He hadn't thought of it as any more than fantastic whimsy for most of his adult life, but he could remember spending the occasional summer afternoon at seven or eight years old, listening for what the trees might be telling him. Now, in the wind he thought he could hear whispered words. He couldn't quite make them out, but the tone suggested cruel and degrading things. They induced pictures in his head that made him intensely uncomfortable and triggered the onset of a migraine, but also fanned the beginnings of an erection. He felt outside of himself, like his mind was a balloon on a string and his body was just a walking shell stuffed with fog and cotton. It made him feel stoned and a little panicky, like his self-control was slipping away. He also couldn't shake the feeling that something important was passing him by, something he couldn't quite access. He thought that maybe if he could just see the owners of the voices, it might somehow wash away the film of confusion that seemed to be accumulating in his skull. Was it really the trees that were talking to him? If so, which ones and why? Why were they telling him things? What did they want from him?

He tried to focus on the path and on the search, to really buckle down and pay attention, but each time his brain tried to hold on to a thought for too long, it felt like a pin was being shoved into his eye. Still, he knew he needed to put the brain-haze and the whispers out of his mind as best he could; he couldn't lose himself looking for evidence of tree people. He had a job to do.

He fanned the glow of his flashlight from one side to another in a clumsy but earnest attempt to examine the area for signs of unit five, as well as clues as to the whereabouts of the missing persons. It was so hard to focus, though. That fog was getting up inside his head every time he breathed in, and it was rapidly turning bad inside him. It made him want to hurt something.

Alvarez couldn't really estimate how far into their trek the two units had gotten before the fog both inside and outside of his head finally began to dissipate a little, at least enough so that Alvarez could see what he guessed was a clearing about twenty feet ahead. The trees looked much thinner there and less dense. Maybe that was where the officers were down. He turned his head to report it in the shoulder-mic but the mic whined back at him. He grunted as the sound sent a needle of pain right through his ear and up into his head.

It was more of an annoyance that he couldn't reach the command post. He didn't think they were too far away, nor did he think the equipment was on the fritz. He supposed it was possible that this place caused some kind of interference. In fact, that sounded pretty likely, given the way his head felt. It was perfectly plausible that some interference, something electric, like live wires or ley lines or something, was the reason for the monstrous and disjointed way in which the plants in the area were growing, the static on his mic, and the headache and crazy thoughts he was having.

He set his sights on the clearing. The sooner they did their jobs, the sooner the officers could get the hell out of there. Who knew what kind of cancers electrical interference like that might cause? The trees all around certainly looked tumorous to him.

"Clearing up ahead," he said, as much to break the uncomfortable miasma of silence surrounding the units as to give the officers a heads-up. It would actually be something of a relief, Alvarez thought, to be in the clearing. The trees felt oppressively close.

It took some climbing over thick, thorny bushes and tall clumps of grasses to make it into the clearing, but one by one, the officers broke through into a small open space that even the trees seemed to hang back from. A faint smell of rotting grass carried on the breeze. There was a low, dull hum like that of incandescent lights, the presence of which fed into Alvarez's theory about electrical interference. He couldn't see anything, though, beyond a foot or two in front of him. Without even the trunks of pines or oaks to break the darkness, it seemed deeper somehow, like it was swallowing them.

The pure, unbroken lightlessness appeared to unnerve the other officers as well. Even Hoss seemed wary. Within seconds, the beams of their flashlights zigzagged like lightning bugs around the area, trying to get a sense of its dimensions. With the fog, though, the boundaries of the clearing constantly shifted. What little plant life they could see, growing in patches across the span of the clearing, looked even more gnarled and dead than the rest of Nilhollow's flora, curling at unnatural angles reminiscent of the hands of desiccated corpses. In truth, it was difficult for Alvarez not to imagine those plants reaching for his ankles, pleading to be pulled out of the ground . . . or possibly looking to drag him down into it. Alvarez studied a clump of what he guessed were maybe ferns under the beam of his flashlight. They set off little alarm bells in his head, those plants. They looked too much like the spines and ribs of children, the way they bent and curved. Most of Nilhollow had a bizarre cast to it—colors and shapes just a little off from what they should be, a little too pale and thin, too much like alien, sentient things. But the plants in that clearing were even more surreal, a stylized Gothic portrait of nature instead of nature itself.

"I don't see anybody," Greer said, tossing up his hands. "In fact, I don't see anything except a bunch of dead plants."

"Me neither," said Hoss. Alvarez had known him for years. He was a serious and levelheaded man, buzz-cut and built like a tank. He'd seen action in Afghanistan a year before, where civilians were used as human shields and young girls blew themselves to bits in public marketplaces in the hopes of taking Americans with them. He had pulled talismans, meant to protect their wearers from jinn, off the charred bodies of dead terrorists and had once faced down a so-called magician in a sun-bleached alley who had hurled down on him every ancient curse a superstitious man might die from. Jack Hoss was still standing. He did not back down and he did not run. But the way his eyes scanned the darkness suggested he felt the same unease that Alvarez did. The wrongness of the place, the unadulterated . . . well, *evil*—it was palpable.

"Well, there's that," Susan Brinks, the Missing Persons Unit officer, said. Her flashlight was aimed at a dark crack in the earth about fifteen feet long and maybe three or four feet wide. In the dim glow, the officers could see some large rocks along the closer edge wiggle free of the dirt and tumble in, widening the chasm by another six inches or so.

"Do you think the officers fell down that?" Gibbons sounded uneasy.

"Not likely," Alvarez said. "I don't think it's wide enough."

Sometime in the last few minutes, the electrical hum had become a low rumble, almost like thunder. It seemed to be coming from the chasm and was of just such a pitch that he could feel it in his chest and head.

"What is that? Can you guys feel that?" Brinks asked.

"Like a bass sound, right? Coming from over there." Gibbons pointed to the chasm.

"I think we ought to radio it in," Greer said.

"Go for it," Alvarez replied. "I had no luck getting through, but maybe you will."

Greer tried, and when the same static feedback whined in his ear, he shook his head. "No luck."

The wind picked up suddenly, carrying away most of the rest of the fog. Clouds shifted somewhere above them and streaks of moonlight passed through the trees, spotlighting the twisted vegetation. The rotting smell wafted stronger in their direction.

"Something's not right here," Greer said. "I think we should go back."

Alvarez turned to him. Greer was a tall, skinny, low-voiced, even-tempered kind of guy. He was never roused to anger or upset by much of anything. Alvarez hadn't known him long, but he'd always come across as a good cop, the kind who genuinely wanted to protect and serve. Alvarez didn't think he was any more the type to run from a situation than Hoss was. However, the look on his face now was of distinct disquiet. He was worried; he felt it, too.

If Greer and Hoss were worried, that was something to stop and consider. It suggested that it wasn't just Alvarez who was beginning to think dismissing the rangers' story had been a mistake.

Alvarez looked at the others. Gibbons, God help him, looked confused and uncomfortable that everyone seemed to know something about the clearing that he didn't. The other two officers, a state trooper named Dave Walton and a local officer named Karen Sykes, looked spooked, and Brinks was chewing on her lower lip, her flashlight jerkily skipping along the leafy canopies above them. It looked like she was searching for something with the desperation of one who had seen or thought she'd seen something she promptly lost.

"Something's not right, Alvarez," Greer repeated. "You know that, right?"

"What do you mean by not right?" Brinks asked him, her eyes and her beam of light still intent on the trees above.

Greer shook his head. "Can't you feel it? In your head, like sinus pressure except all over? In your hands, like the way anger makes you clench your fists? I can feel it in my bones. Something is fucking wrong with this forest, with this spot right here, and it's coming out of that chasm."

The others stood in uncomfortable silence, glancing back and forth between Greer and Alvarez, presumably waiting for the unit leader to respond. From their faces, he could tell they bought into Greer's theory wholesale. Truthfully, so did Alvarez.

He sighed. "Greer's right," he finally said. He had to be careful with how he handled them. Skittish, armed cops were bad news. "We have to focus on what we're doing out here. Two cops, two civilians, and now, most of unit six are missing. Those cops and those civilians aren't here, obviously." He paused. "But something is. This place ain't right, and even if it's just in our heads, it's not conducive to getting the job done. So we head back, meet up with the central command post, and report what we know. Which ain't much, sadly."

"Okay," Gibbons said, and Alvarez could hear relief in his voice. "Okay, good. Let's get the hell out of here."

They were just about to hike back over the tall grasses and get back on the path when a deep roar, loud enough to shake the branches of the trees, erupted from somewhere near the chasm. They ducked and covered their ears. Alvarez turned back to see what was making such a horrible noise and for several long seconds, he just gaped in awe.

On the far bank of the chasm was a tree-creature, just like the rangers had said, but it was huge—easily the size of a small oak. Its humanoid form was made entirely of wood and vines covered in gray-brown bark, and thin branches grew from its back and the top of its head. Its eyes were dual mini-chasms of blue fire. It moved on powerful legs, its roots clutching the earth beneath it and chucking it away as it walked.

"Oh my God," Hoss breathed.

It stepped over the width of the chasm and stopped, tilting its head as if studying the assembled officers. The creature's branch-fingers flexed. Then it leaned forward and its lipless mouth opened to issue another roar. What filled the officers' ears was the sound of a hurricane, the sound of a mountain falling.

Gibbons drew his gun.

Your guns will not help . . .

Alvarez saw it a second too late to stop him. "Gibbons, wait—"

Around them, in the moment of silence just before all hell broke loose, Alvarez heard the trees speaking again, and this time the words, if not all of their meanings, were perfectly clear: *The Kèkpëchehëlat will kill you all . . .*

Then Gibbons fired on the giant tree-creature.

The bullets flew into the wooden torso and the creature jerked a little with each one. The holes filled with sap before sealing over completely with new wood and bark. The blue fire in its eyes flashed. In two powerful steps, the creature closed the gap between itself and Gibbons.

Someone screamed, other guns were drawn, and chaos erupted in that little clearing.

The creature reached down and picked up Gibbons by the neck. The officer kicked his feet wildly, and dropping his gun, began clawing at the rough, wooden fingers. His face paled, then went from red to purple to a kind of blue, his eyes bulging. The creature then took Gibbons's legs in its other hand and folded the man in half backwards.

The snap of Gibbons's spine struck Alvarez as so loud—too loud, even over the din of confusion and fear going on around him. Greer was backing away, shaking his head slowly as if his brain refused to accept what his eyes were telling him. Jack Hoss was circling around behind the thing, gun drawn, and Susan Brinks was aiming her own firearm at the creature's face. Walton and Sykes were facing off with the creature, ostensibly trying to figure out how to get it to release Gibbons without incurring further wrath. They, too, had their guns drawn. No one fired, though. Alvarez supposed no one quite dared.

He had his own gun drawn as well, and considered shooting it in the eye. He thought, with luck and keeping his cool, that he might be able to bury a bullet in that blue fire. It wouldn't save Gibbons now— the state trooper was a mess of bloody flesh and jutting bone—but it might save his own ass, or those of the other officers. He took a deep breath and aimed, coolly exhaled, and fired into the tree-creature's eye.

The bullet found its mark, engulfed by the blue flame, which subsequently shot outward like a blowtorch for a few seconds, then settled back into the socket. It roared again, shaking the earth beneath them, flung Gibbon's crumpled body behind it like it was discarding a wadded-up ball of paper, then turned on Alvarez. The other officers opened fire.

The creature appeared stunned by the onslaught of bullets from different directions, its body taking them in with little twitches. They did no damage, though, other than to enrage the creature. It reached down to grab Brinks around the waist, and as she screamed, it tore off her bottom half in a spray of blood. Her eyes took several seconds to glaze over. She stared at her ruined hips and legs lying on the ground below and heaved. Blood spurted from her mouth and down her chin.

Dropping the two pieces of the Missing Persons Unit officer, the tree-creature turned on Jack Hoss, reaching for him just as the trooper dived out of the way. It tried again but Hoss dodged its hand. It growled, covering the distance between it and Hoss in seconds. Its hand shot out—the thing moved more quickly than Hoss evidently had expected—and pinned the ex-soldier against a tree. He struggled against the creature's palm, straining to pull air into his lungs against the pressure. He managed to wrestle his arm free and shot at the creature's face. It shook off the bullet and scooped him up despite his emptying his clip into its arm and shoulder. Then it threw Hoss into another tree, hard enough to bend the man's body around the trunk with a sickening series of snaps. Then it grabbed Karen Sykes, whose terror had paralyzed her, around the waist, but she didn't scream; even the ability to do that had left her. She looked so small in its hand. Then it shook her like a rag doll. The way her body rocked and dangled in its grasp, the way her head knocked around on her neck, was grotesque and unnatural, and it made Alvarez a little sick to watch. The remaining officers could hear her bones snapping and cracking like a series of tiny fireworks. The sound seemed to echo throughout the forest. When it stopped shaking her, she looked flatter and somewhat shapeless. Her head lolled and her shoulders slumped. When the creature dropped her and kicked her out of the way, she landed in a crumpled heap.

"Cover me," Dave shouted to Alvarez and Greer as he holstered his gun. He picked up a large, sharp-edged rock from the ground and flanked the creature. Alvarez and Greer opened fire. Infuriated, the creature began moving toward them. Dave approached it from the side, and when he got within a few feet of it, he hurled the rock at its knee. Alvarez supposed he was trying to snap the branches of its leg and cripple it. It was strong, but it couldn't keep advancing on them if it couldn't walk.

The rock wedged itself between a root and the wood of its leg. The creature stopped, looked down, and plucked the rock out again, tossing it away like a splinter. The blue fire-eyes narrowed, and it changed direction and in the next second, loomed over Dave. The officer barely had enough time to open his mouth to scream before the creature raised a large root foot and stomped Dave flat into the ground. Alvarez could feel the impact of its foot connecting with Dave's body, and then through it into the earth beneath, right up through his boots. There was a horrific crunch and an ooze of blood from under the creature's foot.

Alvarez and Greer exchanged looks and reholstered their guns.

"Run?" Greer asked.

"Fuck yes," Alvarez replied.

They turned to bolt back over the tall grasses when they noticed a pair of fiery lights, much like the giant tree-creature's eyes, but smaller and bright green. And then another pair lit up next to the first. And then another and another.

Alvarez glanced around the clearing and saw it dotted with similar twin pairs of glowing green eyes.

"No," Greer muttered in panic. "Oh, fuck no."

As the officers' gaze darted between the different lights, more tree-creatures, similar in appearance to the first but smaller, maybe seven or eight feet tall, began to emerge from the woods. Alvarez wondered if they were as strong or as murderously insane as their much bigger brother. He believed it was quite likely.

"Shit," Alvarez whispered. They began closing in.

Then he heard shouts and words from beyond the creatures, a little deeper in the woods, back in the direction that the officers had originally come from. They were human voices this time, not trees. Alvarez prayed they meant some of the other units were close. Then Alvarez saw erratic flashlight beams darting between the trees.

"Officers down!" he shouted as loud as he could. "Officers in need of assistance! Help, goddammit!"

The tree-creatures, even the big one, paused, watching him.

"Alvarez?" came a return shout. More unintelligible words followed, but at that moment they didn't matter. Help was on the way.

"Yes, it's Alvarez!" he shouted back. It hurt his head very much to shout. "We're under attack!"

With effort, he turned back to see the big tree-creature was slowly advancing on Greer, who retreated with cautious and measured steps. Alvarez wanted to help, but the fog in his head was spreading down to his body, weighing him to the spot. He knew there was something he was supposed to be doing in this situation, something police training had taught him about helping fellow officers . . . what was it? He couldn't remember and didn't care. Greer was on his own.

Greer tossed his gun away into the brush and held up his hands to try to placate the thing. "See?" he called to it. "No gun, okay? No gun."

It didn't much seem to care. With a broad sweep of its hand, it batted Greer into the air. His shoulder connected with a cedar about ten feet up and there was the same nauseating crunch of bone that Alvarez had heard with Hoss. Greer cried out and then fell to the ground. It took a great deal of effort for him to get slowly to his feet. He staggered a little to keep his balance, clutching his broken shoulder. That arm dangled uselessly. He glared at the big tree-creature.

"Fuck you!" he shouted. "Fuck you." He spit blood onto the ground.

The larger tree-creature turned to the littler ones and grunted. A few responded with low wind-whistles and growls, and then the two closest to Greer glided across the ground and flanked him. Just as the officers of at least two other units came crashing through the brush into the clearing, the two littler tree-creatures—tree-*spirits*, Alvarez corrected himself somewhere within the fog of his head—drove their sharp, branchlike fingers into Greer's stomach and neck. His eyes grew wide and his body began to shake uncontrollably. His uniform grew darker with his blood. Then his eyes rolled back into his head and his body stopped moving. The creatures withdrew their fingers and shook off his blood.

"What the fuck are those?" an officer shouted from the group gathered at the far edge of the clearing. The officers behind him stood dumbfounded, rooted to the spot. Alvarez saw a number of them try to radio in with their shoulder-mics and wince at the feedback.

He tried to go to them to warn them, but rough, cold wood wrapped around one of his biceps. He turned to see a pair of green fire pits blazing into his own eyes. He tore his gaze away and looked down at his arm. A branch-hand had encircled it tightly.

Alvarez turned his attention back to the far side of the clearing.

The shouts and muttered expletives were increasing in number as more officers started to pour into the clearing from around the trees. They stopped short, too, when they saw the tree-creatures, their hands finding their holstered firearms.

"Don't shoot at them!" Alvarez shouted. At least, he thought he shouted, but he couldn't really tell through the haze in his pounding head. The pain had become a gauzy thing wrapping itself around his thoughts. "No! They'll attack if you shoot! Don't shoot!"

His message was lost amid the chaos. Troopers and local officers alike were pulling out their guns and firing at the bellowing creatures. The creatures in turn laid into the assembled officers like scythes through wheat.

Your strength will not help . . .

The clearing became a cloud of swarming bullets flying into the wooden pulp of bodies that roared and growled, then healed as if never shot at all. The creatures felt those bullets, though. Those sounds they made, like angry winds and falling things, and the fury that emanated from their bodies like a kind of heat, proved that. Their violence was a storm and the officers were in the thick of it.

One state trooper was hoisted into the air and thrown beyond the treetops. His shouts faded until they abruptly cut off. A tree-creature backhanded another officer and she went flying backward into the chasm. With one arm, she held on to the edge, trying to pull herself out. Blood ran down her forehead into her eye. Then thin, ropy vines emerged from the depths and wrapped around her arm and throat. With a violent tug, they yanked her into the chasm itself. All around Alvarez, the tree-creatures were tearing, slashing, stomping, and ripping apart human beings. The clearing filled with screams and the hot stench of blood and decaying plants.

Alvarez noticed for the first time that the chasm depths emitted a coppery glow that eerily illuminated the carnage. Every time those vines could snake out and drag a mangled body, dead or dying, into the chasm, the glow brightened and the roaring hum grew louder. Once, Alvarez thought he'd even heard laughter. Or maybe the laughter was coming from the trees.

It took a few minutes to understand that the laughter was actually coming from *him*.

The fog in Alvarez's head had now engulfed his whole body. Bullets and shouts alike whirled around the wooden forms and the human ones, but he just couldn't feel the sense of danger he had before. In fact, the strange war dances going on around him were pretty damned funny. People looked so silly, all folded up and bent in ridiculous angles as the vines tried to cram them down the narrow throat of the chasm.

It was growing, though, that throat. It was getting wider and longer. Pretty soon, it would be able to extend its fault line right under the feet of the officers and they would just fall back, fall right into it and it would bury them alive or burn them with that copper glow or—

His thoughts were interrupted as something round rolled across the clearing floor and bumped against his toe. It was a head with wisps of gray hair matted to the head by streaks of blood. The face was a mask of shrieking surprise, the upturned eyes glazing. They blinked once and then the light went out in them. He smiled down at the funny thing and kicked it back in the direction it had come.

He turned to the tree-creature holding his arm and with his free hand, pointed to the chasm. The creature whisked him to its edge and Alvarez swayed a little to keep his balance. He looked down into it but couldn't see anything at the bottom except the coppery glow. Wait . . . there was something else, besides the roots of those snaking vines. There was a swirling, amorphous thing like a coal-gray cloud, zipping back and forth like a bug caught in a jar. Was it trapped down there? It didn't seem to be. It seemed excited. It swelled and ebbed, zipped, stretched, pulled together, swirled into a spiral. It was dancing.

Alvarez wondered if anyone else could hear the trees laughing at them and feel all the hideous ideas that the chasm was belching forth—terrible things one could do to children, ways to torture the elderly, how to scar a woman's insides during a rape, how to prolong suffering when killing someone. The cop part of him, now buried deep inside his psyche, was screaming that this was madness and barking commands to pull together and get the hell out of there, but the message was too far away to penetrate the fog. He wondered if anyone else felt the same disconnect from logical thought. His gun dangled at his side. He couldn't fight. He didn't want to. He wanted to cry and laugh and scream all at the same time but his mouth wouldn't work.

Then another rough wooden hand grabbed his other arm. He felt the pressure and heard the tearing before he felt any pain. It wasn't until the sides of his ribs grew warm with his own blood that he saw his arms had been torn off. He looked up at one of the tree creatures, and before he could cry out or sink to the ground, weak from shock and blood loss, the sharp branch-fingers of the creature's hand stabbed into the soft skin beneath his eyes. He felt the fingers moving around beneath his eyeballs, knocking against his sockets. Then everything went dark as the nerves were severed and his eyes pulled free of his skull. He sank to his knees, amused by how the keening of the wind across his empty eye sockets sounded like the voices of the little tree-creatures. He pitched forward. The grass felt soothing and cool against his cheek. The wind blew across the back of his neck. Screams erupted in the dark all around him.

Alvarez used the trunk of his body to drag himself as close to the chasm as he could. Then he rolled himself over the edge and fell down, down, down. The last thing Alvarez thought on this earth before the copper glow enveloped him was that his grandma hadn't ever told him that the trees could be so cruel.

FOURTEEN

Julia, Pete, and Mallon knew they had found the clearing. They could hear unearthly roaring, which Pete and Mallon seemed to be in agreement was coming from the forest king. They explained to her that they thought it was an elemental spirit, a forest god that the essence of the chasm had driven insane beyond all hope of recovery. They heard human screaming, too, and Julia could tell from their faces that it pained them to hear the deaths of their brothers and sisters in blue and not be able to run in there and save them. They could also smell that rot of vegetable matter, the death of whatever part of the forest was still healthy and natural, and the animal smell of hot, spilled blood. Mallon had been right: Nilhollow was bringing them right to its center, right to its throat, because it wanted to devour them. It didn't know they intended to slit that throat and silence its madness and cravings for good.

They had to make it there first. Close to the clearing, Julia's mind was flooded with images from her dream, interspersed with all the ways her ax could dismember a body. She could feel what the effort of lifting and dropping an ax was like in her arm muscles, could feel the phantom sensation of blood splatter on her face. Her ankle blazed white-hot with pain, and she couldn't think of a better way to treat it than to chop the whole damned foot off. When she managed to shove those thoughts aside, it bombarded her with all of her flaws, all of her weaknesses, all the ways that she was a useless burden to the two men beside her. To her, it was more of the same self-doubt that had characterized her entire experience in Nilhollow. She was weary of its attempts, but it was relentless in trying to crumble the last vestiges of her sanity.

Oh yes, they were close to the source of madness in Nilhollow, all right. She didn't know what kinds of thoughts were passing through the men's heads, but she could tell they were struggling with them. Were they imagining killing her? Were they repulsed by all the things the chasm was telling them were her weaknesses? Was Mallon going to drop her on her ass and burn off her face with the blowtorch, or would Pete bury the ax into her back?

The grips of both men tightened around her, and they trudged on. No one spoke.

They reached the clearing, and Julia felt dizzy. Up close it was much harder to fight down the wellspring of panic and despair that threatened to overtake her. She just hoped Mallon knew what to do when they got there, because she wasn't sure how much longer she could hold on.

Pete and Mallon helped her over the high bushes and sharp strands of tall grasses, and the three of them stumbled into some medieval depiction of hell. The clearing was crowded with state troopers, park rangers, and local cops firing guns on advancing tree-beings made of branches and sticks. The tree-beings were ripping off limbs, digging into chest cavities, and hurling bodies against rocks and trees. Officers were running, screaming, wrestling, and emptying clips into the creatures. Mostly, they were coming apart or falling to the ground at the branch-hands of those they were fighting.

And in the middle of it all, those infernal vines snaking up from the chasm were greedily grabbing the bodies of the fallen and dragging them back down into its depths.

"Jesus Christ," Mallon said, taking it all in with a quiet expression of sadness. He unzipped his backpack and handed Pete the blowtorch.

"Anything comes near her," he told Pete, "and you torch it."

Pete nodded dumbly, taking the blowtorch from him. "Captain—"

Mallon clapped him on the shoulder and gave him a paternal smile. Then he pulled out the chainsaw and dropped the backpack at Julia's feet. He took a few steps forward and revved it up. The chaos swallowed any sound it might have made, but its presence was felt, particularly by the tree-creatures. For several seconds, the battles slowed to a stop.

The tree-creatures rustled anxiously, growling and grunting at Mallon but keeping their distance. Julia guessed they had never seen modern technology like that—an ax to the eleventh power, a lightly buzzing, relentless, sawing beast. They appeared to sense it was a dangerous human tool, though, whatever it was.

Mallon strode toward the chasm. He had covered half the distance before a huge tree-creature, much bigger than all the others, with blue pits of fire for eyes, stepped between the captain and the chasm. Julia gasped. She supposed that was the forest king, the one who had gone insane. It was a moving tree-man, a personification of the forest itself, of all that Nilhollow was.

It leaned down and roared so loudly in Mallon's face that it blew back his hair. If he was scared, it didn't show. He closed his eyes until the roar was spent, then opened them and revved the chainsaw again. All around him, the surviving officers cheered. The littler tree-beings watched with the eyes of threatened animals.

The giant tree-creature, unlike the little ones, either didn't understand the tool in Mallon's hand or was too crazy to care. It raised a massive fist and swung downward, intent on smashing Mallon into the earth, but at the same time, the captain swung the chainsaw to meet it. With a hungry buzzing, the chainsaw ate into the meat of the tree-creature's hand and it howled. It yanked back its arm, and several of its long, sharp branch-fingers fell to the ground like so much kindling. Mallon jabbed the chainsaw up and buried it almost all the way to the handle in the creature's arm. It shook itself free only by letting the blade saw from the center of the forearm to the outer edge, and more branches dropped to the ground. Sap oozed up between the splintered and damaged wood, a liquid bandage, Julia figured, while the wound healed.

It thundered in frustration and pain and no small amount of indignation and took a step closer. Mallon moved surprisingly fast, stepping toward the creature and burying the chainsaw into its leg. His arms shook with the force of the chainsaw jerking its way through the massive bark-covered wood and thick roots.

With a bass growl Julia felt in her chest, it grabbed Mallon and yanked him off its leg, shoving him hard across the clearing and bouncing him off a tree. Julia cried out. The assembled officers held a collective breath. The littler tree-creatures grunted and growled, still on guard. Pete shoved the blowtorch into her hands and ran to help him.

The chainsaw skittered across the ground in the other direction, far out of Mallon's reach, and its safety feature shut it off.

The enormous tree creature took a step forward toward Mallon but the bottom half of its chain-sawed leg dangled beneath it, useless. Some of its roots fell away. It growled as sap oozed between both ends to knit them back together.

Mallon groaned and sat up. The bones in his left forearm were poking through the skin like jagged twigs. Pete reached him just then and helped him struggle to his feet.

When its leg was sufficiently repaired, the tree-creature advanced on Mallon and Pete, stalking them like a tiger. Even in its insanity, it understood Mallon to be dangerous, a being with tools that could cause it undue pain, and it was suspicious.

Julia felt numb, encased in a fog. She didn't fully register the fact that she had been moving, that she had been steadily limping in the direction of the tree creature, until she found herself inches behind it. Pete's and Mallon's attention was on the looming, vicious thing above them. They didn't seem to see her. If the other officers saw her, they said nothing. Maybe they knew before she did what she was planning on doing, and didn't want to give it away to either the giant or the littler tree-creatures. After all, if they had never seen a chain-saw, then it was likely they had never seen a blowtorch, either . . .

And then something snapped inside of Julia. Years of anger she had pushed so far down that it had become guilt, tumbled upward. Years of biting her tongue, of accepting her fate, of letting things pass by her because she didn't think she was worthy enough to hold on to them anyway, surged up from the depths of her soul. Like those fucking vines, tendrils of emotion snaked their way all through her, and the fog was strangled to nothingness. It might very well have been Nilhollow's crazy-sickness finally taking hold, or it might have been pent-up years of resentment toward Darren and her parents and all the people who had taken and taken and never given back. Maybe it was her admiration for Captain Mallon and her feelings for Pete. Whatever the catalyst, suddenly she was filled with a rage as hot and bright as the pain in her ankle. This forest had taken so much, had caused so much loss and death. It had ruined lives. It had broken people's bodies, but worse, it had broken people's minds. It had stolen their sense of self, and to Julia, that was absolutely unforgivable. *No more, goddammit. No fucking more.*

She turned on the blowtorch and held the flame to the recently restored leg of the large tree-creature, the flame as blue and hot as that loathsome creature's eyes, and she set the fucker on fire.

It jerked its leg up, away from the perceived source of burning and pain. Its sudden movement startled her, and she fell over. She managed to pull herself out of the way just seconds before the creature brought its burning leg down, shaking the ground. All around the clearing, the tree-beings rustled with nervous energy.

The giant tree-creature, the mad king of the forest, caught fire quickly, a colossal wicker-man flailing as the fire ate into its wood. It stumbled backward toward the chasm, teetering on its edge, and its roar was so loud that the trees themselves shook. It was a primal sound, an ancient sound, a world dying.

The king is grumbling, she thought, and laughed wildly.

The vines reached up from the chasm and dove into the flames, wrapping around the tree-creature's legs. It took many vines, one after the other, taking hold of the creature's legs. Julia thought they were trying to pull the creature down into the chasm and she grunted in satisfaction.

They didn't, though, not exactly. The tree-being, now a fire-being, let out one final roar as the vines yanked, and a bright blue light pulled itself free of the burning body and faded into the sky. The collection of branches, roots, and vines that it had consisted of collapsed in a flaming pile of firewood. The vines pulled the burning wood into the chasm in a flurry of embers that winked out one by one.

The stunned officers said nothing. For several minutes, silence reigned.

Then the little tree-creatures, the elementals of Nilhollow, gathered together. Their movements were solemn and proud. She could feel their emotions, bright like beacons, and those feelings were complicated. There was sadness and relief, anger and respect, weariness and acceptance. Of all the emotions they projected outward, acceptance was the strongest. The little tree-creatures had lived for tens of thousands of years, and they would continue on for tens of thousands more, and time would continue to change things. Things would live, die, and rot away. That was the way of everything.

A mournful song of the wind, a keening, filled the whole clearing. Julia thought she could hear words in it, but she wasn't sure. They were not the words of the clearing, not the endless attacks of hate and fear, the malevolent suggestions of depravity. The words were of inner peace, and Julia found the sentiment endearing, even if she didn't understand.

Then they broke apart into columns of leaves, swirling autumn dervishes that strong winds rushed to carry away. In moments, all traces of the littler tree-creatures were gone.

Julia felt arms around her and turned into them to find Pete had swept her up in a big hug.

"I'm so proud of you. I knew you were tough. You saved our lives," he whispered in her ear. She could hear the smile in his voice, and it made her smile, too, even as her eyes filled with tears.

A voice came from the assembled crowd. "Is it over?" There weren't many officers left. Besides Julia and Pete and Captain Mallon, who was making his way over to the couple with his version of a warm and congratulatory smile, there were six others, ragged and bloody and breathing hard. Each of them was looking at Julia with a mix of amazement and appreciation, and it made her feel good.

Then she noticed another person standing at the edge of the chasm, a tall, gaunt, almost skeletal man with a bedraggled gray beard and long gray hair. His clothes were gold mottled with gray, and his skin was desiccated, a sickly ashen color. The eyes were full of copper light.

Julia felt the world go out from under her, and would have fainted if Pete hadn't been there to hold her up.

I know you, she thought as the world came back into focus. *I dreamed you. I hate you.*

"Who's that?" Pete asked, seeing the recognition on her face.

The figure made its slow and stately way toward Julia. "She knows," the figure said. "So do you, Pete. We've met before, remember?" As the thing walked, Perry's face rippled across its face and then rippled back again.

"You're the Turning of the Earth," Pete said.

Mallon looked at him, surprised, and moved silently away, in the direction of the backpack.

"I am the socks and shoes!" it said with insane, hysterical glee. "The peanut butter and the jelly! I am the degeneration. Yes, yes, I'm what has been called the Turning of the Earth, a force before time and space. And our mutual friend Julia has sent away my best pet.

For taking something, I feel she should give something in return, don't you?"

"Stay away from her," Pete said, stepping between them.

"Oh, Pete," it said, obviously suppressing a giggle. "What are you going to do about it? You can't cut me up into little pieces with your chainsaw or send me up in flames. Destruction begets destruction. And beautiful, freeing madness feeds on madness. Have I always been mad? I don't remember. I don't care. I am the endless loop of endings." The Turning laughed as if appreciating some private joke.

Then suddenly it grew serious. "Give me Julia. I've decided that I want her."

"You can't have her," Pete said. Then he went flying backward, coughing and sputtering where he landed, like the wind had been knocked out of him.

"It's not up to you," the thing said placidly. It turned to Julia and seemed surprised to find Mallon had returned to her side.

She noticed the captain had a few sheets of paper in his hand. He regarded the Turning with cold eyes. Then he spoke to it in a language Julia had never heard before.

To her surprise, the Turning recoiled as if slapped.

"You are not a shaman," it said, but the smug superiority of its tone had changed.

Mallon spoke to it again in that same language, pulling a fistful of something out of his pocket and tossing it in the face of the Turning. It looked to Julia like oregano, but from the way the thing cried out when the flakes touched it, she supposed it must have been something more powerful. Captain Mallon took a step toward the thing and spoke several words in that same language over and over—six or seven times before Julia lost count—and with each iteration, the Turning took a step backward.

"No!" it cried loudly, trying to drown out Mallon's voice. "No!" Around the clearing, the wind was picking up. It blew through the trees, rustling the leaves, and Julia would have sworn that they sounded excited, even triumphant. She figured that whatever Mallon was doing, he was weakening the Turning's hold over the elementals, and they were cheering him on.

Mallon had advanced, matching the Turning step for step in its retreat to the chasm, his deep voice almost chant-like as he unrolled a carpet of words in that strange language, occasionally punctuating what he was saying with a fistful of herbs in the Turning's face. He was armed with something better than a chainsaw or a blowtorch, apparently.

The Turning's head darted back and forth. Julia thought it must be trying to draw strength to fight back, maybe from the people around or maybe from the elementals, but Captain Mallon kept going. As they reached the edge of the chasm, he produced a stone knife from his other pocket and cut his palm. Then he squeezed his hand into a fist and dripped the blood into the chasm, never once stopping or even slowing the flow of words. The Turning cried out and tumbled backward into the chasm, its scream fading for a long time before it finally stopped altogether.

Finally, Mallon's prayer or spell or ritual, whatever it was, came to a whispered end, and he let go of a long and tension-filled breath. He turned to the assembled officers and Julia with a small, satisfied smile. It was replaced by a small "Oh" of surprise as he was jerked backward, and in the next minute, the vine around his leg had yanked him down and he was gone.

Julia screamed. For several seconds, no one moved. No one breathed. Julia's mind refused to accept it. It wasn't fair. After all that had happened . . . why couldn't everything be just fine?

Pete seemed to snap out of his shock and he ran to the edge of the chasm. Several other surviving officers who could still run followed. Julia did her best to limp after them.

Just as they reached the chasm, a hand flipped over the edge and slapped the dirt. It was followed a moment later by the other hand, still clutching the stone knife, its blade sticky with a substance that was clear and kind of jellylike, with threads of loosely clotted blood. It smoked up from the blade.

Hope sprung in Julia's chest at the relieved looks on Pete's and the officers' faces. They reached down and grabbed the arms attached to those hands, and hauled Captain Stan Mallon out of the jaws of the chasm.

Tears of relief spilled down Julia's cheeks as she caught up to the crowd, and she threw her arms around Mallon in a warm hug. Then she limped over to stand next to Pete.

Mallon glanced back toward the chasm and whispered a few more words under his breath, and the fading copper glow far down in its gullet went dark.

Satisfied, Mallon gave a grunt. "Let's get the hell out of here."

Pete looped an arm under Julia's and wrapped it around her back to help her walk. She turned to him, suddenly overwhelmed by her feelings for him, and kissed his cheek.

"I hope that was okay," she said with a shy smile.

He leaned in and kissed her on the mouth, and every part of her warmed at the sensation. They only parted when the giggles and amused coughs reminded them that others were around. They pulled apart, both blushing and smiling.

"Nice work, Grainger," Mallon said with a small smile. "Now let's get the hell out of here."

It took about an hour to make their way back to the road. There were no headaches, no fogs of confusion, and while nothing about the appearance or silence of Nilhollow had changed, the air felt lighter, emptier somehow. She didn't know if it was the security of having others around her or not, but she felt the fundamental change in Nilhollow. The woods would no longer show her things or re-arrange themselves to keep them lost. They were free, and just as Mallon had said, they didn't have to burn the whole woods down to do it. It would probably take decades, maybe centuries for the effects of the Turning to be broken down and replaced by healthy, natural woods, but the forest had a freshness about it that she associated with finally and completely being over an illness.

"Captain Mallon," one of the officers asked. "What was it that you said to that thing to send it back to the chasm?"

The captain replied, "They were words from a time and a people who lived side by side with the trees and their guardians. They were words that there is apparently no written language for. They are only ever represented by these stick configurations, these lattices and pyramids. Three-dimensional representations of words. And apparently, they were words given to these people by . . . well, by those even older than that."

"Okay, I think I follow. But . . . what did you say?"

Captain Mallon shook his head. "Let's just leave it at this: I told the Turning to take a hike."

His tone was such that it invited no questions or further comment. Julia was content with that. Maybe some words were meant only for the speaker and the intended listener. They had worked, had set them and all of Nilhollow free, and to Julia, that was all that mattered.

EPILOGUE

It had been so long since the *manëtuwàk* were truly free that the rest of that night and many others after were spent in the sleep and habitual restricted movement of the past. They were not burdened with violent anger, and by degrees, they remembered more and more of the old days. They blew on the breezes, rippled through the ferns, rustled in the leaves. They felt new vibrancy in the trees they guarded, and over time, they truly reclaimed their forest.

The moving one with the buzzing beast had spoken the old tongue, the words given to the far-moving ones by the ancient forest kings and queens, the gods of the woods. It was the language of the space between worlds, and it had power over forces older even than they were. They had sensed that a far-moving one had explained the sacred meaning of the words to the moving one with the buzzing beast, and had told him that the speaker kept the meaning of the words to himself. To be the chosen speaker meant carrying the import of the words and submitting to a bond to that other world. The speaker would forever see and hear and know things. It was a great responsibility.

Although they seldom saw that moving one, the speaker with the buzzing beast, they did, on occasion, see the moving one they had sheltered, the one for whom the moving ones' spoken word "Julia" was an identifier. She had healed, and she sometimes wandered among their trees and left gifts. She knew the old ways, and so they formed the pathway under her feet so that she would never be lost among their trees again.

In the clearing where the Chasm had been, there was only a sealed scar, crusted over with rock. Little grew from that once blood-soaked ground, and the *manëtuwàk* didn't go there, but they sensed no anger, no rage-sickness. They supposed in time, their forest would swallow it up again as it had once tried to swallow the forest. Change was the way of things, if one were to stay around long enough to see it.

In the part of the Pine Barrens that the locals called Nilhollow, the trees blazed red and yellow and orange, the pines deep green and the shrubs shades of royal purple. The branches waved to each other, and cool winds skipped happily along, bringing news of things from one end of the forest to the other. The ferns giggled again. For the first time in centuries, new flowers and new wild plants grew. Things grew, seeded, and spread more life.

The lesser *manëtuwàk*, the elemental spirit guardians of the trees, were content and they were free.

When the night came, they sang their wind-songs for their little ones about the Julia and the speaker, and the will-o'-wisps glowed and danced in ancient lattice-patterns to light the dark.

CHILLS

MARY SANGIOVANNI

"True Detective" meets H.P. Lovecraft in this chilling novel of murder, mystery, and slow-mounting dread from acclaimed author Mary SanGiovanni . . .

CHILLS

It begins with a freak snowstorm in May. Hit hardest is the rural town of Colby, Connecticut. Schools and businesses are closed, powerlines are down, and police detective Jack Glazier has found a body in the snow. It appears to be the victim of a bizarre ritual murder. It won't be the last. As the snow piles up, so do the sacrifices. Cut off from the rest of the world, Glazier teams up with an occult crime specialist to uncover a secret society hiding in their midst.

The gods they worship are unthinkable. The powers they summon are unstoppable. And the things they will do to the good people of Colby are utterly, horribly unspeakable . . .

Read on for a special excerpt!

A Lyrical Underground e-book on sale now.

ONE

Jack Glazier had worked Colby Township Homicide for going on nine long New England winters, but he had never seen blood freeze quite like that.

It certainly had been cold the last few nights; it was the kind of weather that cast phantom outlines of frost over everything. That hoary white made grass, tree branches, cars, even houses look fragile, like they might crack and shatter beneath the lightest touch. An icy wind that stabbed beneath the clothes and skin had been grating across the town of Colby for days now, and the place was raw.

Jack hated the cold. He hated it even more when his profession brought him out on brittle early mornings like this one, where the feeble sunlight did little even to suggest the idea of heat.

He had caught a murder case—a middle-aged John Doe found hanging upside down from the lowest branch of a massive oak tree at the northeastern edge of Edison Park. The body had been strung up off the ground by the right leg with some type of as-yet-unidentified rope. A crude hexagon had been dug roughly in the torn-up grass beneath the body. Scattered in those narrow trenches, he'd been told, the responding officers had found what they believed to be the contents of the man's pockets, which had been bagged as a potential starting point for identification.

Jack glanced up at the silver dome of sky with its gathering clouds of darker gray and listened for a moment to the low wail of the wind slicing at the men gathered near the body. They worked silently, their minimal conversation encased in tiny breath-puffs of white. The air carried a faint smell of freezer-burned meat that agitated Jack in a way the smell of dead bodies never really did. It made him think of lost things, things forgotten way in the back of dark, cold places and left to rot slowly. There was no closure and no dignity in it.

Of course, he supposed that closure and whatever little dignity he could scrape together for the victims of murder was part of *his* job.

It took an effort to focus on the body again, to duck under the strung-up lines of police tape and move toward it. He found that the closer he got to a decade of dealing with dead, clouded eyes, gelid, mutilated flesh, and distraught loved ones, the more energy it took to give himself over to getting cases started. He wanted them solved—that drive had propelled him to the rank of detective lieutenant and it made him good at what he did—but it was the *starting* of the investigations he had lost the taste for. It was getting harder and harder to stare the next few months of brooding and nightmares in the face.

As for the body itself, the throat looked like it had been cut—bitten, really—and there were lacerations on the naked torso, shoulders, bare arms, and face. Jack, who did his best to suppress his morbidly imaginative streak in these situations yet frequently failed, could imagine the John Doe dangling in the glacial night air, wracked with shivers as his blood poured from his wounds, cooling the fire of life in his body until there was no movement, no feeling. He was an end scene, frozen before the roll of the credits, his screen time cut suddenly short.

All of the John Doe's blood had formed, drop by drop, fringes of crimson icicles from the lowest-hanging parts of his body, as if every part, every tissue of the man had struggled to escape that branch and its pain and death. The overall effect stripped the humanity from the corpse, leaving it a gross caricature of what it once had been.

A uniformed officer whose name slipped Jack's mind—Morano or Moreno, something like that—nodded at him as he made his way up to the crime scene. Crouched beneath the body a foot or so from the outline of overturned grass clumps, Colby's thin, bald, and bespectacled coroner, Terrence Cordwell, was packing up his kit.

"They're calling for about eight to ten inches of snow, starting around midnight. Can you believe that? Probably keep up most of tomorrow," Cordwell was saying to Dave Brenner, his assistant, who had switched from the digital camera to the film. Dave was documenting the churned-dirt hexagon and the body with another series of close-up photos. Both men nodded to Jack as he joined them.

Brenner stepped carefully into the hexagon's center and took a close-up photo of the body's neck wound, a gaping tear like a second frown across his neck, then stepped outside the core of the crime scene, around to the back of the torso. He whistled, holding up his pocket ruler beneath the body's shoulder blades, and took another couple of photos. "Hey, Glazier. Where's Morris?"

Jack crouched and peered closer at the neck wound. It looked deep and uneven, like several serrated sharp objects had torn and gouged at the neck at once. It reminded him again of a bite. "Nephew's baptism. He's the godfather, I think."

"Poor kid. Hey, shit weather, huh? Too cold for May."

"Cold, yeah. Not unheard of, though, I guess."

"No," Brenner offered grudgingly over his shoulder, and Jack heard the whir and snap of the camera taking another picture. "Up north, maybe. But still awful late in the season for more snow around here. It's a sign that the planet is fucked, if you ask me. Global warming and shit."

Jack didn't answer. He wasn't particularly fond of Brenner; the guy always seemed to have one more thing to say than Jack had the patience to hear.

Instead, Jack rose and turned to Cordwell. "So what's the deal with this guy?"

The coroner peeled off his rubber gloves. "No ID, no wallet—but he's got teeth and fingertips, so if he's in the system, we should be able to find him. Dead eight, maybe nine hours. With the cold, it's hard to say for sure until we get him back to the cave. What I can tell you is that he froze to death before he had a chance to bleed out, although the hypothermia was likely accelerated by the blood loss. These lacerations and that neck wound were meant, I'm guessing, to speed up the process. They're animal, most of them. Not certain what kind yet, but we bagged and tagged what I'm pretty sure is a tooth."

"Animal bites? So what, someone fed him to something and then strung up what was left?"

Cordwell shrugged. "More likely, it happened the other way around. Someone strung this guy up and left him to . . . whatever did that to him."

Jack frowned, moving slowly as he examined the body. One of the hands was missing. When he pointed it out, Cordwell shook his head; they hadn't found it. The leg from which the John Doe was strung up was virtually untouched. Jack imagined a man would know that it would have to be kept intact to support the weight of the body, but how the animal or animals managed to avoid it, Jack could only guess. Likely, it was simply too high for them to reach. The other leg was mangled, but not nearly as badly as the head, arms, and torso. Those wounds alternated between slashes Jack figured for a knife and more of those ragged tears, right down to the bone in a lot of places. Jack shook his head at the brutality of it and moved around to the back of the body.

Then he saw the brand. In the entire space between the shoulder blades, ugly, angry pink swells of skin formed a large kind of symbol Jack didn't recognize, featuring asymmetric swirls crossed with an irregular lattice of lines. It looked deliberate; in fact, it surprised Jack that the design was as clearly and intricately formed as it was.

"Hey, Brennan, you get a picture of this?"

"The burn marks? Yeah. Creepy shit. Occult?"

"Maybe. Looks pretty new."

"You know," Brenner said with a careful, measured tone, "if this is some kinda devil-worshiping thing, they'll probably want to bring Ryan in on this."

Jack frowned, glancing at the younger man. "Don't think we'll need Ryan, necessarily."

Brenner shrugged. "Maybe not. Maybe the brand doesn't mean anything at all, other than deluded satanist fantasies of some nut job thinking he's some grand high wizard or something. But you know, if it's not—"

Jack turned the full attention of his gaze on Brenner and the rest of the sentence dropped off.

It wasn't that Jack didn't like Ryan; they'd worked very closely a few years back busting a child sex ring that had strong connections to a radical Golden Dawn sect working out of Newport. She'd also been called in to work with him on collaring a big-name drug dealer in Boston whose specialty product, in addition to persuasive pulpit revelations delivered in an abandoned Russian Orthodox church, was a powder rumored to make devoted users both see and attempt to kill demons. Occult practices, ancient grimoires, devil worship, blood sacrifices, and rites to archaic gods and monsters—that was Ryan's thing, her specialty. She'd worked all over the country as a private consultant to law enforcement evaluating occult involvement and assessing risk, and was known to be efficient and discreet. She also was apparently able, through resourcefulness or mystery connections, to skirt a lot of red tape and paperwork regarding freedom of religious pursuit that usually hung up other investigations. Jack thought she was brilliant, aloof, and intense, but the kind of woman one was dismayed to be inexorably drawn to.

Ryan was good at what she did, although to say she was popular with the people she worked for or with might be pushing it. How she'd come into her line of work or developed a reputation for being one of the country's leading experts in it was something she guarded closely. Jack suspected it contributed to what made her eyes dark and her smile fleeting, and any true attempt at getting close to her impossible. Her experiences formed the ghosts of truly haunted expressions beneath those she offered the world. And Jack thought she was a bottle of vodka and a .38 away from blowing all that she'd seen and learned about the fringes of the world out the back of her head.

Cordwell clapped him on the shoulder, jarring him from his thoughts. "I'll have a prelim report for you in a day or two. Stay warm."

Jack nodded as the men moved away, ducking under the police tape. He saw Cordwell motion to one of the technicians, say something, and then gesture in his direction. Jack assumed the tech had been told the body was ready for transport.

He stood a few moments, his eyes drawing over the details of the body, the contorted features of the face, the wounds already starting to take on that freezer-burn-like quality to match that smell that, when the wind shifted, found its way inside his nose on the back of the cold, dry air. He made his way over to the small blue tent top that had been set up over a folding table, designated as the detectives' safe area. He figured Detective Reece Teagan would already be there, getting a jump start on examining the items Cordwell said had been found in the dirt.

And so he was—Teagan's scuffed sneakers were propped up on the corner of the evidence table as he leaned back in a metal folding chair. He was squinting intently at the contents of a plastic evidence bag with a red label, an unlit Camel cigarette hanging out of his mouth. With his free hand, he absently ran his fingers through his hair, a quirky little habit that sent it up into dirty-blond spikes. When he noticed Jack's approach, he nodded a hello, which sent those spikes drifting back, more or less into place. Jack noticed for the first time that some of those spikes had the occasional strand of gray—not nearly as much as Jack had seen mixed in his own black hair the last year or so, but enough to remind him again just how many cases had come and gone for him with Teagan, Morris, Cordwell, and their winters in Colby.

"Jack. You seen these yet? Right feckin' warped."

Teagan had grown up in Westport and Inistioge in Ireland before going to Oxford and then working as a detective sergeant, and although he'd been almost ten years in the States, his brogue was still strong. It seemed a continuing source of amusement to him that American women swooned and giggled when he spoke to them, calling them "love." His accent and accompanying rakish grin never ceased to earn him confidences, phone numbers, and, when need be, forgiveness from the "birds" he occasionally dated. That he was a pretty good-looking guy beneath the facial scruff, with a lean, strong build to boot, didn't hurt his cause, either.

"How's that?" Jack pulled up a folding chair next to him and leaned in toward the evidence table. Nodding at Teagan's light jacket, he said, "Aren't you cold?"

"Fresh air, mate. Take a look at this stuff." Teagan gestured at the evidence bags. Jack examined the contents of the first few, taking note of some change (thirty-four cents), a key ring with car keys (although the Toyota they belonged to was conspicuously absent), and a receipt for chips and coffee from the nearby convenience store.

"Not sure what I'm supposed to be seeing here. Looks like the stuff on the floor of my car."

"Not those," Teagan said. "These." He slid a few bags over to Jack. The first bag contained what looked to Jack like a chunk of splintered wood about six inches long and three inches wide. He held it up by the bag and turned it over, then saw what Teagan meant. The back side of the wood was flat and smooth, and into it was burned or carved a series of runic marks that formed neat lines across the whole surface. Jack looked at Teagan questioningly, and the other man shrugged.

"Cordwell says this one's a tooth." He handed Jack another bag with a slightly curved bit of ivory substance about five or six inches long. One end held the remains of a rough kind of root while the other tapered to a very sharp point.

"What the hell has teeth like this around here? Is he serious?"

"Damned if I know," Teagan said. He slid another bag toward Jack. "And there's this card, here."

It was the size of a business card, although it was entirely black and there was no writing on it on either side. Jack studied the matte finish on both sides for signs of fingerprints but couldn't even find a smudge.

"Calling card, maybe? Business card?" Jack asked.

"No idea. Though, whoever it belongs to might want to be re-thinking their business plan."

Jack handed it back. "Maybe they can get something off it. Or off that piece of wood there. Cordwell seems pretty sure this was some kind of orchestrated animal attack."

There was a pause. "Cordwell's saying they might call Kathy in on this," Teagan said, his gaze fixed on the piece of wood.

"Yeah, Brennan said the same thing to me," Jack replied. "For her sake, I hope all this black-magic bullshit is coincidental. Last I heard, she could use a break from it."

"Her input couldn't hurt," Teagan said thoughtfully, handling the bag with the wood sliver. "Even if she only identifies this . . . lan-guage, or whatever it is."

"You know superficial involvement, at least in cases, isn't how she operates."

Teagan reined in a small smile. "Yeah, I know."

Jack prided himself in thinking he understood the thoughts, feel-ings, and motivations below the surface—the ones others wore in their eyes and their smiles and nowhere else. He was fairly certain Teagan was in love with Kathy. The way he looked at her, the soft-ness that crept into his voice when he said her name—it wasn't an in-vestigative stretch to see his longing for her, however smooth and subtle he thought he was. Kathy, though, likely had no clue. In spite of their individual eccentricities, or maybe because of them, Teagan and Kathy were probably soul mates, but knowing her as Jack did, he was pretty sure she never allowed herself to entertain the thought. And Teagan . . . he approached his job with the relentless instinct and perseverance of someone resigned to giving up anything like a normal life. To Teagan, there were dead folks and the folks who killed them, the psychology behind how and why, and not much else.

"Well, I'm off. Could eat the ass of a low-flyin' duck," Teagan said suddenly. "We on this thing together, yeah?"

"Yeah, looks like," Jack said, leaning an elbow on the table. "You, me, and Morris. Tomorrow, nine a.m. My office."

Teagan nodded and jogged off to his car. Jack watched him go, then turned his attention back to the chunk of wood in the bag. He took a deep breath, frigid in his nose and throat, and let it out in little white puffs. It was time, he knew, to start the job.

Although the official start of summer was a month away, the forecast of eight to ten inches of snow for Colby, Connecticut, raised few eyebrows, as late in the season as it was. It had been a particularly harsh winter; temperatures often dropped into the negatives and a leaden sky had dumped snow by the foot on a weekly basis for months. When it didn't snow, the rain during the day turned to black ice at night. The children's spring break had been eaten into by the accumulation of snow days. The county had run out of salt for the roads by early March and had been having a tough time acquiring more to clear them.

Still, most people believed this storm would be the last of them for the year, and patiently suffered the weather to exhale its arctic breath one last time over all. The town of Colby warmed up the snowplows and salt/sand trucks in preparation for winter's last hurrah, and the townsfolk swarmed the local supermarkets, the Targets and Walmarts, the Costcos and the gas stations, to stock up on gasoline and supplies.

Most were still blissfully unaware of the body found hanging from a tree in Edison Park, but they felt it, in the vaguest, unarticulated way. They felt the cold trying to wrench their skin from their bones, and they felt something else, too—a kind of forlorn loneliness trying to wrench peace of mind from their souls. Just as they stocked up on food and bottled water, shovels and gloves, they squinted into the night outside their homes before drawing blinds and locking doors, double-checking on the kids in bed and huddling closer to each other than usual. Something other than a late winter was in the air, and it chilled them just as much, if not more, when they thought too long about it.

Though not even the gossips would give voice to it, the people of Colby knew something was coming with the snow.

About the Author

Mary SanGiovanni is the author of *Chills*, as well as the Bram Stoker nominated novel *The Hollower*, its sequels *Found You* and *The Triumvirate*, *Thrall*, and *Chaos*. She is also the author the novellas *For Emmy*, *Possessing Amy*, and *The Fading Place* and numerous short stories. She has been writing fiction for over a decade, has a master's in writing popular fiction from Seton Hill University, and is a member of The Authors Guild, Penn Writers, and International Thriller Writers. Her website is marysangiovanni.com.

Made in the USA
Coppell, TX
15 March 2022